PRAISE FOR *THE AFTERLIFE PROJECT*

"Smart, achingly beautiful, and (yes) important: a gripping novel of climate cataclysm with a cast of characters I cared about deeply."
—Chris Bohjalian,
#1 *New York Times*–bestselling author of *The Flight Attendant*

"A super-smart, super-fun page-turner about a scientist trying to survive alone on Earth in the deep future—and the love of his life trying to travel through time to find him. I can't think of a single page that didn't make me pause to admire a sentence, an image, or a particularly fascinating idea. I loved this book." —Angie Kim,
New York Times–bestselling author of *Happiness Falls*

"The Afterlife Project isn't just a story about the end of the world as we know it—it's an exploration of beauty, and love, and hope in the darkness. If you were a fan of *Cloud Atlas*, you won't want to miss this one."
—Janelle Brown,
New York Times–bestselling author of *Pretty Things*

"This beautiful and heartbreaking book reminds us of what we have, and what we stand to lose. Unforgettable." —Danielle Trussoni,
New York Times–bestselling author of *The Puzzle Master*

"A brave and brilliant imagining of Earth in the years just after a mega-pandemic has killed almost everyone, and ten thousand years hence, when a test subject emerges from suspension to explore a wilderness echoing with solitude. . . . Riveting and wrenching and suffused with beauty—the haunting and intimate beauty of the natural world rendered by a master." —Peter Heller, bestselling author of *The Dog Stars*

"Weed is a fabulous storyteller working at the top of his game. I predict this novel will become a classic." —Joseph Monninger,
author of *The World As We Know It*

"Weed delivers a highly intriguing storyline pulled off through creative worldbuilding and plausible technology . . . a tale that feels wholly original and movingly conveys the full weight of the circumstances while providing a riveting read in the process."

—BookLife by *Publishers Weekly*

"This engaging dystopian tale deftly blends enthralling fiction with real-life fears."

—*Kirkus Reviews*

"The dangers [the characters] endure along the way are set against an unfolding and impossible love story across the vastness of geological time, as the scientists work to keep humans in existence. It may sound like an end-of-the-world tale, but it defines the strength and bravery of human beings and what they will do to preserve this precious thing we call life in the face of overwhelming odds."

—*Middlebury Magazine* (Editors' Pick)

the Afterlife Project

Tim Weed

Podium

Cover design by Heather VenHuizen

ISBN: 978-1-0394-8045-2

Published in 2025 by Podium Publishing
www.podiumentertainment.com

Podium

For Frances Hanchett:
Writer, grandmother, old-shoe friend

the Afterlife Project

PART I

We don't march toward death, it marches toward us
as a summer thunderstorm came slowly across
the lake long ago. See the lightning of mortality dance,
the black clouds whirling as if a million crows.

—Jim Harrison, *Songs of Unreason*

1

Late spring or early summer
10151 A.U.C.T. +/- 18.583 years (estimated)

He crawls up into the daylight, half-seasick and whirling in his mind. Dizzy, brain-fogged, and bone-chilled. Throat and esophagus sandpapered raw from intubation, forehead bruised, muscles stiff and aching, atrophied body pitifully weak and alien-feeling. His grip on consciousness itself feels brittle, as if he's holding on by the slightest branch and at any moment that branch might snap, sending him tumbling backward into the dark.

He finds a water source, a tiny freshwater brook seeping down the hillside through a forest of massive hardwoods and lichen-plastered granite boulders. Lying on his belly on a bed of moss, he tries to gulp some of the tea-colored water but can't keep it down. He scoops another cold handful, uses his lips like a straw to suck a few ounces into his mouth. Holds it there. Swishes it gently. Swallows it slowly. Vomits.

An hour with his chin resting on the mud at the edge of the brook and he tries again. This time it doesn't come back up. Electrical impulses twitch in his aching limbs. His nerve endings tingle as they gradually return to life.

Several more hours sitting and crawling among the ferns, experimenting with different muscle groups, and he feels ready to try a little protein. He finds a snail crossing an algae-slick stone at the bottom of the brook. Has no jackknife, no toothpick, nothing but the nylon-blend jumpsuit on his body, so he uses his primate mouth, suctioning the shell lip and closing his front teeth gently around the rubbery foot. He draws the shell away steadily, careful not to bite too hard, and the stretched creature finally breaks off.

He chews it well. Swallows it, bracing for his gut's reaction. It stays down.

So long away. Liminal memories of an endless whirling passage through total darkness. The whole arc of the species passing through his mind like a slideshow in a conference room in some long-crumbled city. The dawn of consciousness. A blurry snapshot of the beckoning savannah through parted branches. Horses and aurochs painted on a cave wall. The Bering land bridge. New settlements at Abu Hureyra and Jericho. The killing at spearpoint of the planet's last saber-toothed cat. Before anyone had a chance to question what it might mean, Homo sapiens *had traded in its habitual nomadism for planting and harvesting, hoarding and trade. The domestication of cattle. The invention of alphabets and iron smelting—because there was no stopping progress. The rise of the city states: Minoans, Sumerians, Egyptians, Olmecs. Gilgamesh and Imhotep, the Great Pyramid and Stonehenge, Solomon and Buddha. Slideshow running faster now: Lao-Tse, Alexander the Great, Rome and Teotihuacán, Jesus and Muhammad, the Tang Dynasty, Leif Eriksson, Genghis Khan. The whole sordid history of ignorance and savagery, of fumbling in the darkness with occasional lunges toward the light. Maimonides and Alfonso el Sabio, da Vinci and Shakespeare, Zheng He and Isaac Newton. Philosophy and learning, art and exploration, advances in science and medicine, the industrial revolution and the technological revolution, but always the darkness came flooding back. Plague and famine, slavery and prostitution, greed and demagoguery. Wars of conquest, of tribalism and religion and race. The senseless slaughter of crusades and jihads, holocausts and ethnic cleansings and the utter banality of evil.*

Soon it was his own century, the twenty-first. A few flickers of hope, followed by pandemic and renewed violence and accelerating climatological disruption. Bills coming due for those heady decades of optimism and affluence and devil-may-care consumption built on fossil fuels. Deadly weather, raging wildfires, melting icecaps, acidifying oceans. Drought and famine, dislocation and war, fracturing societies, mushrooming authoritarianism. The microbial plagues returned, lethal and unstoppable. Homo sapiens losing its grip. Falling backward into the abyss.

Within a generation, no human voice could be heard across the 197-million-square-mile surface of the planet. No radio, no television, no internet. A few beacon signals persisted from orbiting satellites, but in a moment those signals too would flicker and die out, and the physical remains of human civilization would enter a rapid process of decay. Buildings sparked by lightning strikes, colonized by mold and termites, invaded by water blowing in through broken windows and collapsing roofs. Materials cracking, rusting, rotting, corroding. Exposed plastic bags degrade in fifty years, aluminum in a few centuries more. Glass bottles gone in half a millennium, Styrofoam perhaps a millennium or two. Within five centuries most towns and cities had been swallowed up by forests, dunes, flooding river deltas. Rising oceans eating back their minerals from the rusting I-beams and the crumbling foundations. Alluvial plains forming where cities used to be, leaf litter and soil deposition burying cracked PVC pipes, dead keyboards and LCD screens, the buckled asphalt of roads and parking lots.

A few thousand years more and a sentient observer would be hard-pressed to discover any evidence at all of humanity's brief flourish on the land masses of Earth.

Down below the surface, however, in a carefully prepared limestone cavern, at least one human being had persisted. Twitching and shuddering, bruised by the bands and harnesses that held him in place, conscious of nothing but a vague ache in his limbs as his atrophied body whirled through the darkness like a sleeping customer on a nightmarish, never-ending carnival ride.

Suddenly his oxygen supply had been cut off, and he'd been choking.

His eyes had opened but there was nothing to see in the blackness. A contraction in his gut, then intense pain spreading up through his chest and throat like a powerful fist pulling his vital organs out through his gullet. *It's only the tubes retracting*, a long-unused inner voice reassured him.

Foul stomach acid surged up behind them, burning his throat, and he felt an overwhelming need to throw up even though he couldn't because his stomach had been vacuumed empty. The sphere that had contained him all this time opened slowly, a mechanized Easter egg. The harness released and he dropped in the darkness, his forehead hitting the stone floor with a sharp crack.

The pain accompanying the slow revival of his nervous system had been nearly unbearable. Much worse, though, was the return of specific memory. He could still feel the tender impression of Natalie's lips on his cheek from that one final kiss, awkward because of the tubes running out both corners of his mouth. She'd squeezed his hand and backed away, smiling encouragement, the tears in her eyes glimmering in the bright LED work lights. Then, turning away to signal another member of the team, she'd stepped out of his line of vision forever. The hydraulic closing mechanism had kicked in, the wedge of the visible world narrowing inexorably to a single horizontal line of bright white light: his final glimpse of the twenty-first century. With a hydraulic sigh the vacuum seal had closed, leaving him alone in the darkness for another moment or two before the drugs had kicked in and he'd lost consciousness.

Then he'd found himself awake again, face down on the cool stone, the air filling his slowly recovering lungs moist and redolent of earth and limestone. Natural, unrecycled air, bracingly fresh in his nostrils. Eventually he'd been able to sit up, with his knees hugged in and his head resting on his clasped forearms. After a long time in this position—perhaps another half revolution of the planet—he'd gathered the strength to try his feet. He'd swayed in place, slowly gaining balance. Shuffled forward through the darkness in the direction of his ancient memory of the cave exit.

After some fumbling and a few false turns he'd spotted a beam of natural light slanting in through the access tunnel. Incrementally, he'd dragged himself up through the slanted chimney of rock, laboring and groaning until his elbows finally rested at the edge of the cave mouth, a small bright triangle of sunlight crosshatched by an unruly mat of roots and vines and dead leaves.

It was the sunlight and the vegetation of the deep future, where he will now pass whatever remaining months or years of life fate has granted him.

He spends two nights and one full day shivering in the open air on his bed of moss, drifting in and out of sleep, sipping the tea-colored water, choking down the occasional snail or grub to build his strength. On the second morning, he finds a dead branch to lean on and hobbles off into the forest.

He has a protocol to follow, and the idea of taking steps in a certain direction, of putting things in motion for a specific purpose, is comforting.

The first item is to find a clearing with a wide enough view of the skies. This accomplished, he is stunned if not exactly surprised to find his eye catching on precisely the celestial object he's looking for: Antares. Once a red giant, now easily discernible as a bright white pinpoint in the cloudless morning sky. A supernova.

Beyond a shadow of a doubt, then, it has come to pass.

The simple idea that everything he's ever known could have been so fully erased by the passage of time. Computers, smartphones, the internet. Social media, Hollywood movies, *any* movies. The stock exchange, McDonalds and Starbucks, Coca-Cola, kombucha. NASA, plug-in hybrids, rock-n-roll, jazz. The Roman calendar. Days of the week. Politics. Blueberry scones. Every invention, every creation of the human society he'd once known, not to mention his family and friends, and Natalie and the rest of the Centauri team. Everyone he'd ever admired, everyone he'd ever scorned, all the human beings he'd ever met, and the multitudes he never did. All of them, vanished and expunged. Never to be revisited, except in memory.

It's a lot to take in.

On the plus side, he finds himself surrounded by what is apparently a rich and healthy ecosystem. A humid forest populated by old-growth trees, mostly hardwoods, whose trunks and branches are covered in multicolored lichen as if by a manic tree-climbing Jackson Pollock. The season appears to be late spring or early summer, the forest floor covered in ferns and sedges and mushrooms of every description, with extravagant layers of emerald and yellow-green moss upholstering a complex topography of boulders and crisscrossing fallen logs. Insects everywhere, a symphony of droning and humming and clacking. There are strange wasp nests suspended from many of the higher branches, inverted vase-like paper constructions the size of a mummified infant, the likes of which he never saw in his own time.

The first vertebrates he sees are birds, mostly familiar forest birds. Nuthatches and chickadees flitting from branch to branch, a pileated woodpecker drumming its beak against the trunk of a tall dead tree. No, not a pileated. It's huge for one thing, with a jet-black head under a prominent red crest and a long powerful beak that isn't gray or black but a kind of luminous off-white. He rubs his eyes in disbelief. Could that be an ivory-billed woodpecker? Or has the pileated for some reason evolved over ten millennia to more closely resemble its extinct cousin?

A flock of turkeys struts through the understory, pausing occasionally to pluck beetles or centipedes from the leaf litter. Noticing him, they all stop moving at once and fix him in their cold yellow gaze. Heavier and more massive in build than the wildland turkeys he remembers, these tall glossy-feathered birds are powerfully clawed and primeval-looking, as if trending back to their dinosaur roots. And there's something in their eyes, too. A surprising boldness of attitude. A look of calm curiosity, as if they're more eager to comprehend the nature of this strange new visitor to the forest than they are afraid of him. But this might just be his imagination.

2

The Journal of Alejandra Morgan-Ochoa, M.D.

Spring 2068 C.E., Gregorian (12 A.U.C.T.)

Transcriber's note: In memory of its much-beloved author this account is rendered exactly as written, though in a few instances, where hindsight allows for useful clarification, the transcriber reserves the right to insert additional brief notations. Despite the inevitable small gaps and errors, the following pages represent a fair, accurate, and relatively complete daily record of the Centauri Project field team's activity during the chronicled time. It is our hope that in formatting it for long-term preservation we make it possible for Dr. Morgan-Ochoa's story to be read in a future millennium. If nothing else, let it serve as a fitting coda to what the author herself herein refers to as humanity's "sleepwalking trajectory" on planet Earth.

March 3, 2068 (12 A.U.C.T.)
The Atlantic Ocean

If this were an official ship's log I would no doubt begin with our exact coordinates and bearing, but I don't have that information at my fingertips. I do assume that our "captain," such as he is, can access such data if he needs to, though I would be surprised if he were bothering to track it in any systematic way. Anyway, we've spent the last week stuck and sweltering in what mariners used to refer to as "the doldrums": not a breath of wind, relative humidity around ninety percent, mid-ocean sun beating down with what feels like actual physical pressure on the backs and shoulders of our sweat-soaked tropical-weight hoodies. We have of course encountered this condition before—the dreaded "wet bulb"—but this time it took us by surprise. We didn't expect to encounter it in March, in the middle of the Atlantic Ocean near the latitude of the former cities of Halifax and London, perhaps a thousand miles west of our ultimate destination.

Still, the weather has been more of a discomfort than a danger thus far. We have plenty of food and water aboard, and we all know better than to exert ourselves unnecessarily in such heat. But it has been a miserable week. We need to conserve our fossil fuel supply for true emergencies, and there's not much that can be done about the lack of wind. So we've been spending our time reading and napping in the shade of the bimini covers, cooled by whatever slight movements of air the stagnant troposphere sees fit to provide.

This morning, thank the gods, something resembling a wind has arisen from the west, which has come as bone-deep relief, giving me the motivation to finally begin this account.

And so, dear human reader of the future, I now commence the written record of an obscure, late-in-the-game, seaborne journey that has little chance of success. Although your own existence may be unlikely, I plan to write as if you *do* exist, because what we're trying to accomplish, while also unlikely, is important. Not "important" in the usual sense of the word, referring to a thing that might be socially beneficial, or contribute to an advance of the sleepwalking trajectory that our ancestors liked to call "history."

No. More like do or die, or last-ditch effort. One final roll of the dice for all the human children who have yet to wake up to the glory of a morning sunrise. For all the art yet to be created, the scientific advances yet to be made, love yet to be shared and happy occasions yet to be celebrated. For the chance to strike a long-term balance of sustainability, and for our species finally to assume its destiny as the stewards, rather than the destroyers, of the miraculous web of life that has emerged and flourished over countless eons all across this beautiful, stricken planet.

That kind of important.

So put aside all your doubts, my dear imaginary correspondent. If keeping this journal is to serve any purpose beyond distracting yours truly from the crushing boredom of this voyage—already two months in on a route that could have been covered in one long travel day back when the airplanes still rumbled through the skies—you will certainly come to know it. For now, though, my goal is simply to chronicle the experience as faithfully as I can, whether we succeed or fail, for as long as I'm able to put pen to paper.

We make our slow way across the dying Atlantic, bound for a tiny volcanic island north of Sicily and southwest of the main Italian peninsula. Our vessel is the *Solar Barque*, a 59-foot vintage Hinckley sailing sloop owned by its captain, Ptolemy ("Tollie") Quist, younger brother of my beloved mentor and friend, the expedition's distinguished leader, Dr. Natalie Quist—to whom I'll refer as "Dr. Q."

Dr. Q: lean, petite, mid-fifties, close-cropped gray hair, big round glasses like a 1970s fashion designer. She wouldn't have stood out in a high school teacher's lounge or the check-out line of a discount supermarket to be honest, back when there were such things. First appearances can be deceptive, however. If you looked more closely you would see her as I do, as a figure of unusual luminosity and courage. Those blunt, pleasantly wrinkled, walnut-colored features. That strong chin angled out over the glittering swells, like a petite female version of George Washington peering off into the fog over the Delaware River. When she takes off her spectacles to clean the lenses on the hem of her hoodie you can really see the deep wrinkles radiating out from the corners of her twinkling eyes, a clue that she takes herself less seriously than George Washington ever did. Maybe Joan of Arc is a better analogy, though she would tease me relentlessly if I ever said that to her face.

Daughter of Cornelius Quist, famous tech wizard and billionaire of the twenties and thirties. Childhood spent rotating through various opulent dwellings around the globe, with private tutors, outback safaris, trips to Greenland and Antarctica to watch the dissolving ice caps. At the age of ten she went missing from her family's TriBeCa apartment for three days; her panicked parents dispatched their aides and helpers, who eventually found her sitting in the front row of a conference room at Columbia, where she'd talked her way into a symposium on quantum computing. By the time she was twelve she'd solved a key problem in theoretical physics with an equation for calculating the values of dimensionless constants. Two years later she became one of the youngest students ever at MIT, and by the age of sixteen she'd coauthored a paradigm-shifting quantum field theory that resulted in her first Nobel Prize.

Dr. Q stayed on at MIT for a PhD in physics, focusing on the possibilities for real-world time dilation using insights from quantum mechanics and general relativity. After a stint at NASA she was recruited by the Centauri Project, a small, well-funded team of scientists and engineers created to lay the groundwork for a colonizing journey to an exoplanet orbiting the binary star of Alpha Centauri. A journey that never came to pass, of course; conditions on the home planet deteriorated far too quickly. But the underlying goal—saving our species from extinction—remains her animating passion.

But let me introduce you briefly to the other members of our four-person crew as well. Captain Tollie Quist, already mentioned, younger by three years than his famous sister and considerably less distinguished, sits at the wheel with his headphones on, his body convulsing almost imperceptibly to the repetitive beat of vintage electronica; James Swamp, our youngest crew member, flipping through obsolete bird guides in the shade of the forward bimini with his hoodie up as usual to conceal the severe scarring he received from his close brush with the hyperpandemic; and finally, yours truly, the team's physician, Alejandra Morgan-Ochoa—though you're free to call me Al, as everyone else does—leaning against the rail in my favored spot just aft the bowsprit, glancing up occasionally from this journal to make sure that absent-minded Dr. Q hasn't somehow managed to fall overboard.

The Quists' vast inherited wealth meant more back in the days of banks and stock exchanges. All it means now is that we have the use of the *Solar Barque* and are well-supplied with food, water, and emergency fossil fuel. We do have some leftover technical equipment and a vintage Osprey mountaineering backpack half-loaded with minted gold bars. This helped smooth our way down the Connecticut River a few days after we boarded the yacht by allowing for the temporary removal of a barrier of floating oil barrels blocking our downstream passage. Gods know what use the well-armed river troll who operated that barrier is actually going to make of a dozen bars of solid gold in this day and age, but there's no accounting for taste, and presumably he'll find trading partners who share his fascination for that essentially useless yellow metal.

The truth is, for him and for us, there's no escaping the grim reality of the present. The hyperpandemic was catastrophic on a scale beyond description and imagination. The number of dead will never be known, but it was the physiological changes that were discovered in the surviving population that truly rang the bells of doom for humanity across the planet. Because the microbe was an aerosolized component of the entire troposphere—the air itself—every single human being alive was exposed. Some developed immunities, yes, but even in the most asymptomatic survivors the pathogen had an invisible but irreparable effect. To be precise: surviving human females can no longer ovulate. Surviving human males can no longer generate active sperm. Which is why now, twelve years after the events we commemorate with a new calendar (A.U.C.T.) acknowledging the collapse of the international financial and telecommunications systems and the associated demise of Coordinated Universal Time, we live in a world completely devoid of children.

And we thus find ourselves contemplating a singular probability that has never been experienced since the dawn of our species on the African savannah approximately 300,000 years ago. Unless a solution can be found, *Homo sapiens* will cease to exist.

Unless, that is, the rumors that moved us to embark on this voyage happen to be true.

These rumors, which are really little more than intriguing hearsay in this vast post-telecommunications world, concern a few small, remote, volcanic archipelagos thought to harbor populations with some degree of persistent fertility. That the islands are volcanic is significant: in theory, humans exposed over many generations to the aerosolized ejecta of regularly occurring geothermal eruptions—gas, steam, ash—may possess special genetic immunities to the devastating microbes that were mixed into every cubic millimeter of our lower troposphere twelve years ago. Microbes thought to have originated in geothermally heated groundwater were broadcast far and wide by the series of massive, intentionally triggered volcanic eruptions popularly known as the Pinatubo Solution. (More on this infamous colossal boondoggle later, perhaps. Trust me, you don't want me to go into it now.)

One of these anomalous archipelagos is thought to be the Juan Fernández Islands off the Pacific coast of South America, but getting there now that the Panama Canal is closed would have required us to either sail all the way around Cape Horn and back, or to set off across the North American continent by land, with the uncertain goal of trying to beg or steal a seaworthy boat in what used to be California or Mexico, and returning. Crossing the Atlantic and part of the Mediterranean, as it happens, is a far easier lift, which is why the second anomalous archipelago—the Aeolian chain near Sicily, and specifically the small island of Stromboli—is our chosen destination. When we arrive, our goal will be to locate between one and three fertile females and to bring them back with us across the ocean to the Centauri Project Lab, which is located in the northwestern region of what used to be the state of New Hampshire.

Now the time has come for me to enjoy a few hours' sleep before our captain passes by my berth, ringing his accursed vintage cowbell to wake me in time for my four-hour watch. My plan is to be as diligent as possible with these entries from now on. To recount everything exactly as it unfolds, with the hope that by the time you finish reading these pages you will be in possession of the complete story of our unlikely quest. If we succeed, it will be a story for the ages. If we fail, then you, dear reader, are likely nothing but the fleeting construct of one long-dead woman's overly optimistic imagination.

3

10151 A.U.C.T. +/- 18.583 years (estimated)

It's hard to believe that he's walking over the same ground he once knew so well. As far as he can tell there's nothing left of the Centauri Project Lab compound: the Quonset huts, the reassembled airplane hangar that had once housed the clean room and the storage area for the Time Dilation Sphere systems, the restored historic Round Barn that had once served as the team's living quarters and refectory. He can find no hint of a foundation, no bricks or PVC plumbing or fragments of aluminum siding, no shards of broken glass. Where once there were parking lots, the solar array and wind farm, the gardens and orchards, the rocky pasturelands close-cropped by the Lab's herd of cantankerous goats, the electrified perimeter fence with its automatic security gate—now there seems to be nothing but ferns and moss-draped deadfall, boulders and sphagnum moss and old-growth hardwoods with massive buttressed root flares emerging from thousands of years' accumulation of leaf litter and organic soil. He looks for traces of the old asphalt access road that once connected the Lab to the rural highway into town, but of course there's nothing but uninhabited forest.

Not uninhabited, he corrects himself. Filled with a diversity of life he's never come close to experiencing before, with birdsong and small mammals chittering, and the throbbing many-voiced chorus of pollinating insects, and the high-pitched yip of some unseen larger mammal—probably canine—and the scent of tree blossoms on the moisture-laden breeze, and rays of golden green sunlight filtering down through a dripping canopy supported by trees so massive that any one of their trunks would have merited a celebratory plaque in his day.

A vastly richer ecosystem than the one he left behind, for sure. Which is good to see, because it means that a number of worst-case scenarios didn't play out. The thermal maximum would have come and gone thousands of years ago. The feedback loops must have stabilized too, allowing the super-greenhouse climate to level off and perhaps even to subside somewhat as the carbon worked its way out of the atmosphere and back into the geology. By all appearances the damage to biodiversity hasn't been as terrible as it could have been, though it has certainly been bad enough. Before he'd gone down into the cave the losses had been predicted to range from fifty-five to eighty-five percent of all living species: oceans stripped of life, pollinators decimated, forests silent and full of rot, increasing swaths of the planet rendered barren and uninhabitable. A sixth mass extinction; the unmistakable signature of *H. sapiens*—greed, incompetence, blind stupidity—marked indelibly in the planet's geological record.

What he's seeing now, though, proves that it would have been foolish to worry about the capacity of nature writ large to carry on. A sixth extinction, yes, but perhaps of a less catastrophic magnitude than many had feared. Not on the scale of the End-Permian, for example, when the dominant lifeform for the next million years or so had been a species of bacterial slime. For a professional biologist who'd spent his entire career observing the planet's declining ecosystems with resignation and despair, this feels like a triumph. A good deal more observation and study is in order, but it definitely has the feel of a planet undisturbed by any recent footprint of *H. sapiens*.

With this thought, a tide of loneliness floods in. He hasn't had a chance to mourn the members of the team who were still alive when he'd climbed into that sphere, some of whom he'd known for decades. Natalie first and foremost; Isaac, the Ghanaian aeronautics engineer; Priscilla, the team's long-time communications director; Keiko, the team's IT wizard. And there were those he hadn't had a chance to get to know as well: the junior mechanical engineers, the local couple who'd been brought in to plant the organic gardens and build the Lab's herd of goats, Natalie's brother Tollie, a sometime fishing companion in the small trout streams surrounding Cornelius Quist's mountain retreat, and the beautiful if at times prickly young physician Alejandra Morgan-Ochoa.

Follow the protocol, he reminds himself. *You're here for a reason. It's the only way you're going to keep hold of your sanity.*

In order to do that, though, he needs to find his way back to the cave entrance, which he stupidly seems to have misplaced. He searches for the little stream where he lay for a long time recovering, but he can't find that either, and he kicks himself for not having thought to break a few saplings or otherwise mark his path. Reasoning that climbing a tall tree might give him a better perspective of things, he finds an ancient hemlock growing at the edge of a small clearing with branches low enough that he can climb up into it without too much effort. A family of flying squirrels jabbers in alarm at his approach, streaming out of the tree's upper branches like ruddy paper airplanes. Odd to see them flying in daylight; back in his time, if he remembers correctly, they'd been mostly nocturnal. Well, it wouldn't be the first evolutionary shift he's seen in this place, to be expected after millennia.

He climbs up into the swaying treetop and gazes out over the old-growth forest. The leafy green canopy stretches out in all directions, unbroken except by a few lakes and ponds and the highest point in the surrounding landscape—the reassuringly familiar exposed granite pinnacle of Mount Wingandicoa. The sky above the canopy is cloudless and teeming with birds: flocks of white egrets and honking Canada geese, crows and ravens wheeling, turkey vultures and raptors riding the thermals. He tries to use the mountaintop to triangulate his current location compared to the former Lab site, but it's nowhere near precise enough. He'll have to try to find it walking the forest floor.

By nightfall he still hasn't stumbled upon the cave, and he wonders with increasing frustration if he ever will. He chooses a sleeping place in the thick moss blanketing a flat-topped glacial erratic. It's a comfortable bed if an uneasy one. Insects bite, and hunger gnaws. The night sounds are loud and mostly unfamiliar. Strange grunts and yips and stealthy footfalls in the leaf litter below the boulder.

In the middle of the night he awakes to a chorus of wolf song, loud and heart-stoppingly nearby. It makes sense that this ecosystem would have at least one apex predator. Something to celebrate, certainly. *Canis lupus*, great avatar of the primeval wilderness, its wavering howls heralding the return of something he personally has longed for all his life. Now, though, shivering in his Lab-issue nylon-blend jumpsuit in a bed of damp moss atop an elevated boulder, with the moonless night pressing in, not even a pocketknife to protect himself, he feels vulnerable in a way he's never felt before.

He doesn't sleep well, and when the first hints of dawn provide enough light to see a few hundred yards through the forest, he's up scouring the understory for food. His stomach, apparently, has recovered enough to start functioning normally again, and he's famished. There are ghost-white flushes of oyster mushrooms shelving many of the stumps and fallen trees, and there are wild leeks growing up through the leaf litter. Turning over rocks he finds a rich array of ants, grubs, beetles, and earthworms, though nothing in his previous fieldwork has prepared him for the sensation of eating raw live insects and annelids. He will have to become more systematic in his foraging if he hopes to set the habits for long-term survival.

All morning he looks for the cave. Occasionally he spots a topographical feature that seems to ring a bell—the slope of a ravine, a particular arrangement of boulders—but in truth these surroundings are completely unfamiliar. It's not surprising after ten thousand years of growth, decay, soil accumulation, floods, and landslides. *Ten thousand years*. A nearly inconceivable timespan on the scale of one human life, though barely the blink of an eye geologically speaking. From a rational perspective he understands what his eyes are showing him—or rather, what they're *not* showing him—but it's still a shock to experience how thoroughly all human traces have been obliterated from this previously familiar landscape.

Eventually he finds the Lab site, recognizing a fin of quartz-veined granite that used to jut up out of the pasture behind the Round Barn. The fin was once at least twenty feet higher off the ground, but it's clearly the same geological feature. If he were to excavate on the downhill side he might actually find the foundation of the building where members of the Centauri Project team used to sleep, eat, and drink, and—well—make love, among other things. For now, though, he needs to find that cave entrance. Even with a good visual memory of its location across a sloping pasture a mere stone's throw from the vanished compound, it takes him another hour to locate it among the ferns, boulders, and moss-covered logs of the forest floor, just a few stagger-steps from the silt-bottomed pool in the little brook that sustained him following his emergence.

Set into a reasonably steep slope, protected from landslides and accumulating soil by the overhang of a large limestone slab, the cave opening is situated for long-term viability. Even without the natural camouflage of roots and leaf litter it would have been hard to find. From the outside it has the look of an animal burrow, and a small one at that. A winter den for a woodchuck maybe, or a fox.

The massive TDS and its staging equipment hadn't been disassembled and squeezed down this tiny passage, of course. It had been lowered in by a crane through a much larger cavity that was later roofed in by the placement and burial of several colossal stone slabs. Only firsthand knowledge of that expansive lower chamber would give anyone the confidence to wriggle in through such a constrictive hole in the ground; even now the thought of doing it fills him with dread. But the protocol requires it, and he has his own urgent reasons to confirm what is or is not present in the chamber that he might have missed as he'd made his way up out of the darkness to the surface of the planet in his newly awakened daze.

Still, it takes a major exertion of will to get down on his belly and squeeze himself headfirst into that tiny hole. Despite his best efforts to remain calm, his breathing comes in semi-panicked gasps as he crawls down into the claustrophobic darkness of an entry passage tight enough that he can barely raise his head, much less back up.

It's a relief when he finally senses the ceiling of the cave opening out into the much larger though still pitch-black chamber. There he uses the small ferrocerium rod and striker sewn tightly into the sleeve of his jumpsuit (the only equipment besides the clothing he'd been allowed to bring with him into the sphere), along with some peels of yellow birchbark he's collected to spark a bright, short-lived flame.

Short-lived, but bright enough for him to see what he's come back for—or rather, he realizes with a plummeting in his stomach, *not* to see what he's come back for. The chamber is very much the same as when he last saw it, lit by LED work lights, on the day of his departure. Within it is absolutely nothing else. No new opening, no door or passageway leading back to some newly excavated chamber, and most devastating of all, no second or third sphere. Just blank cave walls and the massive, broken-open eggshell of his own expired sphere. It's not a surprise, not really, though a part of him had dared to hold out hope.

The motion inside the sphere was intense and prolonged enough that it had been deemed unsafe to place any object besides his own clothed body inside it; too much of a risk that such an object could have slipped its housing and battered him to death. Still, the lack of survival equipment waiting for him in the cave surprises him. Perhaps some members of the team *did* leave it there and it was later stolen; or perhaps they'd intended to place it but had for some reason never gotten the chance. The situation had already been dicey when they'd sealed him in; no doubt it had gotten worse in the months and years that followed.

What became of them?

It makes him feel sick to his stomach even thinking about it.

Back out in the daylight he spends a numb half-hour clearing some of the roots and debris from around the opening, then marks the spot by bending two saplings to form an archway and tying them together with vines.

Of course he'd considered the possibility that the team's final efforts might fail. Still, along with the rest of the team, his default assumption had been that each link in the chain of necessary events would click successfully into place. What other choice had they had, really, in the pursuit of their improbable goals? The Centauri Project had represented the best chance, and in all likelihood the *only* chance, to save the human species from extinction. It would have been foolish to dwell on all the things that might possibly have gone wrong.

He doubts anyone else on the team could have fully comprehended, however, in purely emotional terms, what failure would mean for a lone survivor. The irreversibility of the choice he'd made. The high probability that he would never again glimpse the outlines of another human face.

Still, his duty remains clear. Follow the protocol. Which means that he needs to get to work on establishing a viable long-term camp.

4

March 5, 2068 (12 A.U.C.T.)
The Atlantic Ocean

The burning of fossil fuels was prohibited by international law in the year 2047 C.E. It remains so in theory, although of course that doesn't stop anyone with the means of getting their hands on some from using it. The law is irrelevant now, anyway. The damage was done decades before it was ratified, and the signatory governments no longer exist. And with the human species teetering on the brink of extinction, it seems unlikely that anyone is going to have the wherewithal to tap or dig up those fossil forests that still remain underground.

Back in the forties, humanity's doomsday clock was already ticking dangerously close to midnight, driven by the so-called "methane pulse," an abrupt summer thaw of the frozen gas deposits under thermokarst lakes in the arctic circle. Four billion tons of methane escaped over the span of just a few months, bringing atmospheric carbon up to a percentage unseen for fifty-six million years, since the period known as the Pleistocene-Eocene Thermal Maximum (PETM).

Unlike in the PETM though, changes to our climate were unfolding in the geological blink of an eye. Faster-than-predicted melting had already erased the lower-latitude ice fields and now set off a runaway retreat of the destabilized Antarctic ice cliffs. Acidification had accelerated the conversion of large swaths of ocean into the sour, breathless soup we're sailing across today. Virtually every coral reef was bleached dead by mid-century. Enormous phytoplankton blooms, first in the Barents Sea, then all over the globe, caused widespread die-offs at the base of the food chain, and a terrifying reduction in overall marine biomass. In 2050 the consumption of wild seafood was banned by international law. Meanwhile, inland from the shrinking coastlines, rapid warming, habitat decimation, and the long-term overuse of pesticides came together in the so-called "insect apocalypse": a bottom-up trophic cascade leading to the slow-motion collapse of human food systems. The consumption of non-chicken, non-lab-grown meat was prohibited in 2055, but this did little to head off the horrific famines sweeping the globe. The international refugee crisis reached never-before-seen levels, sparking new wars, new genocides, and the collapse of many world governments.

The chain of events leading up to what effectively appears to have been the end of human history began with a seemingly positive development. Policymakers from the remaining world powers finally decided to get together and take decisive action. A newly minted protocol was signed at Davos (the summit had been scheduled for Copenhagen but flooding had rendered that location untenable), and the resulting project—popularly known, again, as the Pinatubo Solution, after the great twentieth-century eruption that had cooled the planet for a few years—became the largest scientific collaboration in history. With operational theaters in Iceland, Alaska, Kamchatka, Indonesia, and Chile, the project used bunker bombs and a scaled-up version of deep-drilling technology that had been developed for so-called hydro-fracking to trigger a chain of large, more or less simultaneous volcanic eruptions. The idea was that the eruptions would jettison a massive cloud of sulfates and other particulates into the stratosphere, blocking out enough of the sun's warming rays to put a temporary halt to greenhouse warming, while the world's scientific and tech elites mounted an all-out effort to develop some kind of technology capable of stuffing the climate genie back into its bottle.

And to a measurable extent, it worked. The next two years were cool, wet, and dark. There were snowstorms on the eastern seaboard such as hadn't been seen for decades. Members of the Centauri team spent our lunch breaks skating on the Charles; some of us drove up to New Hampshire to explore Dr. Q's family property on cross-country skis. News that the polar ice caps were actually *gaining* mass set off a wave of elation across the globe, and many humans—especially those not suffering from acute seasonal affective disorder and other ailments related to vitamin D deprivation—gazed up into the pelting snowflakes with a renewed sense of optimism.

Of course the cooling didn't last. As the sulfates and particulate matter settled back to earth, greenhouse warming returned with a vengeance. And despite a few encouraging technological developments, humanity's fragile hopes were soon shattered by an even deadlier catastrophe.

The precise origin of the pathogen was never pinpointed, though it was thought to have been released during those intentionally triggered worldwide volcanic eruptions. Some theorized it had originated in the geothermal melting of the permafrost around Kamchatka's Klyuchevskaya volcano group; others believed that it had emerged from the disruption of the microbiome of subglacial vents in Iceland, or lava flows interacting with polluted groundwater in Indonesia. Whatever its exact source, the pathogen's nature was clear enough: a new mutation of a microorganism previously unknown to science, with a lifecycle that had once been confined to geothermally heated water features such as hot springs, geysers, and deep-sea vents.

By the time epidemiologists discovered that the disease was transmitted not through person-to-person contact but via aerosolized dispersal throughout the troposphere, more than a third of humanity was dead. Among the recovered, even those whose encounter with the disease had been entirely asymptomatic, the mechanisms of human reproduction were no longer viable.

Across the globe, demoralized human societies entered a rapid process of decline. Governments could no longer cope. Disaster aid was a figment of the golden past. Health care, telecommunications, and most other essential infrastructure fell into disarray and failure, and looting, murder, rapine, famine, and secondary diseases all became rampant. If the planet itself is a living organism, it has an immune system strong enough to rid itself of the species that has been assailing it.

Here on the *Solar Barque*, we have solar panels that can be set up and broken down easily in case of high winds or bad weather, and which we use to run the kitchen implements and recharge the batteries of various gadgets and instruments. The panels are limited in size and wouldn't provide enough juice for an electric motor, which is why we rely on sail, and we carry a vintage internal combustion backup along with several large containers of hoarded diesel fuel reserved for the strictest emergencies.

As to food, our main protein is what we not-so-fondly refer to as "Lab jerky": salt-brined tofu strips sprinkled with various spices and sun-dried to the approximate consistency of old cardboard. In addition we have sacks full of dehydrated fruits and veggies from the Lab's orchards and gardens, and a supply of powdered mushroom elixirs—lion's mane, reishi, chaga—that serve as a substitute for previously imported coffees and teas. These aren't so bad actually, though I would trade a few gold bars for a café Cubano or a hot chai with fresh cow milk. Luxuries that seem impossible these days, like half-remembered childhood dreams.

Now that the wind has picked up, Captain Tollie has been keeping us busy with sailing-crew tasks. As I write this, sitting behind the bowsprit in a rare idle moment, it's a fresh afternoon on the ocean, with the yacht moving along at a good clip over hill-like mid-Atlantic swells. The wind is a constant background roar, the water a perfect bottle-green topped by an ever-shifting tracery of white sea foam, and a fine invisible mist of seawater cools our faces. It's easy to imagine that the ocean passing beneath our fast-slicing hull remains healthy, pristine, and teeming with unseen life.

This is far from true, of course; our week in the doldrums gave us a clear enough glimpse of that. Day after day of drifting listlessly through a languid gyre of brightly colored plastic degrading slowly in the sun. Down to its component nurdles, apparently, to join the underwater smog-cloud that now pervades this planet's oceanic realm. And plastic is the least of it, unfortunately. Humanity's carbon emissions have mostly ended by now, but the built-in time lag means that the seas will continue to warm, and continue on their steep upward curve of acidification, for many decades to come.

We do sail through rafts of jellyfish—Portuguese men-of-war catching the wind with their transparent purple balloon-sails; billions of translucent blobs pulsating through the waters around us at any given hour like a vast army of blind ghosts—but it's hard to know what else might still be living below the surface. It is safe to assume that a staggering number of species that would previously have been swimming or drifting down there are gone forever. But there are no human marine biologists with scuba tanks taking inventories anymore; so again, we have no way of knowing.

Yet even as thoughts like these bring me to the brink of despair, when I glance up from writing these words, the tiny wavelets on the surface glitter beautifully in the sun and the salt spray on my lips tastes pleasant. The wind whistles in the riggings, keeping the sailcloth taut as it propels the *Solar Barque* exhilaratingly up and down one big swell after another, and the sun paints a swath of hammered gold across the dancing surface of the ocean, which has darkened just in the last few moments from bottle green to steel blue.

So why not take solace in the truth that the planet is still a beautiful place? That nature, in some form, will inevitably outlive us? It seems possible, at times, to indulge in the fantasy that everything's going to be okay. That a happy life is still possible. That one still might have a shot, for example, at growing old in the company of a loving partner, or even—because we're talking pure fantasy now—surrounded by laughing children, who will in turn experience the happiness of preparing the ground for their own descendants and heirs.

Ridiculous, of course, this fantasy. Just the cast-off shell of an ancestral instinct I suppose, as dead and meaningless as the memory of taking a long hot shower, or watching a movie on Netflix, or climbing into bed between sheets still warm from the dryer. Pizza delivery, the internet, universally available antibiotics. That grocery store down the block where you could buy olive oil, avocadoes, wild salmon, tampons.

Back in the real world, the system that delivered all these items we once took for granted is long dead and gone. Cities and towns are in full collapse, emptied out or mostly so. The rusting shells of plants and refineries, shuttered post offices and vacant transportation hubs, looted museums and big-box stores picked clean: the rusting, mildewed, weed-covered ruins of a not-so-great civilization.

Indulge me another moment or two, reader, while I nurture these impossible fantasies. Then we will be carried away by this faintly chemical mid-ocean breeze.

Ptolemy Quist spends most of his time at the helm in a swiveling stool shaded by the sun-faded cockpit bimini, listening to electronica playlists on an antique smartphone, a tiny piece of salvaged tech he keeps charged with the yacht's solar panels. He does wear headphones, but he keeps the volume high enough that if you stand anywhere near him you can hear its tinny essence. The driving beat keeps him alert, he says, but I'm pretty sure it's the music's numbing repetitiveness that attracts him. It saves him from having to think.

Tollie. Our surf-shorts-clad skipper with the unruly gray curls and the prominent unshaven jaw. A good-looking man I suppose, in his mid-fifties and athletic for his age, with a weathered bronze complexion and impressively muscular forearms. You can see the family resemblance of course, though in Dr. Q the blunt features are handsomely balanced, like a fine woodcarving in seasoned walnut, whereas in Tollie they're more exaggerated, especially that epic jaw, like an old Hollywood superhero gone to seed.

Their mother died in a helicopter accident when the siblings were still in college. Their father, shattered, retreated to the mountains of northern New Hampshire, where he spent several years buying up all the available acreage around the secluded off-grid compound that later became the Centauri Lab. Before his death he sold the remainder of his extensive properties around the world and converted much of the resulting fortune into minted gold ingots, some of which, as I believe I've mentioned, we have with us to grease the skids on this voyage. Soon after putting the finishing touches on his survivalist Shangri-La, Cornelius Quist died of cardiomyopathy—or, as might have been written in the old days, of a broken heart.

Unlike his brilliant sister, Tollie didn't use his inheritance to become a groundbreaking scientific pioneer. Instead he bought a vintage Hinckley yacht and outfitted it in style, taking groups of wealthy tourists on tequila-soaked sailing tours of the Maritime Provinces and the increasingly sweltering Caribbean. I've no doubt that he went through some exertions in those years—I'm sure there were moments when that job was tougher than it sounds—but I also have no doubt, having come to know Tollie pretty well over the last few months, that he's spent the majority of the last several decades as humanity lurched ever closer to the catastrophic abyss sailing on the ocean, grooving to vintage electronica, and smoking his famous homegrown weed.

You can probably tell that I don't think all that much of our skipper, though I feel duty-bound to state right off the bat that as the owner of the *Solar Barque*, and by far our most experienced sailor, Tollie is an absolutely indispensable member of this expeditionary team.

Seeing as how I've already begun introducing the cast of characters for this little ocean-going stage play, let me continue down the list. Besides Dr. Q and her brother, there are two other team members aboard. The younger of these is James Swamp: half-Jamaican, half-Native American (his father was a certified member of the Mohawk nation), James is an introvert and a dreamer. In his free time he can usually be found poring over obsolete birding guides, as if committing these beautiful creatures' former habits and characteristics to memory will somehow counteract the hard reality that so many of them have been lost to the world forever.

Tall and muscular and somewhat ponderous in his movements, James keeps the hoodie of his Lab-issued jumpsuit constantly pulled up, even when he's out of the sun. He does this to hide his face and bald skull, which are badly disfigured by scarring from a near-fatal encounter with the hyperpandemic. I'm not sure why his constant use of the hoodie bothers me so much, but it does. I understand that he is self-conscious about his appearance, but he's also among friends, and all of us do already know what he looks like and why. It's as if he imagines that a filthy, fraying hood made of vintage Patagonia Sunshade fabric exempts him from ever having to share a personal moment with any of us.

And it's not only the hoodie that annoys me. There's an undeniable power contained within James's big body, a latent athleticism that could be put to impressive use. Unfortunately, he spends most of his time hunched in a deck chair leafing through those bird guides or scanning the ocean through binoculars on some kind of melancholy vigil for survivors of the mass extinction. He's like a grizzly bear with a butterfly net, or Ferdinand the Bull with a hoodie, to which I would not object, except that the success of this mission is going to depend on neither butterfly nets nor Ferdinand-the-Bull sensitivity. It's going to call for alertness, cold-eyed pragmatism, and, most likely, very bold action. When the moment comes, assuming it does, we're all going to need to display a certain pitilessness, even cruelty, in the name of a much greater cause. I have to resist the urge to tell him to straighten up in his chair.

It's not my place, though. He's twenty-eight years old and I'm thirty-five—only seven years difference. Not some kind of hierarchical superior, and not even close to a mother figure.

Which brings me to the fourth and last member of our voyaging crew: your faithful correspondent. A physician by training, the entirety of my career has unfolded in times of increasingly dire global crisis, meaning that I've been exposed and perhaps in some ways desensitized to the realities of mass trauma and death.

Once upon a time you might have called me Cuban American—back when there were places you could still call Cuba and the United States of America. I was born in Havana, in the middle of the third decade of the twenty-first century on the Gregorian calendar, the only daughter of a Boston-born Anglo-American journalist (my father) and a Cuban installation artist (my mother), both of whom achieved a certain measure of international renown in their youth. I won't mention names because no one can be expected to remember them now, much less in the hypothetical deep future where you, my hypothetical reader, reside.

I was only seven years old when we had to leave the island. I remember hurricane sirens, roofing tin tumbling demonically past in the rushing wind, the terrible sound of loudly splintering trees, and a strong tide flowing like a filthy, corpse-strewn river up the avenue in front of our house in Miramar. I remember the stink of it.

My father's extended family were from Boston, so that's where we ended up. I attended college and medical school there, and after my parents died, I eventually met Dr. Q there. She was in her late thirties by then, already considered one of the great scientists of her generation. I was a third-year medical student interviewing for a prestigious summer program focused on women in science. I remember quaking with nervousness as I shrugged on one of the Centauri Project's white lab coats hanging in the foyer of the original lab on the MIT campus. But there was no need to be nervous; from the beginning she went out of her way to put me at ease as I entered her glassed-in office, which had a big window overlooking the clean room where they were at the time assembling a prototype of her greatest invention, the Time Dilation Sphere (TDS). I don't remember much about that first conversation, though I do remember walking out of the lab feeling highly exhilarated and hopeful about the future, despite all the ominous news stories dominating the airwaves at the time.

Two years later, she lured me away from a residency at Brigham and Women's hospital to work as a medical advisor to the Centauri team. This was around the time that the international geo-engineering catastrophe known as the Pinatubo Solution was taking effect, before the onset of the hyperpandemic. Dr. Q hadn't made it public yet, but I'm pretty sure she was already contemplating moving the entire Centauri Project to her father's off-grid compound in New Hampshire. When she made the move I was invited to come along as a core member of the team, and I've been with her ever since. It has been the honor of my life.

As the team's only surviving physician, my sole responsibility is to provide medical advice and care to my fellow voyagers—all of whom, I'm happy to report, are for the moment in excellent health. With the world as it is today, however, we all live under the constant threat of coming down with an array of serious illnesses, and my most important job is to administer a daily regimen of immune support: vitamins, zinc, probiotics, and an antiviral prophylaxis. Tollie jokes that my job is to come around twice a day and make everyone feel like throwing up. He's not far off the mark, though of course I do it for their own good.

People who don't know me well (i.e., most people) probably think of me as prickly and somewhat lacking in a sense of humor. I'll cop to being prickly at times, though not to being humorless. If I sometimes project the impression of coolness, or unassailability, it's only because I've had to armor myself. Despite what I mentioned above about having been desensitized by catastrophe, my secret flaw is that I am in some ways far *too* sensitive. My radar is attuned to what others are thinking and doing, and I often find it impossible to turn that radar off. I don't tell you any of this out of pride. In fact, I wish that I had a different kind of personality.

Earlier today, for example, Dr. Q and I were sitting together reading on the cushioned benches in the shade of the forward bimini. Both our colleagues were out of earshot, and I confided to her some of my concerns about James. The way he'd hesitated this morning before complying with my repeated requests that he do the breakfast dishes. How he's seemed unusually quiet in recent days, keeping himself hidden in the privacy of his pulled-up hoodie. That when it comes down to it, given his general attitude, I'm not a hundred percent sure that we'll be able to rely on him if things get dicey.

Dr. Q listened carefully, both of us gazing out at the undulating swells. When I finished speaking she met my eyes, and instead of her usual look of fondness or amusement, her expression was one of deep exasperation.

"For heaven's sake, Al dear, none of us is perfect. Can't you just give it a rest?"

5

10151 A.U.C.T. +/- 18.583 years (estimated)

Near sundown he climbs another tree to get a view of the mountain. Exhaustion is hitting him in waves now. He's weak, undernourished, lightheaded, still reeling from revisiting the empty cave chamber. Still, he's ready to move on to the next item on the protocol: locating or creating a secure long-term refuge. This will be a task for tomorrow, however. For tonight, he settles on another moss-covered glacial erratic, this one higher off the ground in a grove of tall white pines. He gathers a few armloads of leaf litter to add to the moss, resulting in a reasonably comfortable bed, but he can't fall asleep. He watches the branches of the immense pines swaying back and forth in the night breezes above him, the crescent moon appearing and disappearing behind the swaying needles. The rich tapestry of stars above the canopy is unquestionably pristine now—no light pollution from cities, spotlights, satellites, jet traffic—but he finds it difficult to savor.

A memory of barbecuing on a summer night back at the Lab. Himself at the grill with an apron and a spatula; the other team members sitting around lantern-lit picnic tables behind the Round Barn, with the same moon rising over the pasturelands. The smell of paraffin and roasting meat. A whole chicken marinating in home-brewed beer, and a dozen eggplant fruits from the Lab's garden, the leftovers of which he would leave on the grill overnight for Natalie to scoop out in the morning to make her famous baba ghanoush.

Another memory: a summer night at his childhood home in the foothills west of Denver. His father grilling ears of corn and a thick steak, the grease sizzling off it and drawing up the flames. His mother sitting on the bottom stair of the deck, her hands busy knitting a sweater or checking messages on her cell phone, smiling, teasing him gently about something, he can't remember what. His childhood feels so distant now. Like a dream, or a half-remembered passage from a book he'd once read.

He'd lost both parents seven years before the hyperpandemic. One of the megafires that incinerated Denver's Front Range foothills in the summer of '49. The stairs his mother had been sitting on, the deck itself, his childhood home, all the other houses in a twenty-mile radius—converted, one windy night, into fine white ash. He hadn't been home for nearly five years by the time the fire hit and had plenty of excuses for his lack of attentiveness. He'd been busy with fieldwork, writing his dissertation at MIT, falling in love with Natalie. Air travel was prohibitively expensive, reservations difficult to arrange. In the end, though, these were flimsy excuses. He'd been flying to South America at least twice a year for research; it wouldn't have been that hard to arrange for a layover in Denver. He's never quite overcome the sense of guilt he feels for that lack of attentiveness. His grief for his parents still feels unrealized, like an amputation undertaken in his sleep, without his prior knowledge. A phantom ache that hits him at the oddest moments and never really goes away.

He forages at the edge of a swamp in the lowlands, harvesting cattail shoots and a leopard frog he manages to trap with his bare foot. It's wonderful to see a frog, or any amphibian, and he feels a momentary twinge of regret as he strangles it. He rinses it in swamp water and contemplates the best way to eat it. In the end he only manages the legs, which he rips from the body with his teeth, spitting out the mangled bones and cartilage. He keeps the meat down, and with his shrunken stomach filled for now, sets off for the mountain.

It proves to be slow going. The hike used to take about an hour and a half walking directly from the compound, but back then the lower terrain was open pastureland with a well-marked trail up through the forest to the summit. Now he must pick his way through downed logs and undergrowth, with his atrophied muscles aching and barely up to the job. So he takes his time, resting often, and reaches the still-treeless rock pinnacle by midafternoon.

It's exactly as he remembers it. An uncanny air of permanence seems to suffuse the place, as if some gas radiating up from the lichen-covered slabs and abutments has allowed the mountain to resist the passage of time. He even finds the original U.S. Geological Survey marker driven into the highest crag, its lettering illegible now but the characteristic little brass disk still clearly recognizable. For a moment the discovery feels pulse-quickeningly momentous, like the first step in the solution to a difficult puzzle. In the next breath he's transported by a memory of standing in this exact place with Natalie, early in their relationship, on a visit to her father at his compound years before it became the Centauri Project Lab. A breezy autumn day, couples and families sprawled out on the boulders picnicking and gazing out at the view. A group of teenagers clowning dangerously with their cell phones at the edge of the cliff. Natalie skylined a few yards away, young and beautiful, wearing a sky-blue down vest, her supple prematurely gray-streaked hair blowing in the wind that alternately hid and exposed her face. He said something to her, possibly to get her attention so he could snap a picture with his phone, and she turned slowly, smiling in that special way she used to have, her friendly yet distracted eyes slightly magnified by the big lenses of her spectacles as a compartment of her mind pondered, no doubt, the solution to some stubborn problem in quantum physics or practical engineering.

The image fades, and he's alone again on the granite peak amid the lichen and some lowbush blueberry scrub and a few thickets of wind-blasted krummholz. Three large birds circle the mountain, turkey vultures is his first thought, but upon more careful examination their shapes show them to be some sort of raptor, a large hawk or eagle of the same unfamiliar species he spotted from the treetop, enormous and black with a surprisingly huge wingspan.

The sun is veiled by a translucent scrim of overcast and the surrounding topography has a three-dimensional look, somehow miniaturized, as if he could just reach out and trace the valleys and ridges with his fingertips. Stretching out in all directions is the old-growth forest, the tall crowns of dark-needled hemlocks and white pines standing out from the spring-green canopy of hardwood leaves. Tracing the bottom of a long valley to the west glints the snakelike ribbon of what they used to call the Connecticut River. A series of gentle ridgelines echoes off westward across what used to be Vermont, with the white blur of an approaching rainstorm obscuring the profiles of the more distant Green Mountains. This mountaintop has a fifty-mile, three-hundred-and-sixty-degree view, and he can make out no artificial clearings or other signs of human life. It's getting cold.

Climbing down from the summit, about a third of the way down the mountain perhaps, he finds a ledge of protruding granite with a south-facing aspect and a good view of the forest below. The ledge is smooth and sun-warmed, cupped by the mountainside and framed by yellow birch and hemlock saplings in a way that gives it a nice feeling of combined refuge and outlook. Up against the mountainside the root ball of an ancient hemlock partially toppled by the wind provides a ready-made sleeping grotto naturally sheltered from the rain. A good place to set up a long-term camp, he figures. Protected by the mountainside from north winds and stalking predators, it has an expansive view and there is the advantage of a small spring water rivulet trickling downslope just a short walk away.

He gathers firewood and birchbark peelings and sparks a flame with the ferrocerium rod. He finds a rotting log covered with oyster mushrooms, breaks off a green branch to roast the tender white fungus over the fire, and turns over rocks, forcing himself to eat a few of the squirming invertebrates he uncovers. After the meal he sits cross-legged on the sun-warmed ledge, watching the red sun sink below the horizon as three or four species of dragonfly zigzag in and out of his view.

The team threw Nick a candlelit party in the dining room of the Round Barn the night before he left. The gates of the compound had been sealed for months. There was only one radio station still operating in the local service area; no power grid, no internet. They were living on hoarded soy protein, eggs from the Lab's chickens, milk and cheese from the Lab's goat herd, fruit and vegetables from the compound's extensive gardens and orchards, many of which had first been planted decades earlier by Cornelius Quist. They had a backup generator and a utility room stacked with carbon nanotube batteries charged daily by the Lab's large solar array—though they'd turned off all but the essential appliances for this occasion. The candles felt just right, warm and intimate and redolent of ritual. The whole team was there, what was left of it at that point, a dozen people of various ages and genders sitting around the long farm table, a summer breeze wafting in through the screen windows, the warm flicker of the candle flames giving everyone the look of apostles or prophets. There was a dash of excitement in the air, despite the deteriorating conditions outside the gate and the well-founded dread of everything that could possibly go wrong. There was a feeling of destiny, and determined resolve.

He said his goodbyes to those he wouldn't be seeing again, and he and Natalie went to bed one last time. They made love tenderly, shed some tears, talked for hours, and managed to fall asleep for a few more hours.

At dawn, accompanied by the team's young physician, the brilliant and unsmiling Alejandra Morgan-Ochoa, they walked uphill across the pasture to the cavern, which was at that time not a cavern at all but an excavated, mostly covered pit with a metal staircase leading down into it from a hole in its ceiling yet to be roofed in and buried. The space felt especially desolate that morning, lit by industrial work lights, with the sphere lurking in a corner like the egg of some huge magnesium-alloy spider.

Natalie threw a switch and the sphere emitted a hydraulic sigh as it cracked open. Nick climbed in and began strapping himself into the webbing as Dr. Alejandra, who looked about twelve but in reality was in her early twenties, pulled his limbs this way and that, tightening various nylon straps and harnesses and inserting various needles and tubes connecting the cryoprotectant control system to key points on his body: wrists, throat, inner thigh, temples. When that was done the young doctor said her brisk goodbyes, wishing him good luck and good health on behalf of all humanity.

He took a few deep breaths, attempting to clear his mind. It had been his intention to remain calm and professional despite the obvious risks of death, oblivion, and solitary exile. *Keep a cheerful outlook*, he told himself, *just as Natalie would do if our positions were reversed.* But that was easier said than done.

Contorted awkwardly around the feeds and harness, Natalie held him in a long embrace. Then she kissed him on the lips, keeping a tight hold on his hand as she carefully extricated herself from the tubes and webbing. "Think how fascinating it will be, Nick. Witnessing all the changes."

He nodded, fighting back tears. "I wish we could witness them together."

She produced a fleeting smile, the work lights glinting on the big lenses of her glasses, and gave his hand one last squeeze. "We'll find you some company, don't worry. And you'll have the honor of helping to give our species a chance to get it right this time."

Tears streamed down both their faces. She flipped a switch and the pharmacological cocktail began to flow through his veins. He thought of one last thing he wanted to tell her—something about keeping an eye out for each other in their dreams—but by then it was too late. She tightened the straps of the respirator over his mouth and flipped another switch, and the tubes extended themselves like a braided snake down into his gullet. His field of vision contracted like the aperture of an old camera closing in, and he was plunged into the dreamless darkness that would be his dwelling place—assuming the sphere functioned as intended—for the next 10,150 years of coordinate time (plus or minus 18.583 years). When the cold fusion reactor had run its course, the tubes had retracted and the sphere had dumped him unceremoniously onto the cavern's cold limestone floor.

Was the team unable to locate another viable subject? Apparently so. Did an even more deadly variant of the microbe sweep through, or had some other unforeseeable disaster put a premature end to the whole enterprise? He knows the team would never have given up of their own accord. Not while Natalie lived and breathed.

And a single thought keeps cycling through his mind, despite his best efforts to keep it from intruding. *How did she die?*

6

March 7, 2068 (12 A.U.C.T.)

The Atlantic Ocean

On a chain around her neck Dr. Q wears a small magnesium-alloy key. This key fits the locking mechanism for a TDS—an acronym that will surely be familiar to you if you're reading this account.

Not that Dr. Q will ever be using this particular key again. It's more of a symbol now, a talisman of personal loss and professional hope. Once a TDS has been sealed it cannot be opened until the cold fusion reactor runs its course. If you were to attempt it, you would set off an uncontrolled nuclear reaction that would wipe out any living thing within an estimated fifty-mile radius. Vaporizing the occupant too, of course.

That is to say, vaporizing Dr. Nicholas Hindman, Dr. Q's close colleague and romantic partner, former chief astrobiologist for the Centauri Project, the aforementioned failed effort to lay the groundwork for interstellar colonization of which, nominally at least, our little voyaging crew is the only surviving remnant. Alpha Centauri's proximity—twenty-five trillion miles, only 4.5 light-years away—put it at least theoretically within reach of a manned vessel from Earth. The target exoplanet, in orbit around that nearby star, had long been considered the most reachable planet whose climate fell within the so-called Goldilocks zone—meaning that it exhibited a temperature range suitable for human habitation. The latest astronomical observations had revealed that it almost certainly had an atmosphere and oceans too.

Unfortunately, interstellar travel at or near lightspeed never progressed beyond wishful thinking. Even with the most advanced pre-collapse technology the journey would have taken approximately ten thousand years. Building a vessel large and energy-intensive enough to sustain three or four hundred generations of humanity was never a practical option, which is why the Centauri Project's efforts were focused on methods for sustaining the lives of a limited number of human colonists aboard spacecraft not much bigger than the probes that already existed: *Voyager*, *Pioneer*, *New Horizons*, and others launched by China and India during what proved to be the final era of human space exploration. A way had to be found to keep these interstellar colonists alive for ten thousand years, either by coming up with much better technologies for long-term suspended animation, or by circumventing what the physicists call "coordinate time" altogether.

Which is where our beloved Dr. Q came in, and the invention that vaulted her into the ranks of scientific immortality. The TDS is driven by a mechanism I don't have the energy or sophistication to attempt to explain, other than to say that it consists of a vacuum-sealed magnesium-alloy sphere—actually a pair of closely nested spheres—powered by a self-depleting cold fusion reactor. A quantum computer housed between the nested spheres has the ability to decouple them from each other, so that while the outer sphere remains stationary in the coordinate universe, the inner sphere operates as a completely isolated system whose wave function can be persuaded to believe that it is accelerating through space at a rate in which whatever is contained within it is traveling at lightspeed. Or something like that.

The point is, combining insights from Einstein's theory of general relativity and the quantum physics concept known as a Schrödinger box, the TDS allows a human subject to exist in a state of cryogenic suspension for only a few decades of subjective time, while outside the sphere approximately ten millennia of coordinate time fly by. The quantum computer is precisely calibrated with the cold fusion reactor, so that (theoretically at least) when it runs its course and the quantum recoupling is complete, the subject will be revived, the vacuum seal will be released, and the sphere will open of its own accord.

The effort to find a new home for humanity in the stars had to be abandoned after the wholesale collapse of international political and economic systems in the wake of the Pinatubo Solution and the hyper-pandemic it caused, but an advanced technological biproduct of that lost dream—always assuming it functions as designed—has given us a way to transport human subjects into the deep future here on Earth, by which time the microbe and all its mutations will have worked their way through the troposphere and been re-ingested by the greater planetary biome.

The technology remains untested to completion, of course, and no one knows for certain if it's going to work. There remains a significant chance, even if everything else goes according to plan, that by the time the vacuum seal releases and the sphere cracks open its occupant will have been reduced to a desiccated skeleton, or a pile of dust. But everyone on the team agreed that it was worth a try.

Several problems remained to be figured out. A robust life-support system had to be designed for inside the sphere, including a slow-drip IV to provide the basic nutrients and protectants a subject would need to survive the slow entry into and even slower exit from cryo-hibernation. One-way, stationary time travel requires a geologically stable setting, like a natural cavern removed from any active fault line. Fortunately for us, such a cavern already existed on the grounds of the relocated Centauri Lab compound. Our engineers agreed that it could be expanded and rebuilt, leaving in place the cave's narrow original entrance beneath a stone overhang where it was likely to remain open to the surface despite ten millennia of soil deposition.

Dr. Hindman's background in extremophile microbiology made him an excellent candidate for an interstellar mission as a younger man, but by the time the cranes lowered the first TDS down into the excavated cavern pit, he was in many ways not an ideal colonist of the Earth's deep future. He was already middle-aged for one thing, in excellent health but physically average in most respects. He did bring one qualification to the table that was impossible to overlook, however. Most likely as a result of all the time he'd spent in the field breathing fumes from craters and steam vents and other volcanic features in his observations of chemosynthetic microbes, he'd developed robust antibodies in advance of the pathogen—which was, again, loosed upon the world as a result of a series of forced volcanic eruptions. Assuming he survives his time inside the TDS, Dr. Hindman remains the only human male we've encountered post-collapse who's still capable of producing viable sperm.

When he climbed into that sphere eleven years ago, the odds for the survival of humanity looked better than they do now. At the time, our educated opinion was that up to .0001 percent of the global population, men and women, had retained their fertility. It was just a matter of finding a few of these, we thought, at least one of them female, and convincing them that as a way of ensuring the survival of the species it was their duty to colonize the deep future alongside Dr. Hindman. Unfortunately, our percentage estimate seems to have been wildly optimistic. Perhaps a few seconds of subjective time have passed for the unconscious Dr. Hindman by now, but for the rest of us eleven long years have gone by, and we've spent nearly every day and month of those years chasing down leads. Some have been more promising than others—we've had a few near misses—but so far every last one has led to a dead end. The two inactivated spheres sit empty back at the Lab compound, gathering dust in a reassembled hangar we procured from a nearby municipal airport.

Dr. Hindman was supposed to have been our opening move, not the entire game. So we press on. We're not too worried that anyone will disturb the compound, which is being looked after in our absence by reliable caretakers, or the underground chamber where Dr. Hindman (or—let's be honest—whatever's left of him) whirls endlessly through the uncanny night of quantum-altered spacetime.

Gods willing, everything there will remain more or less as we left it, and we'll return with at least one viable female subject in tow.

March 11, 2068 (12 A.U.C.T.)
The Atlantic Ocean

The wind's gone slack, and Tollie's making trouble again. I'm continually struck by the contrast between Dr. Q and her younger brother. While she's been a high achiever all her life, driven by the most honorable goals imaginable, Tollie has consecrated himself to pleasure-seeking. While she's one of the most brilliant minds of her generation, he seems content to play the mischievous, happy-go-lucky, joke-cracking bon vivant. He loves to go around pushing everyone's buttons. He seems drawn to turmoil like a moth to flame.

I don't question his commitment to the mission, really, and it's hard for me to believe that he can truly be as unconcerned and frivolous as he often appears. As far as I can tell his true loyalties are squarely with his sister. When she asked him to provide his yacht and sailing knowhow for this expedition, I doubt he hesitated even for a moment. The rest of his friends and family are of course long gone—as is the case with most of us—and I imagine there's only so much homegrown marijuana one can smoke before a solitary life begins to lose its meaning. Tollie's a gambler by inclination, and I suspect he found the longshot nature of our quest appealing. It's a good thing he did, because without this wind-powered, solar-supplemented sailing vessel we would never have made it this far.

As I may have mentioned, our rations aboard the *Solar Barque* are overwhelmingly vegetarian. Other than on very special occasions when we might boil up a freeze-dried mylar soup packet left over from Cornelius Quist's survivalist stockpile, the taste of actual meat is a distant memory. This was the reason for today's flareup. It seems that our fun-loving Ptolemy wants to go rogue on the European mainland. Specifically, he's announced that when we reach the coast of Spain, he intends to go ashore with his antique Remington .30-06 hunting rifle and hunt us up some fresh game.

The rest of us are dead set against this plan, needless to say, which violates an unwritten directive at the heart of a voyage that has been years in the making. We want to avoid setting foot on any alien shore until we arrive at our destination.

Let me explain. It's not just the risk of infection. All of us are hyperpandemic survivors, with hard-won antibodies to the offending microbe, which spreads primarily through the air itself and not through human contact. The medications I dispense every day are intended to protect us from new variants, and from a whole host of other pathogens that we have to assume continue to circulate through human populations all over the globe. But our concerns go well beyond disease. Among survivors, from everything we've seen and heard, civic-mindedness is a quaint relic of the past. Food and water are scarce, famine is rampant, and many of the niceties of what we used to call civilization have long since gone away. Cities and towns are crumbling disaster zones, and roadways are impassable jungles overgrown with weeds and brush, where dead bodies are left to rot. This is what societal collapse looks like, I'm afraid.

Naturally, in many places, a particular kind of human being has stepped in to fill the void. Local strongmen in other words, or if you have a taste for more antique-sounding vocabulary, gangsters, warlords, chieftains. It doesn't really matter what you call them, and I don't think I need to spell it out any further. It's simply not worth the risk of going ashore at any point on this existentially important journey except in a true emergency. This is a policy I'd assumed we all agreed upon, but apparently Tollie didn't get the memo.

It was over dinner at the low table in the shade of the forward bimini—a typically unappetizing meal it must be admitted, of grilled Lab jerky, dehydrated peas, and a pitcher of tepid water from a vitamin-supplemented tank—that Tollie announced his intention to head up into the coastal mountains of Spain with his hunting rifle. His intention, in other words, to jeopardize the entire mission for a taste of real meat.

James and I stared at our plates, aghast. Even Dr. Q appeared upset, though her reaction was clearly leavened by the affectionate lens through which she always sees her younger brother. "There won't be any game animals left, Tollie, dear. They'll all have been hunted out years ago, just like everywhere else."

"You don't know that," he retorted, with a dismissive wave of his hand. "The mountains south of Granada have always been sparsely populated. It's crappy soil for agriculture, there's hardly any water, and I doubt there are more than a handful of human survivors. The place is probably overrun with feral goats, rabbits, maybe even some wild boar. Why all the glum faces?" he interrupted himself, glancing incredulously around the table. "Aren't you guys as tired of soy jerky as I am?"

Dr. Q shook her head. "Stop talking nonsense, brother dear. This is not why we came. You could get us all killed."

"Don't come with me. Just stay on the boat, rest up for a few days. You deserve it, all three of you. I'll just mount a quick little excursion. With any luck I'll come back with a load of fresh meat. Maybe a few bottles of old Spanish wine too, if I can round them up—and even some olive oil. Think about how good *that* would taste."

James and I kept our gazes fixed upon our half-finished plates. I don't think either of us felt that it was our place to speak up.

Also, it's clear that he's already made up his mind. Maybe Dr. Q will be able to talk him out of it in private before we actually get to the coast of Spain, but if she can't, there's not much we can really do. The *Solar Barque* is our sole form of transportation, and while the rest of us have picked up some new skills on this voyage, Tollie's knowledge of sailing and navigation is indispensable. We'd be stuck without him.

7

10151 A.U.C.T. +/- 18.583 years (estimated)

Nick's academic fieldwork had taken him to plenty of wilderness areas, though back then he'd always carried his own food: freeze-dried soup packets, pasta, quinoa, and the like. Hunting and gathering, that's the protocol now. A long-term camp for stability and security, but strike the right tone from the beginning by keeping a light footprint.

Technically he could have brought along a few more tools for hunting and processing food sewn into his clothing, but again, the motion inside the sphere was drastic and constant and the technical members of the team had not been able to assure themselves that anything sharp or heavy wouldn't eventually work itself free and end up severing some vital wire or tube, poking out his eyes, or slowly bludgeoning him to death. It did occur to him that they might have hidden an equipment cache of some sort inside the cave, but he's now conducted a fairly thorough search and found nothing. In pure survival terms this isn't really a problem though. In the months before she'd sealed him into the sphere, Natalie had insisted that he develop a thorough understanding of foraging practices and learn to make his own simple tools.

Beyond oyster mushrooms, the slopes around the ledge contain a plenitude of edible fungi: chanterelle, boletus, green agaric, turkey tail. As to plants, there are plantain, trout lily, white pine pollen cones, purslane, and ostrich ferns, though he's already missed this year's fiddleheads. There are blueberries flowering above the tree line and a great abundance of nut-bearing hardwoods throughout the forest—oak, beech, hickory, black walnut—which will mean no lack of nutrition that's easy to harvest and store come fall. His main staple in the meantime will be the cattails that fill the shallows of the lowland lakes and ponds, every part of which can be eaten at some season of the year. He's not above the invertebrates either—the snails and crickets and grasshoppers—though he would prefer not to rely on them as a regular source of protein until he can devise a more appetizing way of consuming them.

He spends half a day making a storage cellar, excavating a pit in the mountainside and capping it with a flat slab of schist he rolls down from the slope above. He makes a set of spears from ash saplings, sharpening them with a piece of flint, rubbing the points with pine sap, and hardening them in the fire. The next morning, waist-deep in tea-colored water below the inlet of the closest lake, he spears a smallmouth bass bigger than any fish he's ever seen except in photos, black and glinting in the gnat-filled air as it thrashes out its life on his spearpoint. He cleans it with a sharp flint, strings it on a cattail stalk, and brings it back up to his camp to roast it slowly over a bed of embers, storing the leftover meat in his pantry under the rock.

There are a great number of birds and mammals in the forest, including some species that come as a surprise. Peccaries for example, a large rodent he thinks may be a South American nutria, and snuffling along across a grassy bluff near the lakeshore, a scaly anteater or pangolin that must be the descendant of escaped exotic pets.

He finally gets a closer look at one of the huge black raptors he's glimpsed soaring high above the canopy, this one gazing down at him from a perch in the lower branches of a massive white oak. He has no idea where this species might have come from—or what it might have evolved from—but it's the biggest bird of prey he's ever seen, with a massive hooked beak and sleek blue-black feathers like a crow. And again, as with the turkeys, something in the massive bird's eyes gives him pause: a scornfulness and uncanny intelligence that sends a chill up his spine. As if some of the creatures in this new landscape might be evolving not only larger bodies but also more penetrating minds.

In the next moment, however, he dismisses this line of thinking. No doubt it's just his own heightened perceptions caused by the extreme solitude. Looking into the eyes of any other living being is bound to be a more charged experience than it used to be.

Weeks go by. It's hard to get close enough to kill anything with a spear, but eventually he figures out that patient stillness, rather than exhausting pursuit, yields the best results. Once he's internalized this lesson he takes several creatures in quick succession: a pigeon, a turkey, a long-bodied, dark-furred squirrel.

He cures the pelt by scraping it with the sharp flint and stretching it taut over the fire on a framework of saplings, and before long he's collected a pile of cured animal skins: woodchucks, more squirrels, a young deer he finds trapped in the briars near a beaver dam. He makes thread out of gut and a needle from a heron bone, and uses the deerskin to fashion himself a pair of moccasins to replace the worn-out tennis shoes he'd been wearing in the sphere. His Centauri Project jumpsuit is filthy and getting threadbare at the knees and crotch. Eventually he'll have to make more clothing for himself, but for now he just sews the remaining deerskin and the woodchuck and squirrel furs into a wraparound cloak for the cold weather he knows must be coming. His frequent comings and goings wear a footpath down the mountain to the valley. In the mornings especially he enjoys the walk. The simple act of striding down a familiar trail refreshes his sense of purpose, and the smells of a rich forest ecosystem please him. Not just earth but *living* earth: moss and duff, ferns and sedges, microorganisms and mushrooms. The trees breathing. Every leaf its own little oxygen factory.

At the end of each day he stares out from the ledge, scouring the view for any signs of human presence: a reflected flash; a wispy column of smoke. Except what his own fire produces, however, there's no smoke in the whole panorama, and the only flashes are from lightning, or from the setting sun's reflection winking on the small lakes and ponds bejeweling the forested lowlands.

In the middle of one night he's startled awake by the dream-memory of an overnight flight from Santiago to New York. He'd been jolted into consciousness then too, heart pounding, trapped inside the flexible metal cylinder as it hurtled through the darkness somewhere over South America, shimmying and juddering alarmingly in the turbulence. Now, in the shelter of his little grotto with half a sky of bright stars glittering in his view, the memory of airline travel seems implausible. Then again, human technology had a way of making seemingly implausible things happen. His own renewed existence is proof enough of that.

He'd taken a three-month leave from the Centauri Project to wrap up the decades-long study of extremophiles in Chilean steam vents that he'd begun as a PhD candidate. Absorbed in his observations and cut off from the world in a remote study site, he'd completely missed the onset of the hyperpandemic. Traveling home was like reentering a different world. Santiago was a chaotic tangle of riots and looting, stopped traffic, smashed windows, buildings on fire, people dying off in droves. He was fortunate to find himself aboard one of the last commercial flights ever scheduled. There were sick people on the plane, ashen-faced and struggling for breath, some of them coughing up blood. The pilot wasn't bothering with any of the usual niceties like making announcements, turning on the fasten seatbelt signs, or adjusting his altitude to avoid turbulence. He was taking the fastest possible route to New York, because the world was ending. Human civilization was in freefall, and everyone knew it.

The drive from JFK to Boston was harrowing. Cars abandoned on the side of the highway, some burned, some with drivers slumped over the wheel or curled up on the nearby pavement. Most of the gas and charging stations were already shut down, malls and convenience stores had been looted and set aflame, big columns of black smoke stained the filthy sky. Several times he had to detour to avoid stopped traffic. The secondary roads were thronged with panicked refugees, most on foot or bicycle. You could see who was sick the moment you glimpsed their face.

The cellphone networks were down or jammed, so he couldn't call ahead. He made it back to the apartment on Memorial Drive in

Cambridge and found to his indescribable relief that Natalie was well, part of the percentage of the population, like himself, who remained asymptomatic.

"Don't unpack," she said. "We're moving the whole Lab and whoever's left up to my dad's old place."

They made the drive north to New Hampshire the next day in Natalie's bumper-sticker-plastered vintage plug-in, leading a motorcade of two fifteen-seater vans and three huge flatbed trucks. At the compound the electric gate slid open and the surviving members of the Centauri team eased their vehicles through.

The gate has long ago rusted into nothingness. Whatever remains of its constituent parts is buried under meters of soil along with the splintered asphalt of the former access road. But he's never really left.

A huge quarter moon smolders through the leaves of the branches that frame his view. It occurs to him that his sense of distance is altered. The world feels so much larger. Almost inconceivably vast.

Six weeks have gone by since his arrival. He's explored the mountainsides and the surrounding lowlands thoroughly by now, doing his best to memorize the character and topography of the forest by walking out in ever-widening circles. The farther he walks, the harder it becomes to convince himself that the entire planet isn't wilderness now. The noun *wilderness*, he reminds himself, is a synonym for "abandoned place." Deserted place. Place devoid of human presence.

It's a feeling that's grown stronger since his emergence, so that he's almost come to assume it. Now though, staring out at that big lonely quarter moon inching up from the horizon, he reminds himself that to give in to his intuitive sense that there's no one else would be a dereliction of duty. The protocol is clear enough on that score: Check the cavern for other active spheres. Establish and provision a secure, low-impact, long-term camp. Then start looking for other survivors. The first item on the list had been heartbreakingly easy to check off. Now that the second is accomplished, he needs to turn his full attention to the third.

Given the fact of the Centauri team's failure to activate another sphere—a failure that was not surprising to him given the obstacles they'd faced—it is now his job to look for signs of other remnant populations that may somehow have been able to survive and reproduce. And the best place to look isn't here in this inland valley, but a hundred-odd miles away to the south and east.

Humans have always been drawn to coasts.

8

March 14, 2068 (12 A.U.C.T.)
The Atlantic Ocean

The weather is finally calm. My apologies for not writing earlier. The last forty-eight hours have been a trial, including a few moments when we all expected to sink to the bottom of the ocean. I may have mentioned that we set out from the Centauri Lab in early January, hoping to minimize our exposure to the annual rogues' gallery of mid-Atlantic hurricanes and super-hurricanes. Until a few days ago we'd been lucky enough to dance between the raindrops, so to speak. I'm not even sure whether what we just came through was technically a hurricane. Whatever it was, I'm glad it's over.

It began with rising winds under a sky weighed down by brooding purple clouds. Then the swells started to grow, soon becoming big hillsides of bottle-green seawater with lacy foam peeling off in the wind. The spray off the water was unrelenting, and our clothes were soaked through by the blasting wind even before the rain hit. Tollie's laid-back attitude evaporates in times like this, thank the gods, and he wasn't shy about screaming orders at us. We took in all the sail except part of the jib, which he needed up in the wind to keep the *Solar Barque* crosswise to the swells. The bowsprit would crash through the top of one wave and we would plunge like a roller-coaster car into a deep valley before being lifted up on the next.

Soon the wind increased to an alarming high-pitched shriek, and the swell grew more colossal still, and we were like a tiny cork bobbing on a howling seascape of huge, watery, rolling mountains. The deck was awash with foaming green seawater that sucked at our ankles and knees as it flowed across the teak and poured out through the scupper holes. At a certain point Tollie lost control of the rudder and the *Solar Barque* turned sideways into a series of huge breaking waves. We tilted sickeningly, going almost vertical, with seawater flooding in over the port rail like an unstoppable cataract. This was the first of several moments when I for one was convinced we were done for.

We managed to right ourselves without capsizing, but another huge wave broke over us and to my horror, as if in slow motion, I saw Dr. Q lose her grip on whatever she'd had hold of and slide feet-first down the deck. I lunged, in the process losing my grip on the shroud I'd wrapped around my arm. We tumbled down; a tongue of pouring seawater flipped her over the rail and into the churning green maw of the ocean. I managed to catch the rail and grab her by the wrist before she disappeared, yanking her small body back up as the yacht righted itself again.

A third huge wave hit, tilting us up on our side again to bring the deck nearly vertical. I struggled to keep hold of Dr. Q's wrist—the force of gravity and the seawater pouring down was nearly too much, and I felt the elbow I'd crooked around the rail slipping. In that moment a strong hand gripped my forearm.

"Got you, Al. Don't let go of her."

It was James, the wet hoodie clinging to his scarred face and skull. Having had the foresight to secure himself by looping a shroud around his waist, he now somehow found the strength to drag the two of us across the now downward-rolling deck to the mainmast, to which he very efficiently tied us.

The storm raged for hours, and Tollie was mostly able to keep the bowsprit pointed into the wind. We didn't capsize, in other words, and everyone managed to stay aboard, though by the end we were all exhausted and chilled to the bone, our lips blue and our teeth chattering. But what stands out most in my mind as I write this—all dry now and bundled up in three big beach towels under the bimini—is how calm and cheerful Dr. Q remained the entire time, even when the rest of us were convinced that this little sea journey was about to come to a sudden end.

Tollie's competent skippering and James's moment of unusual decisiveness were amazing and admirable actions, but I can't help thinking that it was our expedition leader above all who got us safely through that storm. Panic is the deadliest killer in any emergency, and she exudes an air of confidence and calm optimism that's infectious in a way that's difficult to fully articulate. It's almost as if she can see into the future. As if she knew from the beginning that none of us was going to drown.

Impossible, of course. We're talking about an eminent scientist whose entire career was built on logic and empirical study, and I very much doubt that she draws her emotional strength from some mystical notion of preordained destiny. But it has to come from *somewhere*. And it makes me wonder, not for the first time, despite having worked so closely with her all these years, if I'm not still missing a key piece of the puzzle when it comes to our beloved Dr. Q.

March 15, 2068 (12 A.U.C.T.)
The Atlantic Ocean

A quiet day on the *Solar Barque*. This morning Tollie connected the windvane autopilot and donned snorkeling gear (with a hooded full-body wetsuit to protect him from jellyfish stings) and went down to check the hull for cracks after its exertions during the storm. The rest of us gathered on the cushioned benches under the bimini to brainstorm a concept we've somewhat facetiously decided to call *The Afterlife Handbook*, a reference to the codex discovered at Deir el-Bersha in the early 2000s, which is (if indeed it still exists) the oldest book in the world.

Our idea is not to create, as those ancient Egyptians did, a field guide to the land of the dead. Rather, we have in mind a compendium of knowledge that might be helpful in establishing a sustainable human culture on deep-future planet Earth. To be clear, this exercise is built on a whole series of optimistic assumptions. But in a best-case scenario, if such a codex were printed on some highly durable material, it could help steer this human culture of the deep future away from some of the mistakes that have brought the current version of humanity to such a disastrous pass.

I wrote down our initial ideas, and I will copy them out for you here. This is obviously just a partial list, but we feel that it represents a pretty good start:

- A history of the rise and fall of "Humanity 1.0," with the hope that it might be seen as a kind of cautionary origin tale
- Easy-to-follow instructions for no-char, bio-till agriculture as a long-term sink for carbon dioxide
- A catalogue of herbal medicines and cures, with an emphasis on ecosystems similar to climatic predictions for ten thousand years from now and beyond
- Instructions for the creation of penicillin-based antibiotics
- Diagrams of DNA and the solar system
- Instructions for basic weather forecasting, including an explanation of cold fronts, warm fronts, occluded fronts, and the effects of terrain on local precipitation
- The most important formulae underpinning modern physics and applied mathematics (though we do have some doubts about this and it will require further discussion)
- A pervasive theme or leitmotif regarding the importance of living in balance with nature, possibly with the Native American concept of the "honorable harvest" as a through-line
- A second pervasive theme or leitmotif discouraging the adoption of fossil fuels, possibly in the form of recurring warnings about the inadvisability of burning anything that has been dug up from underground

Transcriber's note: As human languages tend to mutate at such a rate that they become largely unrecognizable after five or six centuries, it was also later decided that apart from mathematic formulae all information contained within the codex should be diagrammatic and/or pictorial rather than written.

The memory that lingers most in my mind as I write this, a few hours after our brainstorming session, is that of James's surprisingly animated contributions to the discussion. It may be that I'm more predisposed to give him the benefit of the doubt after he saved me and Dr. Q from drowning the other day. In any case, he spoke with a level of passion and authority that I never would have expected, contributing useful insights and showing flashes of a dry sense of humor that was also completely new to me. It's almost as if Mr. Swamp's true self has finally begun to emerge, tentatively but unmistakably from beneath the hoodie, like the shoot of a sun-damaged houseplant peeking up from the soil and a layer of its own dried leaves.

There was even one moment toward the end of the session when he became so animated that he didn't notice that the ever-present hoodie had fallen back to reveal his entire face and head, which isn't nearly as ugly or disfigured as he must imagine it to be. In the next moment he caught me staring at him, and his face darkened with embarrassment as he quickly pulled the hoodie up, giving me a quick apologetic nod as he did so. I wanted to tell him that everything was okay, that we were all friends, he really wasn't such a bad-looking guy, and he certainly didn't have to keep himself covered up for his shipmates' sake. Not wanting to single him out in front of everyone else, I just shook my head and tried to say all that with my eyes.

I don't think he got the message; the hoodie stayed up.

Anyway, it was a productive discussion, and an unexpectedly illuminating and hope-inducing one. In the event that we actually follow through and create this little codex, the plan is to find a way to entrust its care to the subject or subjects chosen to occupy the next activated TDS, who will presumably have internalized the wisdom contained therein, and will pass it down with a measure of reverence to the first generation of new humans, who will in turn pass it down to the next generation, and so on. Of course we'll have to locate a subject or subjects first. But every day, gods willing, we're getting a little bit closer to that goal.

March 17, 2068 (12 A.U.C.T.)

The Atlantic Ocean

It's evening now, two uneventful days having passed since my last entry. The wind is gentle but steady, and the soft creaks and groans of the yacht's timbers and the water splashing against the hull are the only sounds as we make our way. A huge crimson sun smolders on the horizon, and the sea is dark indigo, an achingly beautiful shade of almost-purple that's giving me a new appreciation for Homer's fondness for the phrase *wine-dark sea*. Say what you will about the mess we've made of this planet. At least we can still count on dazzling sunsets.

I'm sitting alone, with my back to my usual stanchion behind the bowsprit, enjoying the mild salt air as I attempt to sort through the unexpected feelings that seem to have arisen within me. It appears—and I share this with you, my hypothetical reader, in the strictest confidence—that since our brainstorming session the other day I've actually developed a bit of a crush on our youngest crew member. Which is odd. We've actually known each other for a long time, and as I think I've made clear, my feelings for James Swamp—when I've had time to consider him at all—have been feelings of irritation, mostly because of his stubborn unwillingness to ever share what's going through his mind.

His inclusion in the Centauri Project team began as something of a personal project for Dr. Q. It was she who discovered him curled up outside the Lab's access gate one morning during the last cycle of the hyperpandemic; she who brought him to me in the infirmary, his head and face covered in suppurating scabs, shivering, feverish, clearly in a state of septic shock, and very near death. His whole family in New Haven, Connecticut, had perished, and he himself had barely survived his own brush with the pathogen. He was only twenty-one at the time and had somehow made it all the way north on his own, only to collapse on our doorstep. This was seven years ago, four years after we'd sealed Dr. Hindman into the activated TDS. There was still a great deal of suffering and death both inside and outside the Lab gates around that time—we lost half our surviving team members during that final deadly surge—and Dr. Q's decision to bring him in was controversial. It wasn't as if he was the only survivor outside the compound in need of rescue. But she took pity on him, having seen something about him that apparently made her believe he would someday become an indispensable member of the team. As I hinted a few days ago, although she's the most eminent scientist imaginable, her thought process sometimes doesn't appear to follow pathways that are strictly logical.

Anyway, James recovered, and he's been with us ever since. There have always been plenty of chores around the compound suitable for a physically strong man—moving rocks, digging holes, repairing windmills and solar panels and generators. It was only after nearly a year with the team that he finally let slip that he had a talent for coding. Our software engineer had died in that last cycle, and to function properly the Lab depended on the smooth and continuous operation of a self-contained network. And this is how, just as Dr. Q had predicted, James *did* become indispensable.

Which didn't mean I liked or even trusted him. In fact, his long initial silence about his coding skills irritated me to no end, and I'm afraid that I actually spoke to him about it in a fairly inhospitable way. After that we did our best to avoid each other, which wasn't hard to do as he spent most of his free time in solitude—playing obsolete computer games on his laptop, leafing through his bird guides, or trudging moodily around the compound's expansive pastures and hillsides with a pair of binoculars, hoping to catch a glimpse of something other than a crow or a starling.

Now though—suddenly—I can't seem to get him out of my mind. Those strong hands, those dark eyes. The way he stops to collect his thoughts before he speaks, and the peculiar timbre of his voice, low and gentle. That little apologetic nod he gave me as he pulled his hoodie back up, and the current of partial understanding that seemed to pass between us.

I realize it must seem strange that I've known him all this time and have never had this kind of reaction. Then again, if I'm going to be absolutely honest (which is one of my goals in these pages), I have to admit that my own jealousy and/or territoriality may have blinded me to some extent about the true character of Mr. James Swamp. Because he's always been Dr. Q's personal project and she, in a certain way, has always been mine.

So what's changed? I don't know. Am I in love? I don't think so. An episode of infatuation, though? A schoolgirl crush for a woman in her thirties? Apparently, yes. I'm hoping it will pass quickly though, like a minor virus of the spirit.

The strangest thing just happened, taking into consideration what I was writing about. Dr. Q wandered up to the bowsprit and took a seat beside me on the deck. I put my pen down, and the two of us sat and watched the sunset paint the undersides of the mackerel clouds a brilliant rosy pink.

"I appreciate that you're giving James the benefit of the doubt, dear," she remarked. "I know you weren't thrilled about the idea of him coming along."

"He seems to be pitching in well enough," I replied warily, taking a sip from my water bottle to hide my discomfort. "He did basically save both our lives the other day, for example."

"Indeed, dear, he did. You're absolutely right." She nodded enthusiastically, gazing out over the darkening sea. "I remember you were fairly adamant about not inviting him to join the team at first."

"It was a difficult period. We'd lost so many. Why him? Why not someone else?"

"I understand."

"I do feel differently now, though."

"I can see that."

"You can?" I was slightly dumbfounded to be having this conversation with Dr. Q, a woman whose intellect and leadership I respect more than that of any other living person.

"Of course I can, dear. I'm not blind."

I blushed. She seemed to pick up on my reluctance to talk about it, and we sat awhile in awkward silence as the dusk set in, making no further mention of James or my feelings about him. Anyway, what advice could she possibly offer me? I have no intention of acting on this little infatuation. Now is hardly the time to indulge in such distractions.

A light wind has begun to luff the sails, and the yacht is moving briskly over the inky water. Dr. Q has gone belowdecks, which is just as well because it's time for my evening rounds. According to Tollie, we're within two or three days of entering the Mediterranean, and I expect to have new impressions for you soon.

Transcriber's note: Given the events that will be unfolded in the pages to come, "Dr. Q" has cause to regret not taking advantage of this moment to be more encouraging with Alejandra. I knew very well, for example, that James Swamp's feelings for our physician were long-standing and intense. He was in fact deeply in love with her, and had been for years. Alejandra is exactly wrong here, in other words. This would have been exactly the moment to act, as "Dr. Q" damn well should have advised her.

9

10151 A.U.C.T. +/- 18.583 years (estimated)

He takes two water skins, several flint-knapped stone blades, and a generous supply of smoked meat, dried mushrooms, and cattail rootstalks wrapped in oak leaves, and bundles it all in a deerskin roll to which he affixes a comfortable deerskin shoulder strap. Choosing his best spear, he descends from the ledge at dawn, and by midafternoon arrives at the banks of the river that used to be called the Connecticut. Dense stands of knotweed cover the lower-lying banks—the invasive plant has clearly established a permanent niche for itself—but the river itself appears to be thriving. It's much clearer and faster-moving than he remembers: minnows flash in the seams and eddies, mayflies stream up from the surface in great shimmering clouds, dragonflies orchestrate their virtuoso maneuvers along the riffles and the slower runs, geese and mergansers huddle silently on cobble-strewn bars. The open lane of blue sky above the river teems with swallows and fly catchers, looping and circling as they feed. Spotting him, a family of foxes slips quickly away into the brush on the far bank.

He makes his way downstream, sometimes following open stretches of riverbank, sometimes sticking to the forest within earshot of the river. Near sunset he startles a huge bull moose wading in the shallows. A pleasant surprise, as he'd once heard that the species had gone extinct. Like many of the animals he's seeing, it must have found a refugium somewhere in the boreal forests of what had once been Canada and spread southward again after the thermal maximum subsided.

He sleeps in trees, or on prominent bluffs with a clear view of all approaches. He has no trouble with predators, though for half a day an immense, mournful-looking wolf stalks his progress downriver from the opposite shore. Once in a while he finds a crumbling abutment from an old bridge or waterwork. Mostly, though, it continues to surprise him how much he *doesn't* see. How thoroughly the human footprint has been erased by nature, eroded, covered over, and washed away.

It takes him a week to reach the confluence of the Connecticut and the river he believes used to be the Deerfield. From there he sets off to the east, trekking through the forest in the direction of the sunrise. But the way eastward is blocked by a region of vast swamplands, some of which he eventually has no choice but to take off his moccasins and wade through.

The swamps are flooded lowlands filled with the sun-silvered skeletons of ancient trees. The water is tannin-stained, like very dark tea, mostly ranging from shin to neck deep, and teeming with microorganisms, amphibians, fish, and who knows what else. Snapping turtles probably, though he doesn't see any. In sunnier spots the surface is blanketed by European frog-bit, *Hydrocharis morsus-ranae*, like millions of tiny, emerald-green lily pads.

It's almost impossible to see where he's stepping, and despite his own attempts at self-reassurance, he grits his teeth nervously as he makes his way across first one and then the next unavoidable expanse, his bare feet sinking into the suctioning mud. Stepping into an unexpected hole, he plunges in over his head, soaking the deerskin bundle. The silt bottom is especially soft and in a panic he has to kick and thrash to free his feet, after which he frog-strokes to the nearest peninsula of solid land to dry off and regain his equilibrium.

After that he chooses to swim rather than wade whenever the water is more than waist deep, with the bundle held awkwardly above his head. The foul-smelling muck, the aggressive mosquitoes, not being able to see beneath the frog-bit and the surface of the melancholy black water—the truth is, he feels his enthusiasm wavering, and a tide of loneliness and self-pity floods into him. But the protocol is clear, and along with his basic curiosity it gives him the impetus to continue making slow progress toward the coast.

On the evening of his fourteenth day out from the ledge, his sixth day crossing the swamps, soaked and foul-smelling, he finds a camping place on a high and pleasantly breezy knoll shaded by swaying white pines. He spends the night up in the branches of one, caressed by the breeze and blessedly above the range of the mosquitoes.

In the morning, investigating an opening in the pines at the edge of the knoll, he comes upon a curious mound. A buried building is his first thought, though a closer inspection reveals an outcropping of solid schist at the base of the mound that has kept the forest from growing in. At the top of the mound a matched pair of marble posts poke out of the moss, waist-high, pure white, identically tapered to fingertip-like points.

He drops to his knees and uses his hands to peel away soft layers of moss. The peaty soil beneath the moss is fairly loose too, and he removes more of it around the posts, which turn out to be irregularly shaped, though still nearly identical, with smoothly rounded stubs protruding from the sides in a serrated fishbone pattern, like the leaves of a ric rac cactus. The digging is easy, though he's gripped by a strange mix of feelings: urgency, anxiety, dread. The posts turn out to be connected to a larger, egg-like dome of the same pure white marble. He stops digging and sits back on his heels, exhaling slowly several times in an effort to quiet his pounding heart.

He knows exactly where he is. This is the site of the deCordova Museum and Sculpture Park, near what used to be the town of Lincoln, Massachusetts. If he were to continue digging he would uncover the remains, fully intact from the look of things, of a monumental work of art that is deeply familiar to him, with vivid personal associations that are nearly overwhelming.

Allowing himself to replay the past will only sharpen his despair, so he does his best to push the memories back. But they keep flooding in.

He and Natalie were at the sculpture's unveiling. The artist, a brilliant and multi-talented emeritus professor of theoretical physics at MIT, had been one of Natalie's favorite mentors. The occasion was well-attended, on a pleasant spring day, with an open bar in the courtyard of the sculpture park and a white-shirted catering staff of MIT undergrads circulating through the crowd with trays of locally-sourced hors d'oeuvres. The press was there, and scores of dignitaries from the soon-to-be decimated ranks of the cultural meritocracy: scientists, artists, curators, philanthropists, state politicians, even a famous Hollywood actress. It was a festive public gathering, among the last he ever attended, before the decades-long chain of catastrophic events made such gatherings inconceivable.

He remembers filing slowly up a winding staircase cut into the schist. A live chamber quintet played an ironic funeral dirge as the coverings were pulled teasingly off. He and Natalie found a bench in the shade of a blooming cherry tree to gaze up at the newly revealed sculpture. It was a monumental head, an enormous marble egg crowned by rickrack antlers in stylized homage to Actaeon, the mythical Greek hunter who'd been transformed into a stag and eaten by his own hounds as punishment for glimpsing Artemis bathing in the nude. The head's huge marble eyes were hauntingly blank. Its mouth was open, giving an uncannily good impression of a scream, presumably as the hunter was set upon by his disloyal hounds.

The artist himself had broken away from a group of admirers to make his way down the stone steps to talk to his favorite protégé, and the three of them had shared a pleasant conversation. Nick can no longer remember exactly what the old physicist had said about his work. Was Actaeon a stand-in for humanity, and were the treacherous hunting dogs, growling bloodthirstily in the implied background, technology, industrialization, or capitalism? Where was the naked goddess Artemis in all this? He has no idea, thinking back.

In truth, he probably hadn't been paying much attention, intoxicated as he'd been by the proximity of Natalie herself. The relationship was freshly minted at the time, and all his senses were attuned: to her scent, to her low-pitched voice, somewhat unexpected coming from that diminutive frame, to the way her slim curves filled out the sleeveless black cocktail dress she was wearing that day. It was the first time he'd ever seen her in a dress—normally she wore jeans and oversized thrift-shop cardigans or men's oxford shirts—and this had undoubtedly blocked out most of his other impressions.

Regardless of the artist's intentions, his monumental marble head with its rickrack antlers and terrifyingly soundless scream was a work of expressionist art that captured something essential about the moment. A moment in which humans were losing faith in their capacity to alter the course of history. Most still hoped that the scientists would be capable of inventing solutions to the looming crisis—either to save human civilization on Earth or possibly to start anew somewhere else—but that optimism was getting harder to sustain with every passing month.

In the preceding decades, despite increasingly frequent international conclaves attempting to address the problem, the planet's surface had been warming ever faster; faster indeed than at any other moment in known geological history. Rapidly receding coastlines, megadroughts, biblical floods, cyclones, killer heat waves, more hectares of forest consumed each year by raging wildfires. Collapsing ecosystems, trophic cascades, periodic outbreaks of zoonotic disease providing deadly foreshadowing of the hyperpandemic to come, and, especially painful for a career biologist, accelerating rates of extinction. The polar bear, the African elephant, mountain gorillas and orangutans, walruses and Bengal tigers, humpback and beluga whales, Adélie and chinstrap penguins, pandas and leatherback turtles—the grim tally went on. And these were just some of the more iconic representatives; thousands of other species were consigned to oblivion as well, many of which had never been described by science.

Those with means, including Natalie's billionaire father, were buying up remote properties in high latitudes, stockpiling supplies, and taking themselves off the grid—but this was no solution. Global financial shocks and persistent economic recession, dire poverty, an increasingly severe global refugee problem, bloodier and more frequent wars, ethnic cleansings, a growing taste for anarchy on one hand and authoritarianism on the other—the elaborate civilizational infrastructures humanity had built to sustain itself on the fragile home planet were failing. Even before the hyperpandemic, it had become increasingly clear to scientists and policy experts that the time when Earth could be counted on as a safe home for hundreds of millions of humans was rapidly coming to an end.

It was in this context that the Centauri Project had recruited Natalie, a brilliant young doctoral candidate, to research a colonizing mission to the stars. A few months after the unveiling of the Actaeon head, she'd recruited Nick as well. He'd never thought of himself as an astrobiologist, but his fieldwork on chemosynthetic extremophiles did fit the bill rather well, and he received a formal invitation from the Centauri board to join the first class of prospective interstellar colonists. His thesis adviser was adamant in urging him not to do it. Going to work in the private sector, for what was then considered a fringe scientific enterprise, would disqualify him from tenure-track consideration at any major university. But at this point he would have followed Natalie anywhere, and all his instincts clamored for him to join the team. It was a move that felt like destiny.

In the end, the Centauri Project's mission failed—though in a certain sense the jury's still out, he reminds himself—and everything the gathered luminaries had been celebrating on that long-ago afternoon at the deCordova Museum and Sculpture Park, the whole edifice of accumulated human knowledge and achievement—is now gone with the wind. Given that he already finds himself forgetting many details of his own core academic training in biology, not to mention details pertaining to the great landmarks of human cultural development like Dante, Confucius, or the theory of relativity, Nick considers himself a poor vessel for preserving its buried memory.

He and Natalie drove up to the event from Boston in her little plug-in, a beat-up old Honda jalopy plastered with bumper stickers celebrating out-of-date political causes along with nerdy puns about black holes and particle physics. It was a sunny late-spring day, only a month or two after they'd first met. Arriving early, they strolled the perimeter of the sculpture park, passing through a corridor of majestic oaks into the wilder and more densely grown part of the reserve.

They found a dry hillside overlooking a small lake, a fenced-off municipal water supply that has long since been absorbed in the swamplands that stretch out in every direction from the pine-covered knoll where he now sits. He'd borrowed a linen tablecloth from the caterers, which he spread out for them over a patch of springy moss.

"When did you become such a barbarian?" she remarked, glaring at him through the oversized lenses of her spectacles.

"I didn't mean to imply that we have to do anything naughty. We can just take a snooze while we wait."

"You're far too literal, dear. You don't really want to take a snooze, do you?"

He smiled, coloring. "I guess that wouldn't be my first choice."

"Luckily, I have a particular fondness for barbarians. Especially in natural settings."

She turned her back to him on the tablecloth, laughing at his clumsiness as he unzipped the cocktail dress.

It's an intense memory and a happy one, though in the end it only serves to increase his loneliness and sharpen his despair. He does his best to purge it from his mind.

At least he knows where he is. The deCordova had been half an hour's drive from Boston. Maybe two or three more long days of travel if he keeps up a good pace, and the swamps aren't too deep.

10

March 20, 2068 (12 A.U.C.T.)

The Mediterranean Sea

We sailed through the Straits of Gibraltar this morning. We caught a distant glimpse of Africa, and to the north, got a closer look at the Rock of Gibraltar, whose famous profile is exactly as it appears in the old photos. So we've now passed through the Pillars of Hercules, into the Mediterranean Sea of ancient myth and legend. Mare Nostrum to the Romans, cradle of the Greeks and the Phoenicians and I forget how many other ancient civilizations that came before. To think of all the human history that has unfolded on the shores of this sea. Just being here boggles the imagination.

We've also had our first glimpse of mainland Spain, staring at it through our binoculars as we sailed eastward along a ruined coastline that must have been densely populated back in the day: crumbling cinder-block apartment buildings, the shells of defunct hotels and seaside restaurants, many scarred or gutted by fire. There were a few more recent constructions as well, ramshackle huts made of buckling plywood and rusting tin; a few tatters of dirty cloth or a threadbare plastic tarp flapping in the breeze. But even these newer structures looked abandoned, and we saw no other sign of current human occupation. After we'd all had our fill of looking, Tollie steered us farther south, out to sea and away from the coast.

He continues to agitate for a landing, however. Ranting and raving about wild boars and feral goats, abandoned almond orchards and fat green olives. Waxing poetic, too, about the city of Granada, where he spent a study-abroad semester in college, and whose historic core district was designated, he reminds anyone who will listen, as a UNESCO World Heritage Site, back when there *was* a UN. And of course he talks about the great Alhambra itself, the red palace-fortress of the medieval Nasrid emirate, a landmark of human history, where the Moors held sway for more than five centuries, designing aqueducts and fragrant gardens and miraculously engineered gravity-powered fountains that are in all likelihood still babbling away as they always have.

As Tollie is the owner of this vessel, and our expedition leader's brother, we have no choice but to defer to him. But he's also personally appealing in an odd way. He's in his mid-fifties, and there's a certain gravitas that goes along with that seniority. As the son of a billionaire, he has an intrinsic self-confidence, combined with an outlook of sunny optimism similar to his sister's, that can be difficult to resist.

Still, I do wish Dr. Q were less willing to indulge her younger brother's boyish whims. Blood is clearly thicker than water with them, which is understandable in an age when so few of us can claim any living relative at all. But the fact that, for the sake of a few good meals and his own nostalgic amusement, he's willing to put our entire mission in jeopardy—after we've successfully crossed the broad Atlantic Ocean, I might add, at considerable risk to ourselves—well, I find it sort of incomprehensible. It'll be a wonder if he doesn't get us all killed.

It appears that Dr. Q has decided not to press the argument. Perhaps she hopes that common sense will prevail and that he'll eventually relent, but honestly, I don't see that happening. Barring something drastic, it actually appears that we'll be looking for a landing place in the next few days.

Having written all this—and you may find the next part surprising—I must admit that in some respects I understand where Tollie's coming from. Our diet is relentlessly, soul-crushingly dull. In my capacity as the team physician I find it concerning to note how much body weight each of us has lost since we began this journey . . . especially Dr. Q, who never had much surplus fat to begin with. A few days of onshore exertion accompanied by a refreshing change in diet might be exactly what all of us need.

And it *would* be fascinating to get a peek at the Alhambra.

11

10151 A.U.C.T. +/- 18.583 years (estimated)

Two days after leaving the sculpture park he finds his path blocked by yet another swamp. He ties the deerskin bundle to the spear, balances it on his shoulders, and wades in up to his waist. The water smells slightly odd; at first he can't tell why. The bare branches of a grove of drowned trees are studded with the unkempt nests of a heron rookery. Dozens of osprey ferry the open sky, several with good-sized fish squirming in their talons. Shoals of minnows roll beneath the surface in silvery glints, occasionally breaking to scatter ahead of some larger gamefish that is corralling and hunting them down. When a flock of terns starts dive-bombing the hapless minnows from above, it dawns on him that the water smells different here because it's brackish. This swamp is an estuary. Somewhere it is connected to the sea.

In the split second after he makes this observation, something moves in the corner of his eye that freezes him in place. It's a fast-moving object just under the surface of the black water, leaving a V in its wake as it heads straight for him. At the point of the V, cutting through the water, wet and glistening in the hazy morning sun, is the raised triangle of a dorsal fin.

A current of panic reverberates through his arms to his fingertips. Suddenly the world has gone still. Even the birds fly off, as if making room for what's about to take place.

He staggers backward. The resistance of the muck bottom trips him up, and he loses his footing. For a moment he goes under, flailing and choking in the brackish water. Electrified by panic he regains his feet, recovers the half-sunk bundle, and splashes back toward dry land. The predator nearly catches him, veering off through the shallows to disappear with a rolling boil back into the depths of the estuary.

He rests on his hands and knees in the reeds, retching up the foul-tasting water. After a time he gets to his feet and stares out over the swamp, which, aside from the antics of the baitfish and diving birds, is glassy again, as black and inscrutable as obsidian. He has no idea what creature that dorsal fin might have belonged to. A shark he assumes, or a small-toothed whale that has adapted itself to hunting in the brackish shallows.

It makes no difference. He's not getting back in that water.

Shaken by the encounter, and nearly ready to succumb to despair, he considers turning around, back to his mountain aerie, high and dry, the closest thing he has to a home. The truth is, he's harbored the same awful intuition from the moment he climbed out of the cave. An intuition telling him there's really no point in going on with the protocol.

His instructions are clear, however, and this latest swamp is an estuary, meaning that the coast can't be too far away. This remains the most likely setting to discover some clue—perhaps even a decaying ruin—as to what might have befallen any generations of fellow humans that might have clung to life on Earth.

He fights his way south, through a tangled forest of scrub oak and brush, and eventually east along a kind of tidally saturated causeway. Eventually he comes to a saltmarsh, like a broad green meadow, though in reality it's much less pleasant to walk across than a meadow would be, as the seagrass has its roots in the same grasping muck that lines the bottoms of all the swamps. On the far side of the saltmarsh his progress is halted yet again, this time by a deep tidal river. But on the opposite bank is an area of high white dunes, and the shifting wind brings the sound of pounding surf to his ears.

He wades in, keeping a nervous eye on the fast-moving flow. Thigh deep, chest deep, neck deep, raising his arms to keep the bundle dry. His feet lose contact with the sandy bottom and he tries to kick toward the dunes, the strong incoming tide sweeping him upstream. Eventually he does make it over to the dunes, where the sand is pleasantly dry and hot on the callused soles of his feet.

When he crests the dunes, he's rewarded with a view of the vast sparkling ocean. It's a surprisingly emotional sight: the dull roar of surf breaking on a pristine beach stretching out into the distance in both directions, pewter-green rollers glinting in the sun as they rise, curl, and come crashing down into the fizzing backwash. Crashing in, fizzing out, leaving a strip of wet, khaki-colored sand at the tideline, where sanderlings sprint back and forth in their frantic quest for sustenance. Seabirds everywhere in fact: ospreys wheeling, terns riding the wind like delicate origami, herring gulls and black-backed gulls, petrels, willets, turnstones, oystercatchers, cormorants, shearwaters, and something like an albatross. Out beyond the break, the swells are dotted with the glinting heads of seals, and white-feathered gannets fold their wings to plummet, one after another, into the schools of baitfish that glimmer in shoals just beneath the surface. A pod of dolphins erupts a few hundred yards out, leaping joyously as they make their way north along the coast.

Forget about loneliness. Put aside despair. The sight of this thriving ecosystem is a balm to his spirit, to the still-raw psychic wound of having witnessed the rapid decline of the planet's oceans in his own time. The last of the coral reefs gone by the time he'd finished high school. Algae blooms, hot zones, garbage gyres the size of continents, mass death washing in on the putrid tide. He retains a few happy memories from early childhood, but as time went on any visit to the shore became a depressing and actively unpleasant reminder of all that had gone wrong. Beaches littered with single-use plastics, medical waste, the desiccated skeletons of strangled sea creatures. Jellyfish concentrations made swimming or body-surfing inadvisable on most days—and who would want to swim anyway, in a sea redolent of chemicals and the putrefying carcasses of dead fish, sharks, and seals?

The scene unfolding below him now stands in heartening contrast: the raucous chorus of piping and screaming seabirds; the onshore breeze laden with the distinctive smell of living seawater; a wandering tideline of black seaweed and yellow kelp, driftwood logs, copious shells, witch's moneybags, and not a single scrap of plastic in view. Out on the sparkling swells in the distance, he can even make out the waterspouts of a small pod of whales. It's a staggeringly beautiful shoreline, rich with life, and it would make a perfect seasonal base for a band of semi-nomadic hunter-gatherers.

And yet the whole beach, as far as he can see, is unmarked by a single human footprint.

He wanders north and west along the coast for two weeks, keeping to the beaches when he can, cutting inland to wade and swim across bays and estuaries when he must. He manages to avoid further encounters with marine predators, and does end up discovering many remnants of past human occupation: sea glass, fragments of ceramic tile, chunks of asphalt worn into smooth cobbles by the sea. But there's nothing recent.

One afternoon near the mouth of another river he chances upon the ruins of a twenty-first-century neighborhood partially uncovered by the wind in an area of migrating dunes. Uprooted slabs of asphalt, crumbling cement foundations with traces of rusted-out rebar, PVC tubing, even a colorful piece of plastic he's somewhat stunned to identify as a faded fragment of an old Dunkin' Donuts sign, which flakes and crumbles in the sea breeze when he tries to pick it up. The only useful thing he finds is a coil of heavy copper wire, seven or eight feet of which is still in good condition. Stowing it in the deerskin bundle for potential future use, he continues on up the coast.

He climbs a rocky bluff to gain a longer view and stumbles upon the rubble of a large stone ruin. Could it be the Mormon tabernacle of Belmont, a prominent landmark right off Route 2 on the way into Boston? He remembers the building well, a miniature cathedral, impossible to miss, built from the same whitish granite as the honed blocks now poking up through the sea lavender growing atop the bluff. Driving past the temple, the Boston skyline would reveal itself in the lower distance: the Prudential, the John Hancock, the Millennium Tower, Fenway Park, the iconic old Citgo sign—all still vivid in his mind's eye, though of course the city is long gone now, collapsed and corroded far beneath the waves.

If he remembers the projections correctly, in the IPCC's middle-of-the-road scenario sea-levels have risen between 150 and 250 feet by now. Goodbye Boston, goodbye Concord and Lexington, the Old North Church, Faneuil Hall. No more Head of the Charles regatta; no more Boston Common swan boats; no Beacon Hill or Financial District or Chinatown; no Harvard or MIT or that wonderful little Portuguese restaurant in Davis Square. Nothing at all but sand and rocks and the sun winking on the ocean as it seethes and crashes onto pristine beaches and rocky promontories.

He lingers on the coast for a few more weeks, eating well on speared fish and kelp and a bountiful harvest of shellfish: quahogs, oysters, mussels, razor clams. At the edge of a marsh he finds a dried-out salt pan where the encrusted crystals glint like diamonds. He collects as much as he can realistically carry and wraps it in bundles of knotweed leaves. Salt will be a big plus for preserving food, and a life-altering improvement in the palatability of his diet. In the end, however, he finds no trace of living humans, nor indeed of any remnants that might have survived beyond his own time. He can think of no other obvious place to look for them either, and although the eating is good on the coast he has no desire to linger permanently. It is thus with a sense of numb despair that he decides to make the journey back to the familiar ledge overlooking the valley that was once the site of the Centauri Project Lab.

He walks due north for several long days before turning west, with the idea that if he can find higher ground in what was once southern New Hampshire, he may be able to avoid some of the swamplands.

It takes him several weeks to get to what he believes is the approximate location, but with no GPS and a less-than-perfect homing instinct he ends up circling through the forest for another week. Finding the familiar mountain and valley begins to strike him as a pointless exercise—it's not like anything is waiting for him—and a few times he nearly makes the decision to give up. But when he thinks about exactly what this would entail—choosing a manner of death and then taking steps to make it happen in the least miserable way possible—he forces himself to keep walking.

Finally, one hot breezy afternoon in what he estimates is early September, malnourished and demoralized, he climbs up into the swaying top branches of a tall white pine and spots the unmistakable profile of Mount Wingandicoa in the distance. Two days later he comes to a faint trail through the forest he recognizes as having been worn by his own feet and follows it back up to the familiar ledge.

PART II

It is almost as though in our very bones were felt ancestral memories of the way we have come, and the feeling like magic touches us once more so that we repeat with something like terror in our voices, "It can never be done again."

—Loren Eiseley, "The Fire Apes"

12

March 27, 2068 (12 A.U.C.T.)

The Mediterranean Sea

Dear hypothetical reader,

I realize there have been moments in this account when I've adopted a lighthearted or half-joking tone regarding whether you actually exist. But I want to make it clear that your existence actually matters very much to me. Because if you *don't* exist, it's probable that all our efforts have failed. Unfortunately, after the experiences I'm now going to do my best to recount for you, that outcome seems more likely than ever.

If you *are* reading this, I hope that you have a more generous capacity to forgive your fellow humans than I do and that you will teach your children and grandchildren that there is a better way to live.

And I must apologize for my recent silence. So much has happened over this past week that it stretches out in my mind like months.

Another extended sail along the southern coast of Spain seemed to confirm our first impressions that the entire region is uninhabited. It's no wonder, really. By all appearances most of what used to be known as the Costa del Sol has become a sunbaked, waterless desert. This part of the Mediterranean had been losing population for decades pre-collapse due to water shortages and frequent deadly heatwaves. A high percentage of those who remained were likely to have perished in the hyperpandemic, and it appears that most of the survivors must have moved northward into regions less assailed by the extreme heat and chronic drought that have clearly become the defining features of the climate here.

The Mediterranean is clear and sapphire-blue but pretty much devoid of life as far as we can tell. With the demise of irrigation systems, all the land visible from off shore is also dead or mostly so—desiccated shrublands in the lower spots, a few fields of brittle yellow weeds, but mostly just barren hillsides rising abruptly from the azure sea. The skeletons of what used to be an enormous complex of tomato-growing greenhouses cover many of these hillsides, shrouds of plastic sheet flapping free in the hot breeze like disintegrated cobwebs.

Tollie's plans had taken on a clearer shape. He proposed to anchor at a former beach resort he knew of on the coast due south of Granada and trek up through the foothills and over the crest of the Sierra Nevada mountains, shooting any game animals he might see on the way. Depending on how things looked, he would then descend into the city of Granada, "quickly" visit the Alhambra and the historic Albaicín neighborhood, then return to the coast by the old trans-Sierra highway. He estimated the whole circuit would take between three and five days, and the rest of us, with the exception of at least one person to stay and guard the yacht, were welcome to either come along or remain on the coast. It was up to us.

I fear that my initial resistance to the scheme eroded pretty quickly. Tollie's evocations of the smells and tastes of fresh-roasted meat had awakened within me an irrational yearning, however unlikely it seemed that he would actually chance upon anything he could shoot. Even more convincing for me, however, was that the city of Granada had always loomed large in my imagination. My mother used to speak with great pride of her ancestors who were *Marranos*, Sephardic Jews forced to convert to Catholicism after the reconquest of Granada in 1492. The idea that I might actually lay my eyes on this legendary city, and especially the Alhambra, one of the wonders of human civilization, was in the end impossible for me to resist. It was an opportunity that would almost certainly never come my way again.

In my opinion, James, as the most junior and by far the most intimidating-looking crew member, was the logical candidate to stay behind, but Dr. Q was having none of it.

"I've *been* to Granada, dear," she said. We were sitting by the bowsprit, with our feet up on opposite rails as Tollie steered us toward the shore. “Besides, I'd rest easier knowing that both you and James were there. Tollie's notoriously bad at split-second decisions.”

“But I really don't like the idea of leaving you here by yourself.”

“Nonsense, Alejandra, dear. I'm perfectly capable of looking after both myself and the yacht. You three should go. Have an interesting adventure together! You can tell me all about it when you get back. The truth is, I could use some time alone. I can always get in the kayak if I feel the need to explore.”

In the end I agreed, though I still didn't like the idea. In addition to being my mentor and long-term employer, Dr. Q is the closest thing I have to a mother or older sister. The prospect of leaving her behind filled me with anxiety.

The spot Tollie chose for our landfall seemed to be a good one, a deep cove protected by an archipelago of half-submerged boulders. On the landward side were the ruins of a multistory hotel built into a cliff; according to Tollie this was once a gathering place for the international yachting set. The hotel's façade and picture windows had long since fallen out, leaving a hollow grid of crumbling concrete clinging to the cliff, with rusted rebar jutting out from it like broken-off taproots. Along the top of the cliff was a fringe of weedy vegetation. We could see nothing beyond that, which also meant that in order for anyone to see the *Solar Barque* they would have to walk right up to the edge.

Dr. Q helped the three of us—Tollie, James, and me—lower first our expedition packs and then ourselves down into the waiting dinghy.

“Please don't go ashore alone,” I said, squeezing her hand before releasing it.

“And if you *do* go ashore,” Tollie added, “take the Glock with you.” At breakfast he'd handed her his pocket pistol and a box of bullets, which I suppose should have given me confidence, but the fact that he'd thought it necessary at all left me even more anxious than before.

“But there's really no need for you to go ashore at all,” I insisted.

“Not unless Mr. Tolstoy becomes fatally boring, dear,” she replied, smiling, and holding up an ancient hardcover of *War and Peace* from the yacht's well-stocked library.

James rowed us across the cove, Tollie in the prow gripping his high-powered Remington hunting rifle with a look of undisguised delight on his aging cartoon-hero face. I kept my binoculars pressed to my eyes, scanning the top of the cliff for any movement.

James ran the nose of the dinghy up onto the narrow strip of sand at the base of the cliff, which was marred by a tideline piled with garishly colored plastic rubbish; Tollie hopped out and helped me ashore. We pulled the skiff up against the cliff, flipped it, and camouflaged it with a pile of sun-bleached detergent bottles and dismembered plastic toys. After one final parting wave to Dr. Q—already lost in her novel; we had to shout to get her attention—we hoisted our expedition packs and set off.

The ruined hotel's staircases were still intact, and it was easy enough to find our way up and out through the rubble-strewn corridors to the former resort town's main square. Most of the buildings were in various stages of collapse, with drought-tolerant vegetation growing in the medians and coming up through cracks in the pavement: ragweed, tumbleweed, desiccated pampas grass rustling and rattling in the hot wind.

From the beginning I had the distinct feeling of being watched, perhaps through binoculars or a rifle scope: a prickling sensation in the hairs at the back of my scalp and neck. I don't know if we actually *were* being watched at that point, though it's certainly possible.

We crossed a weed-grown highway and climbed up into the parched, steeply rising foothills above the town. Following the paths of least resistance we eventually found ourselves on a clearly defined trail—so clearly defined, I speculated that it might constitute evidence of a continuing human presence.

"I haven't seen any boot prints in the dust, Al," Tollie said, reading my thoughts. "And I *have* been looking. It's bone-dry up here. No doubt it takes a long time for the vegetation to grow in."

We trudged on in silence, all of us sweating and puffing for breath after the sedentary weeks at sea.

"What's our plan if we *do* run into people?" I asked after a moment.

"Great question." Tollie stopped in the middle of the trail and took out a handkerchief to wipe his face. He was always happy to chat, especially if, as in this case, it gave him an excuse to rest. "We'll be polite, and assume their intentions aren't hostile. It's probably a good idea for you to do the talking, Al—my Spanish is a bit rusty. In the absolute worst-case scenario, we do have an insurance policy." He raised the hunting rifle and narrowed his eyes in an exaggeratedly hardboiled expression that I suppose was intended to be funny.

I caught James's eye and he gave me a barely perceptible grin beneath the hoodie, which made me feel a little better. I'm not sure how explicit Dr. Q had been with him, but it was clear our highest responsibility for the next few days was preventing Tollie from doing anything stupid.

Several hot and dusty hours later, in the shade of an overhang beside the trail, we came upon something that seemed to confirm our fears: a relatively recent human encampment complete with a fire ring and a scattering of litter from looted commodities: broken glass, grimy plastic juice bottles, and dust-coated cans with labels in Spanish that could still be read: white asparagus, sardines, olives stuffed with garlic. To me the campsite looked like it had been abandoned months rather than years ago, though as Tollie pointed out it was hard to judge with certainty given the dryness of the climate.

It was without question the clearest sign we'd yet had of a surviving human population. Assuming the humans who'd camped here hadn't perished in the meantime, it brought up several uncomfortable questions, such as where they were at the moment, and what they were living on now that pre-collapse shelf goods had undoubtedly become difficult to find. Because despite Tollie's undying optimism and frequent stops to scan the terrain with binoculars and rifle scope, we had yet to see anything resembling a game animal. A lone crow; a small flock of starlings; a cockroach inching along the ground in the shadow of a roadside shed with a caved-in roof. Otherwise nothing but scrub, rocks, and echoing stillness, with an occasional tumbleweed rolling across the trail in the parching wind.

Tollie's immediate goal was the Alpujarras, a collection of tiny villages founded high on the slopes of the Sierra Nevada range by the Nasrids fleeing the reconquest of Granada in 1492. Following the old access road we walked through three of these deserted villages, ghost towns now with broken-out windows and ancient wooden shutters creaking on their hinges. The cobbled main streets were creepily silent, the dark and steeply sloping alleyways between the houses seemed perfect hideouts for an ambush. We didn't linger.

The villages were built into steep mountainsides planted with what were once well-irrigated almond orchards. The region used to be famous for its air-cured jamón serrano, and Tollie thought it might be a good place to look for feral pigs. It was not. Some almond trees still clung to life, though they bore no nuts as far as we could tell, which of course makes sense as there are so few remaining pollinators. We humans have made sure of that. Most of the trees were dead, mummified by the sun and the constant dry wind into haunting silver-gray tree sculptures.

We saw no feral pigs. Not even a squirrel. There were oak forests in a few moist ravines, but no acorns, and many of the trunks and branches were rotting under a kind of velvety crust of cobalt-blue fungus. In the end, Tollie did manage to put a bullet through the breast of an elderly crow, which we cooked over a small fire on a trail overlooking the villages. I devoured my portion of the stringy roasted meat with relish, feeling slightly guilty that Dr. Q was missing it.

We made camp on a rocky slope with a panoramic view of the sun-gilt Mediterranean, with the coast of North Africa somewhere in the hazy distance beyond. Tollie took advantage of what he called "the golden hour" to go hunting again, leaving James and me to set up our tents and build a fire. There was plenty of dry wood in nearby ravines, and we soon had a respectable if smoky campfire.

It was the evocative smell of the woodsmoke I think, and the cheerful snap and crackle of those bright yellow flames, that put me in a sentimental mood. Or maybe it was just being out under the sky on that pleasantly cool boulder-strewn mountainside, with the last rays of the sun slanting down to pick out the elaborate branching folds of the buff-colored foothills and the glittering platinum expanses of the sea below. In any case, I began to feel the stirrings of something I hadn't felt in years, and an array of powerful and nearly forgotten emotions came rushing back in—loneliness, affection, physical lust—an intoxicating brew of feeling that drove me to plunk myself down beside James in a way that was far too purposeful, and far too close, to be misinterpreted.

He didn't meet my eyes. I don't think he dared. After a moment, he did pat my knee, which gave me an excuse to slide in closer. He put his arm around me, and I let myself soften into his side, which felt surprisingly large and powerful beneath the loose-fitting fabric of the Lab hoodie, like a warm tree trunk, or the flank of a bull, or maybe the torso of some strong and graceful marine mammal like a beluga or an orca. And we sat that way, still not looking into each other's eyes, but basking—or at least *I* was basking—in the sensations of being held by someone, and in the novelty of this newly discovered current of attraction that existed between us.

"You sure this is okay, Al?" he asked softly after a moment. I could tell from the uncertainty in his voice and the slight tremor in his side that he was as nervous as I. Probably more so, given that I was a senior colleague who'd been markedly cool toward him over these past however many years—and at times, being honest, even a little unfriendly.

"No," I said. "I mean, I don't think—" But there were no words I could come up with that didn't echo in my own mind as either sappy or gratuitously cynical, so I didn't finish the sentence. Instead I abandoned all caution, closed my eyes, and sought out his lips with my own.

It was only a moment before we heard Tollie's footsteps crunching loudly on the scree below us. We both sprang guiltily to our feet and busied ourselves with camp tasks. The Great Hunter had come back empty-handed of course, and there was no more communication between James and me as we prepared a meager dinner for three from the food supplies we'd brought with us from the yacht.

In the days that have followed, as I will recount for you, the need to cope with ongoing crises was such that there have been no further opportunities for intimacy. But I *am* sure that that moment by the campfire forged a connection, at least that's what I keep telling myself. Despite the fact that we haven't spoken about it directly since that moment, I flatter myself in the belief that his feelings are similar, and I must admit that this turn of events has filled me with an unaccustomed, unreasonable, probably illogical sense of hope. Illogical, because given the current state of the world there isn't likely to *be* much of a future for James and me. And if there *is* to be a future it will have to wait, leaving whatever feelings and desires that may have arisen between us to bide within the private confines of our own hearts. Because for two members of a team about to enter the most critical stage of a perilous and existentially decisive mission, this is really not the moment to be pairing off and losing focus.

In any case, it's now time for me to do my rounds so I can get some sleep. I'll continue the story of our little Granada expedition tomorrow, because there's still quite a bit left to tell.

Transcriber's note: I'm not sure Alejandra's last point is entirely accurate. Pairing off doesn't necessarily mean a loss of focus, and in some cases it actually leads to *increased* focus. Even busy people engaged in a critical mission have a right to their happiness, do they not? To the transcriber's regret, however, she was not fully aware of the situation and never had a chance to discuss the matter directly with the writer.

13

10151 A.U.C.T. +/- 18.583 years (estimated)

A drizzling fog on the trail up the mountain. Light wind, trees dripping. He's making his way up to the ledge after another monotonous day of foraging. Yellow leaves flip and spiral on their way down to the forest floor, presenting one side, then the reverse, as they chase one another to the ground. At the edge of the trail he sees a striking new mushroom, a purple knob poking up out of the wet duff like an erect phallus.

Above him on the hillside, he hears a thud of footfalls. Thinking it might be a bear, he hides himself on the downhill side of a moss-covered boulder. The footfalls pause, then start up again. Whatever it is is clearly coming down the mountainside toward him. The rhythm of the footsteps is odd, though, and strangely evocative of something.

When the creature comes into view, he's gripped by a dawning amazement. *A human.* A woman. Tangle of dark curls. Clear olive skin. In her late thirties perhaps, rawboned but not malnourished, with strong hands and deep laugh lines around her eyes.

He was wrong to have given up hope. They have sent him a companion after all. But where was her sphere? Or does she belong to some remnant of humanity that has clung to life through all these millennia?

Tears blur his vision as he steps out from behind the boulder. "Do you speak English?"

She stares blankly. He holds out his hands, palms up, in a universal gesture of harmless intent. She mimics the gesture, smiling. It's a very beautiful smile, though a few teeth are missing. But she appears calm, and unsurprised to see him.

Suddenly they're holding each other, the generous breasts beneath her deerskin tunic flattening into his chest. He buries his beard in the warmth of her shoulder; takes in the fragrance of her body, her hair. The scent is stirring, and deeply familiar. He has to clench his teeth to keep from sobbing.

She takes him by the hand and leads him to a bed of moss by the side of the trail. Shrugs out of her tunic and motions for him to come. Her hands are rough and callused, but the rest of her is silken and hot. She pushes him back onto the moss. Straddles him, guides him into her. Gasps for breath, then urges him on with a string of shockingly filthy language.

After, they lie side by side on the moss, staring up at a bright tapestry of stars above the canopy. Odd to see stars so bright in the middle of what had been a drizzly day—and he sits up, suddenly confused. "So you speak English."

She lifts her head, staring up at him. Her eyes flash bottle-green, the way a cat's eyes catch a flashlight, and it's only then that he realizes he's in a dream.

In the next moment he's awake, shivering beneath a pile of furs in the bone-chilling damp of his pitch-black grotto at the back of the ledge, with the sound of a hard rain echoing through the forest.

In the morning the dream still feels real to him. The crinkle of her eyes; the feel of her clear dark skin; the smell of her hair. Even the sex, clearly a subconscious projection of his own unmet emotional and physiological needs, remains as detailed and graphic in his mind as if it had actually happened.

He remembers reading about how the collective unconscious is the repository for the dreams and myths of all humanity. Was this dream a proof that the repository still exists? Or was it just a ghost of the distant past, the reflexive firing of an individual synapse long ago cut off from the species-wide nervous system?

14

March 28, 2068 (12 A.U.C.T.)

The Mediterranean Sea

We had a breakfast of cold Lab jerky and canteen water and hiked up to the barren, rocky summit of what Tollie informed us was Mulhacén, the highest mountain on the Iberian Peninsula. As we started making our way down the other side toward Granada, we began to see more signs of a human presence. There were footpaths etched over the scree fields and trampled through the weeds. We came upon a recent firepit and a scatter of wrappers from a trove of what seemed to be recently scavenged snack food—cookies and crackers, possibly from an old vending machine hidden in the bowels of a hollowed-out cement ski lodge. I couldn't rid myself of that constant tickling sensation at the back of my neck, like phantom spiders crawling up under my hairline.

Looking back, I'm not sure why I didn't insist on turning around and heading down to the yacht. It was clear by now that there were going to be no game animals. We were about to make a needless descent into a ruined urban environment populated by human survivors most likely living under difficult, even desperate conditions. My internal alarm bells were ringing, but for whatever reason I didn't speak up. Part of it was probably just curiosity. I was still longing, against my better instincts, to get a glimpse of the Alhambra. A larger part of it undoubtedly had to do with what had happened the previous night between James and me.

We'd made a connection, and despite the doom and gloom of my earlier entry, it was a connection that felt (and still feels) quite important to me, though tenuous, like a spell that could be broken if I said or did the wrong thing. I didn't want to risk coming across as my usual bossy self, putting a damper on everyone's fun.

Our first view of the Alhambra was magnificent: a colossal, multileveled palace on a lofty perch above the valley of Granada; a complex of towers and fortress walls that glowed reddish-gold in the late afternoon sun and seemed to rise organically from the ridgeline, like cliff faces in a geometrically arranged escarpment. Tollie reminded us that the Moors were geniuses of civil engineering whose handiwork is still functional, especially their aqueducts and other waterworks, and we could see from the lush vegetation around the base of the fortress that this was at least partially true. The rest of the city is in ruins, and the whole broad valley has, like most of the surrounding region, reverted to a parched desert. But the Alhambra, in addition to being high and strategically well-situated, appeared to be a genuine oasis, and a natural gathering point for human survivors.

I must admit that for a moment I imagined we might actually figure out a way to sneak into the palace and see with our own eyes everything Tollie had enthusiastically described. The scented gardens; the interior rooms full of elaborate plaster arabesques; the arched windows open to the cross-breezes that trickle down from the Sierra Nevada; the marble courtyards and bubbling fountains and even the ingenious marble toilets with a steady stream of spring water flowing beneath them.

Studying the fortress more closely with the help of our binoculars, however, we saw that the bases of its ancient stucco walls were marred by grimy black graffiti, and that there were garbage middens beneath many of those picturesque windows, mountainous piles of befouled paper and plastic refuse avalanching down into the ravines below. The rest of the city looked even worse. Streets choked with garbage and rubble and the usual hardy weeds growing up through cracks in the stone; windows broken out or boarded up; many buildings reduced to shells, charred and collapsed. I'm not sure what I expected to see in Granada. Not this. Not a squalid ruin of a city that told a story of mass death, anarchy, and violence. Though it really shouldn't have been a surprise. The identical post-collapse pattern seems to have replicated itself all over the globe.

Through our binoculars we finally spotted our first Spaniards: four dark figures skylined atop the tallest towers of the Alhambra, seated comfortably on plastic chairs of the sort that might once have belonged to an inexpensive outdoor café. Lookouts, obviously. Male, above a certain age, lean and leathery, with ponytails and graying beards that moved in the breeze under battered straw sun hats, dressed in tattered black jeans and faded t-shirts bearing the logos of defunct music groups. One was missing an arm; another's cheeks were badly marked, like James's, with the telltale scarring of a close-call hyperpandemic survivor. All four were well armed, with automatic rifles strapped across their shoulders in a way that looked disconcertingly comfortable, as if they never took them off.

"Maybe they're friendly," Tollie said.

James and I put down our binoculars and turned to stare at him, incredulous. These Spaniards did not look friendly at all. They looked lean, battle-scarred, and dangerous.

"They might be able to tell us a lot if we could find a way to approach them," he suggested. "Exactly how things have gone down this part of the world for the last twelve years, for example. Which would be good information to have."

"So it's historical research we've come all this way for? I thought your main interest was in securing us a supply of wild meat."

He colored a little, scanning the palace walls with his binoculars. "Well, I'm curious, Al. Aren't you?"

"Curiosity is not a good reason to take that kind of risk." I glared at James, irritated by his all-too-typical reluctance to voice his opinion.

"Al's right, Tollie," he said at last. "The mission has to come first."

"Which is exactly why I think we should go down there and try to learn what we can. Who knows what we'll find out? It could be something useful to the mission."

"Tollie!"

"*What*, Al? Come on. I'm not suggesting we walk right up to the gates of the fortress and turn ourselves in. We can slip into the city unnoticed, take a look around, see what we see, then head back to the coast."

I remained adamantly opposed. James supported me, though not as forcefully as I would have preferred. Tollie likes to appear clueless, but he's surprisingly good at reading people, and he must have detected a whiff of indecision.

"How about we just camp here for the night?" he suggested. "We can watch their comings and goings, and in the morning we can decide whether we want to go into the city or head back. Okay?"

I went along reluctantly, and James did too, though in the end it didn't matter what either of us thought. Tollie had already made up his mind that he was returning to Granada, his old college stomping grounds, with or without our company. His only real concession was waiting until the next morning to let us know.

It's difficult to express how frustrating Tollie's insistence was, but what were James and I supposed to do? Stay at the campsite waiting to see if he would come back alive? Go straight back to the yacht to explain to Dr. Q why we'd abandoned her devil-may-care brother, our indispensable navigator and skipper, to whatever fate awaited him in the ruined city?

Which is how, with our backpacks loaded and the early-morning sun already hot on our shoulders, we found ourselves following him down into the valley, using the cover of ravines and embankments to keep ourselves hidden from any eyes that might be watching from the fortress. As had been our practice throughout the expedition we walked single file: Tollie in the lead with his loaded .30-06, your faithful correspondent second in line, and James last, with an eye to our flank.

We entered the city at a point to the southwest of the Alhambra, on a relatively narrow street that led to a neighborhood of hollowed-out apartment buildings that we hoped would block any sightlines from above. It was melancholy and unsettling to walk through the weed-grown, rubble-strewn shell of what had once been a thriving modern city: the burned-out hulks of cars and buses; the rusting poles of defunct street and traffic lights; piles of sun-degraded plastic garbage at the feet of crumbling, graffiti-covered walls. Most of the windows in the buildings that still stand have been broken out; even in this dry climate the interior spaces appear to be in a state of rapid decay, cracking in the heat and occasional frost and under attack from termites, fire, and dry rot.

Eventually we came to the narrow stone plaza that marked the edge of the city's historic core, with the massive red walls of the Alhambra blocking out half the sky along the crest of a clifflike ridge to our right and the tile-roofed hillsides of the Albaicín neighborhood rising steeply to our left.

"UNESCO World Heritage Site," Tollie intoned, unable even now to resist playing the tour guide. It was fairly stunning to think that the human species had once had the wherewithal to create an international body to declare such historically and architecturally significant places worth preserving in perpetuity.

Odd word, perpetuity. But let's continue with the story.

At the head of the plaza was a sixteenth-century church with a tall, delicate bell tower of golden brick inlaid with beautiful blue-and-white tile. Tollie used the barrel of his rifle to pry open the big iron-clad double door, one half of which swung outward on its hinges with a loud creak. When nothing emerged, he slipped inside.

James and I stood uncertainly in the blazing sun until our personal tour guide popped his head out again, beaming enthusiastically. "No one here," he said. "Come check out the cloister. I think you'll find it interesting."

The shade and relative cool inside the convent were a relief, though it did smell sharply of rodent dung. Tollie led us back to a dusty courtyard with a dry fountain at its center and a second story held up by a forest of columns. It was the carvings at the capitals of the columns Tollie wanted us to see: a Renaissance menagerie of realistic-looking imaginary figures; some with human faces and the bottom parts of fish or birds or snakes; some with human bodies and the heads of donkeys or gape-mouthed demons with curving horns. Tortured shapeshifters howling in transports of joy or extreme agony as they looped their limber bodies into impossible-looking yoga poses.

If the circumstances had been different I might have been tempted to linger, but that was when we heard the front door of the convent creak open. We looked at each other, wide-eyed, and hurried back to see who it was.

As our eyes adjusted to the darkness, we made out a stooped human figure loitering in the narthex just inside the door. We approached cautiously, Tollie in front with his hunting rifle raised, but the Spaniard put up his hands, and he appeared to be unarmed. He was younger and softer-looking than the lean guards we'd seen on the fortress walls, wearing cut-off sweat pants and a t-shirt, with a gap-toothed grin and a scraggly, goat-like beard that was oddly reminiscent of the figures in the Renaissance carvings we'd just been looking at. He was bald but unscarred, with big gentle eyes and a calf-like demeanor that created the impression of harmlessness. He seemed to be mute, his speech consisting of a series of very enthusiastic but unintelligible high-pitched groans. But his body language—wringing his hands and bowing obsequiously—was intended to make clear that he didn't represent any kind of threat. After a moment he started making urgent gestures toward himself and the door as if he very much wanted us to follow him outside.

Tollie lowered the rifle, smiling and nodding in sympathy with our new friend. For a moment I wondered if he'd been right all along. Maybe I'd been overly suspicious. Maybe coming here really would lead to something other than danger and disaster.

Cautiously, we followed the Spaniard out into the bright sun of the plaza. From there, trailing along at what we considered a safe distance, we followed him up a narrow cobbled street deeper into the core of the old city.

The situation was making me nervous again. Our new friend loped energetically ahead of us, turning every once in a while to reassure us with his toothless grin and beckon us on. The street was bordered by a chest-high masonry wall above the fetid trickle of what was previously a small river meandering along the bottom of a steep ravine. To our right rose the high walls of the Alhambra, to our left the steep hillside of the Albaicín neighborhood.

Tollie pointed to an ancient staircase slanting up into the brick-and-stone Nasrid architecture and informed us excitedly that this led to the exact location of his semester-abroad apartment. He vowed to bring us back and show it to us later in the day.

In front of us we could see the ravine bottom open out into another oblong plaza directly beneath the Alhambra, so that the golden-red towers almost seemed to lean over it. I think James and I got the same feeling at the same time: a prickling intuition of menace that caused us both to stop in the middle of the street.

Tollie turned with a look of impatience. "Come on, you guys! It's going to be fine."

"Ven, ven!" our guide agreed, urging us forward in the first comprehensible syllables he'd uttered.

"En seguida," I assured him, raising my binoculars. James already had his to his eyes, scanning the plaza ahead, where a small crowd had gathered, perhaps two dozen survivors. A welcoming party by appearances, made up primarily of middle-aged men with the same lean underfed look as the guards we'd seen earlier, with a few sharp-shouldered, hollow-cheeked women lingering in the shadows.

"Ven, ven!" our guide repeated, walking back toward us with his hands raised in supplication. But his toothless smile looked strained now, and in the distance behind him the welcome party had spotted us and were shouting friendly greetings and beckoning us forward. Scanning their faces through the binoculars, my blood went cold. The friendliness of their expressions, their broad encouraging smiles, were exaggerated, distorted, and patently insincere. All the men and a few of the women were armed, not with guns but with long blades tucked discreetly into their belts. Machetes, bowie knives, carving knives . . .

"We need to run," James said. "Right now."

Tollie opened his mouth to argue, but in the next moment our toothless friend stepped up with surprising quickness and grabbed hold of the .30-06 barrel. He tried to wrench the gun away, but Tollie drove its butt hard into his stomach, and the strange young Spaniard collapsed in a heap on the cobblestones, whimpering pitifully.

We were all in full retreat by then, with the welcoming party streaming down the cobbled street after us. Tollie screamed to take a right at the stone staircase he'd pointed out before, and because we had no good alternative, we followed his advice.

The Albaicín is a medieval rabbit warren of steep cobbled passageways, winding staircases, blind corners, and dead ends. Out of shape as we were, and with our backpacks weighing us down, it was a tense, tortured, and lung-burning uphill jog. We did have adrenaline on our side, along with the motivatingly fresh memory of those ominous-looking faces down in the plaza. Tollie's instincts, for a change, were good. The neighborhood was built for walking, not driving; any visible windows had been boarded up, and although the roofs of many of the houses had collapsed, most were surrounded by high walls, making the narrow streets labyrinthine and confusing. It's an easy place to get lost. Any Spaniards still trying to find us must eventually have given up.

Tollie led us over the crest of a hill to an ancient Moorish arch, where he actually tried to take advantage of a moment's rest in the shade to give us another history lecture. James and I were having none of that, and we hurried him along down the hill into the wreckage of the modern city, then out of Granada altogether along a highway of cracking asphalt and half-collapsed concrete beam bridges that Tollie was pretty sure would offer the most direct route back to the coast.

Unfortunately this is not the end of my narration concerning our little Andalusian excursion. In fact, the worst is yet to come. But medical duties call once again so I'll have to finish it tomorrow.

15

10151 A.U.C.T. +/- 18.583 years (estimated)

Nick flakes himself an adze from river flint, makes a spade with the scapula of a cow moose, and carries these tools down to the Lab site. He uses a stick to mark out a rough quadrant and starts chopping with the adze at the root network. The tough woody laterals, and the fine intermeshed root hairs working with their mycorrhizae partners to do the complex ongoing work of the forest. Transporting the water in and up. Photosynthetic growth. The deployment of nutrients and sugars. The cleanup and recycling of dead organic material. Beneath the roots the soil is black and friable, deep layers of accumulated humus full of annelids and beetles, grubs and millipedes, microorganisms in untold multitudes. The incredible concentration of life in every square foot of soil in an old-growth forest.

Sweat pours from his body as he digs down through the layers. By the end of the first day he has a chest-deep test pit, neatly squared off. No artifacts yet of course. For that he figures he'll need to remove at least a few more cubic yards of dirt. He's hoping he'll come across something that will allow him to piece together what happened to the surviving members of the Centauri team, and Natalie in particular. As futile as it might seem, he feels the need to conceptualize how everything might have played out.

As an undergrad he'd spent a term at an iron-age site in Portugal, so he knows the basic techniques of archaeological excavation, and he also understands that the probability of finding anything meaningful is low. But with no pressure to preserve or document, all he really needs is time, of which he has plenty to spare.

After three weeks of grueling daily work interrupted only by foraging, hydrating, sleeping, and frightening off a few curious predators, he has completed six deep pits. He knows he's reached the right stratum at the bottom of one of these when he finds, in quick succession, a fragment of an old solar roofing tile, a nest of copper wiring clinging to a piece of dirty fiberglass insulation, and the broken-off neck of a wine bottle, a Rioja probably, pillaged from Cornelius Quist's original wine cellar for one of Natalie's signature candlelit dinner gatherings. Next he finds the stainless-steel blade of a butcher's knife in nearly perfect condition apart from a spot near the cracked remnants of the handle where mineral soil has become embedded in the alloy, and a large cast-iron skillet, dirt-encrusted and partially corroded, but still useable.

The familiar feel and heft of these last two objects provokes a leaden feeling deep in his gut. Muscle memories of using this very knife to mince garlic from the Lab's garden. Of using this very skillet to cook countless omelets from the eggs of the Lab's wandering flock of chickens.

He stops digging and sits on his heels in the dirt, his vision blurred by tears.

It's not as if he didn't know what he was doing. The whole point was exactly this: dig right down to the ghosts. But he isn't prepared for the force of emotion that comes from holding these objects in his hands. What happened to the compound before it went into its final cycles of degradation, he wonders. Did everything collapse from rot, or was there a fire at some point? Or perhaps the whole place was looted by gangs of increasingly desperate survivors? If that were the case, what happened to any members of the team who were still alive?

A sort of dam in his mind breaks, and his memory starts a rapid scrolling of images of Natalie: Natalie at the door of the clean room, professionally radiant in her white lab coat; Natalie on a mountaintop, the wind sifting her fine salt-and-pepper hair; Natalie in winter, wrapped in a green cashmere throw she'd knitted herself, reading a novel, with her cheek resting on her palm as she flipped another page; Natalie on a quiet summer night, sipping a glass of Rioja on the screened-in porch of the Round Barn, cross-breezes filtering in through the screens, her big-lensed glasses glinting in the flickering candlelight. And he realizes that all this time, out of some protective instinct no doubt, he's been resisting the urge to visualize her. To actively remember her. To mourn her. To accept that he will never again hold that small frame in his arms, never again smell the fragrance of her favorite cedar oil soap on her recently showered skin. Natalie's been dead for millennia now. An objective fact. And yet, somehow, emotionally, it doesn't feel quite real.

All the things he's been busy with over these last few weeks—pacing out the quadrants, hacking through roots, the endless moving of earth—it's as if his subconscious mind has been doing everything possible to make contact. To dig her out. As if her heart were actually still beating down there under the dirt.

He supposes that in a certain way she *is* still alive, in his memory at least, where, unlike in the real world, time runs both forward and backward. For now, memory is a place that feels more real to him than his actual physical surroundings. And it's certainly less lonely.

They met standing in line at a café on the MIT campus. His first impression was of a typically self-absorbed STEM grad student in her mid-twenties, petite, eyes inwardly focused behind big-lensed round glasses, dictating something complex and vaguely mathematical into her phone.

At two parallel registers they uttered the same phrase simultaneously: "Black tea with coco-creamer and a blueberry scone, please." The coincidence inspired a quick exchange of glances, nothing more. Given the limited number of items on the menu it probably wasn't so unusual for two customers to make the same order at the same time, but it struck him as uncanny that they'd spoken the words almost in unison.

It was a warm morning in May. The café's outdoor seating consisted of a dozen cut-granite boulders arranged in a circle on the mowed grass, like a low-slung Stonehenge shaded by riverside sycamores, a mystical and bucolic scene somewhat marred by the blur and whoosh of plug-in traffic on Memorial Drive, only yards away. There was still hope in the air at the time, he remembers, especially on the campuses of MIT and Harvard where everyone was confident that a solution to the environmental crisis stalking the world was almost within reach. That humanity would soon be able to engineer its way into a new era of enlightened planetary stewardship.

The only open seats were on the same crescent-shaped bench hewn into one of the blocks. They sat, placed their teas and scones on the honed granite surface, and stared stubbornly at the screens of their phones for a few minutes. In the end, they surrendered to their fate and began a conversation.

He'd underestimated her. She was not self-absorbed at all, nor was she judgmental, as he'd assumed she would be, about the fact that his field was biology, a discipline some considered to be middling or humdrum at a university famous for cutting-edge research in the hard sciences. But she listened to him with avid interest as he told her about his dissertation on extremophiles in geothermal steam vents. Gazing out across the streaming traffic to the small boats thronging the steel-blue expanse of the Charles River, he listened just as intently, though with less comprehension, to a simplified account of her work on entanglement and other experimental problems in quantum physics.

Judged purely on appearances, Natalie wouldn't have stood out in a crowd. She was small-boned ("spindle-shanked," in her own words), just over five feet tall, with a tawny complexion and curly shoulder-length hair, salted even then by a few strands of premature gray, held out of her eyes with two or three cheap plastic barrettes. She had a way of dressing that privileged comfort over fashion: generally she wore Birkenstocks, over-sized cardigans she'd knitted herself or found in her periodic scavenging trips to local thrift shops, and loose-fitting, straight-hipped vintage jeans, often patched at the knees or embroidered with a few bright flowers. But despite her diminutive stature and no-frills fashion sense she possessed a larger-than-life aura impossible to ignore, as if her whole being were lit from the inside by some hidden source of light.

Nick hadn't been the first to notice this of course, nor would he be the last. She'd be constantly fending off admirers as long as he'd known her. But the encounter was unforgettable for him, like a mild and unexpectedly pleasant electrical shock.

After that first coincidence there was no good reason for their paths to cross again. Their departments were on opposite sides of campus, and they moved in different social spheres. But he couldn't get her out of his mind.

He googled her, of course, and learned that she'd neglected to mention that her father was Cornelius Quist, or that she herself had gained a reputation as a brilliant young physicist. Of course her greatest discovery was still ahead of her then, but she was already the author of dozens of groundbreaking studies, and it was clear to anyone paying attention that she was going to win at least one Nobel Prize.

A few weeks later they noticed each other standing in the same line at the same campus café.

"Black tea with coco-creamer and a blueberry scone, I presume?" Her voice was lower-pitched than he remembered, almost husky, and she enunciated her words in a refined, slightly English-inflected accent that came from having spent parts of her childhood in London and Hong Kong. Her unruly hair was pulled back from her forehead by the same utilitarian plastic barrettes. Her expression was friendly but slightly disoriented, like a bespectacled river otter recently emerged from pursuing trout through the shadowy depths of the Charles.

It was a hot, sun-blasted day in early summer. They found a seat on the same granite bench in the shade of the riverbank sycamores and sat talking long after their teas and scones were finished. Natalie was a bookish polyglot with a photographic memory. Out of sheer curiosity she'd mastered eight or nine world languages and scores of scientific disciplines. A passionate talker but also a good listener, a self-proclaimed nerd who also possessed humility and social intelligence, Natalie seemed to have a special knack for seeing the positive in even the darkest situations. This was a skill that would persist for as long as he knew her, and it would be useful in the midst of the catastrophes that were to shadow humanity in the decades to come.

He fell in love with her almost immediately. With her voice and her laughter and her denim-clad hips, and those unfathomable eyes and the simple way she moved across a room. His main desire was to be in her presence. It was the only thing that could ease the ache of his feelings for her, feelings that seemed to have commandeered his entire being like a chronic virus or a bittersweet addiction to a strong new drug.

They shared confidences. They became close friends, and he assumed, due to her consuming passion for her research, that friendship was all she wanted. That she didn't have the bandwidth for an actual love affair. So he kept a respectful distance, and listened, and talked when it was his turn, and kissed her cheek when they met, or hugged her if more than a day or two had passed. But it turned out he'd misread the situation.

It was late summer, a Saturday. They were out walking on the Esplanade. The Charles teemed with crew sculls and small sailboats, and across the river the skyline of Boston was filled with huge rotating windmill blades and construction cranes busy with the expensive and ultimately futile project of installing solar windows on all the skyscrapers. He was feeling ill-tempered as they walked along the river, and suddenly she stopped and turned to peer up into his face. "Is it because we haven't slept together, Nick? Is that what's eating you?"

He felt himself reddening. That was of course exactly what had been bothering him, though he'd been barely willing to admit it to himself, much less to her. Now he worried that insisting on it would be the end of their friendship. "Look," he said. "I'm fine with a platonic friendship—just as long as we can spend time together. There really doesn't have to be any physical element."

She frowned and shook her head disapprovingly. Then she took him by the hand and marched him back the way they'd come, to the five-story brick residence hall on Memorial Drive where she lived. She led him up three flights to her small, neat apartment, which had a prominent view of the old Citgo sign, an icon from the days when the petrochemical companies had been cornerstones of the global economy.

He stopped her at the door. "Natalie, please. The last thing I want is for you to have sex with me just because you don't like to see me in a bad mood. Believe me, I'll get over it."

"Nonsense. You're not very good at reading the room, are you? And you're far too polite for your own good, Nick. I've been wondering when we were going to get around to this."

She pulled him inside the apartment. He saw no further need to protest.

In September she drove him up to New Hampshire to meet her father, whose name and reputation he of course already knew. After the loss of his beloved wife, Natalie's mother, Cornelius Quist had built himself an off-grid hermitage, complete with the latest technology in home security and renewable energy, on a remote tract of pastureland surrounding the distinctive structure of a large nineteenth-century round barn. The young lovers spent a weekend hiking the countryside and sipping single-malt scotch with the old tech entrepreneur at a firepit behind the barn, within a stone's throw of a certain natural cavern Mr. Quist had adapted to house a neatly stacked fortune of gold ingots. Despite his Howard Hughesian reputation, Mr. Quist had an excellent sense of humor and was a perceptive and engaging conversationalist who clearly doted on his brilliant daughter. Nick liked him immediately.

After that, for a time, research demands took them in different directions: back out into the field in his case, to comb the meltwater pools of subglacial steam vents in southern Chile for extremophiles; she to Beijing for a month, followed by a six-month stint at the European Space Agency headquarters in Paris. But when that was over they found it surprisingly easy to pick up where they'd left off, and the relationship continued.

Perhaps that first separation in some way helped prepare them for the inevitable. As they would find out before too long, their work with the Centauri Project gave their relationship a built-in expiration date. His health was good, and his work on the microbiology of so-called analog environments put him on the shortlist for any interstellar colonizing mission. Natalie, meanwhile, was far too valuable to waste on such a speculative enterprise, so they knew almost from the beginning that the day and hour would come when they would have to say goodbye forever. Death parts everyone eventually, but in their case it was different, because if all went as planned they would both live on for a time after the separation.

Natalie, immersed in the contemplation of relativistic time, was sanguine. "We're used to thinking of all parts of space as existing at once," she would say, "even if we're not there to experience them. Well, it's the same with time, Nick. Past, present, future: all are in continual existence, even though we don't experience them that way. So what there is between us already exists at the point in four-dimensional space-time where we're having this conversation. Which is, in a thoroughly real and mathematically provable sense, eternal."

Her optimism and indefatigable spirit were strong enough to sweep him along with barely a second thought, and their time together dwells in his memory as the most blissful decades of his life, despite the increasingly cataclysmic circumstances gripping the planet. Now, though, he's beginning to wonder if he really gave enough thought to how permanent separation from her would actually feel.

16

March 29, 2068 (12 A.U.C.T.)
The Mediterranean Sea

Another uneventful day, not too hot, with a steady northwest wind that Tollie says is the Mistral. He thinks we're somewhere around the longitude of Marseilles, though perhaps having learned his lesson he's now keeping us far away from any visible shoreline. As promised, I'm going to use today's entry to finish the Granada story. I should be clear that the events I'm going to narrate now were disturbing for all of us, but it is my firm intention to track the progress of this voyage as faithfully as possible. Consider yourself warned.

Thirsty and shaken after our hurried exit from Granada, we found a small spring by the side of the highway from which to refill our water bottles. From there we trekked up to the top of a high foothill with a view down into the city and left our packs under the roof of an old concrete bus stop. As the sun sank toward the horizon, we peered through our binoculars down into the interior courtyards of the Alhambra.

A crowd had gathered in the plaza outside the Renaissance palace at the heart of the ancient Moorish fortress. There were perhaps sixty or seventy people there, the same lean, rough-looking men and women in salvaged pre-collapse clothing we'd caught a glimpse of down in the city. They'd gathered in the square around a blazing bonfire of broken-up wooden furniture. But there was something else in the center of the square: a sort of low wooden bench with a figure kneeling in front of it. Three armed men in battered straw hats stood behind him.

"Holy shit," Tollie murmured. "I think that's our friend from the convent."

Adjusting the focus of my binoculars I saw that it was indeed the man who'd greeted us at the convent, and then tried so earnestly to lure us into a trap, though his face was now asymmetrically distorted, badly swollen and bruised from what looked to have been a severe beating.

Two of the men standing behind him pressed on his head and shoulders, forcing his chest down onto the bench. The third drew a long blade out of a scabbard at his belt—a machete like those once used to cut sugar cane or tall grass. Was it possible that he was about to—

No. It couldn't be that.

But that was exactly what it was.

The guard with the machete stepped back to perform an oddly self-conscious flourish, twirling the blade and glaring meaningfully up into the mountains, as if he knew we might be watching through binoculars. Then he pivoted, slashing the blade down. Our erstwhile friend's toothless head parted easily from his body, bouncing once on the flagstones and rolling a few yards before the blood even began to spurt from the severed neck.

Gasping, I tore the binoculars away from my eyes.

"Fucking hell!" Tollie exclaimed. James was silent, still staring through his binoculars, but what I could see of his face had gone quite pale.

"Holy crap," Tollie said. "What now? Are they going to—are they getting ready to—?"

I forced the double lenses back to my eyes. Only for a moment; that's all I could stand. But it was long enough to see what the Spaniard with the machete had begun to do, moving athletically, with the well-practiced skill of a butcher, while the other two erected a kind of iron spit or rack beside the fire. Most of the onlookers had cups or old plastic water bottles in their hands. Three women went around with plastic buckets, ladling some kind of home-brewed spirit into them, and the crowd conversed animatedly, as if this were a celebratory pig roast.

Only instead of a pig it was a man. With whom we'd exchanged friendly greetings earlier in the day. Whose toothless grin and obsequious vocalizations I still can't get out of my head.

On the mercilessly sun-blasted journey back to the coast I was plagued every moment by the fear that our single-file trek over the mountains was being watched closely from a distance. We paused often to scan the terrain behind us, and though we saw no evidence of pursuit, a film loop of that horrific scene in the Alhambra courtyard kept playing and replaying in my mind. I couldn't shake the feeling of dread, of pervasive danger and evil intent.

The former highway, fractured and deteriorated though it was, allowed us to make better time than we had on our way north, and we actually had a distant view of the Mediterranean after a single day of walking. It was such a relief to crest that ridgeline just before dusk, and to glimpse that expanse of empty midnight-blue ocean stretching out to the horizon. Empty except for the *Solar Barque* that is, which we assumed was still placidly hidden in the little cove at the foot of the ruined cliff hotel.

Unfortunately, however, this is not the end of the story.

At dawn the next morning we were getting ready to make our final push, warming ourselves by a small campfire, when something like a lightning-propelled hornet zipped in to strike Tollie's right shoulder with a sickening *plunk*. He yelped, grabbing the shoulder with his other hand as the thunderclap of a rifle shot rolled down over the coastal foothills.

James screamed for us to take cover as he reached for Tollie's Remington. I grabbed our cursing captain and led him to an outcropping, and we hunkered down as best we could while James—demonstrating a practiced ease in handling the rifle that took me by surprise—peered through its scope, trying to pinpoint the location of our attackers.

I helped Tollie out of his old denim shirt, which was ruined by a rapidly spreading stain of dark purple blood. He was white-faced and trembling, understandably in a state of shock. It turned out not to be a worrisome wound—certainly not as worrisome as it would have been if it had hit a few inches one way or the other. The bullet had entered just above the left collarbone, missing the clavicle itself and the subclavian artery and exiting cleanly on its own. It would need to be thoroughly sanitized back at the yacht, but for now I tore up the shirt and fashioned a tourniquet to stanch the bleeding. In truth we had more pressing worries, such as how to get down out of the foothills and across the cove to the yacht without being picked off by more long-range rifle shots.

We started moving down the mountainside, staying low and seeking cover as we descended among rocks and gullies and thickets of dry scrub, but it was a hair-raising time as we really had no idea where our attackers were located, other than behind and above us. Fortunately there were no more shots fired for the time being, and we dared to hope that they'd given up and gone back to Granada.

By midafternoon we'd made it into the old resort town and down through the ruins of the cliff hotel. Tollie had shaken off his initial shock enough to produce a nearly constant stream of curses; his shoulder was in a painfully swollen state, and his handsome unshaven face was pallid from pain and loss of blood. He was beginning to show signs of coming to the end of his endurance, and I worried that he might pass out, though for a man in his fifties under these circumstances, he'd shown remarkable staying power. James and I made him lie down on the beach while we uncovered the dinghy just where we'd left it, buried in plastic and sea wrack on the small beach below the hotel. We flipped it right side up and dragged it down to the waterline, then went back to help Tollie get in.

And it was in that moment that the hunting party showed themselves, lining up at the crumbling balcony atop the cliff. They were seven or eight in total—we were too busy to get an exact count—all men, dark-bearded, hollow-cheeked, ominously underfed. All had long blades hanging from their belts, and several had firearms. One had a long-range sniper's rifle mounted with a large scope, which he worked to attach to a tripod at the edge of the cliff.

"Get in, Al, get in!" James yelled. He was already in the prow with Tollie's rifle; I pushed us off and jumped in, taking the oars.

The first shot was surprisingly loud in my ears, and it took me a moment to realize that it was James who'd fired it. Later he told me that he hadn't been shooting to kill; he just wanted to give us more time to row. And he was successful. Glancing up I saw the others crowd around the sniper, who sat on the ground, grimacing and holding his arm.

"As fast as you can row, Al!" James yelled, but I was already rowing as if our lives depended on it—which they unquestionably did.

A second Spaniard sprawled behind the rifle tripod and took several shots, but it seemed that he wasn't quite as good at aiming as the one James had hit. Two bullets raised little spouts in the water ahead of us, and a third left a splintered fissure in the dinghy's fiberglass hull, above the waterline. After that they decided not to waste any more precious ammunition for the moment, probably because they'd seen something new that we ourselves had not.

I nudged the nose of the dinghy up to the yacht. James clipped the bowline to the stern ladder, and we helped our gray-faced skipper aboard. I tended to his wound in the shade of the cockpit while James hauled in the anchor, and we readied ourselves to put up the sails.

It was only after this flurry of activity, with Tollie settled on an extra cushion on the stool with his good hand on the wheel, that I went belowdecks to check on Dr. Q. It struck me as odd that she hadn't come up as soon as she'd heard us. I assumed that I would find her napping or absorbed with typical abandon in whatever it was she was reading or thinking about, but that was not the case. In fact, Dr. Q wasn't aboard the *Solar Barque* at all. The kayak was missing, so apparently she'd gone off to explore the coast. Worse yet, Tollie's pistol lay abandoned on a shelf beside her bunk. My body shook with panic.

After a hurried discussion, we decided to head east along the coast, on the logic that we'd come in from the west and she would have been more interested in exploring something new. Rather than take the time to put up the sails we opted to use some of our emergency fossil fuel supply. Tollie gave James instructions for starting up the old combustible motor; it wheezed a few times but came to life with a burst of loud coughing, and we were soon motoring noisily along the coast as close to shore as we dared.

We'd chosen the right direction. Soon we spotted the cherry-red slash of the kayak pulled up among the boulders beneath a half-ruined stone watchtower (built by the Romans or even the Phoenicians according to Tollie, still enthusiastic enough to play tour guide despite his weakened state). With our binoculars we located her right away, a tiny brown figure poking around in the rubble at the base of the tower, the big round lenses of her spectacles flashing unmistakably in the mid-afternoon sun. One of the greatest minds of her generation, so lost in reverie among the tumbled stones of ancient human history that she hadn't heard the sound of distant gunfire or even the approaching putter of our emergency motor. It might have been an amusing prospect if it hadn't been so worrisome. Because the hunters—well-armed and purposeful-looking—were hurrying along a hiking trail that ran parallel to the rocky coastline. They had almost reached her.

James and I jumped up and down on the foredeck, waving our arms and screaming to get her attention, but she was lost in thought, strolling with her hands clasped behind her back as she gazed down at those old rocks, pausing occasionally to pick up a pebble or wipe away some dust.

"Ugh! Do we need to fire bullets to get her attention?" I asked in frustration, but James had gone below and came back up a moment later with the yacht's signal horn. This made an extremely loud and stress-inducing noise, and Dr. Q jumped. She saw us, held out her arms in a questioning gesture, and finally started making her way down through the broken rocks to the kayak.

Meanwhile the hunters were rounding the last bend in the trail. I felt a dropping sensation in my stomach, because it looked like there was no way she could get the kayak down to the waterline in time. But in the next moment there was a loud explosion beside my ear and the lead Spaniard appeared to lose his balance. He teetered, then fell from the cliff, his forehead striking the point of a sharp boulder with a sickening finality.

The Spaniards scrambled for cover. Dr. Q dragged the kayak down into the blue water and lowered herself into it. Ears ringing, I turned to James, who was peering through the scope of Tollie's smoking .30-06. It seems that our shy young bird-lover is also a crack marksman, with an excellent sense of timing.

And now, dear hypothetical reader, I must attend to my patient. His shoulder wound seems to be healing well, though he continues to experience swelling, tenderness, and intermittent pain. You might think that he deserves some lingering discomfort as punishment for leading us into such a foolhardy excursion, though medical ethics prevent me from ever saying such a thing aloud, especially as I myself deserve a major share of the blame for not arguing more forcefully and consistently against it.

But I have to admit, I don't wholly regret the experience. I've discovered a new appreciation for my male shipmates for one thing—for James Swamp, obviously, though our interactions are currently limited to the occasional "accidental" meeting of glances or the "innocent" physical contact of a friendly pat on the shoulder or a hand brushing a forearm—but also for Tollie Quist, who it turns out possesses a few admirable qualities along with all the exasperating ones. We all have our flaws, myself very much included. But I'm beginning to realize that this little crew of four is the closest thing I have to a family. And for a family to function well you have to look beyond the shortcomings of each member, and find something not only to respect, but to cherish. I'm determined to give that my best shot.

Our way now lies straight across the Mediterranean, with no further detours or distractions, following a straight bearing well south of the Balearic Islands and Sardinia and well north of Africa, to the Aeolian islands north of Sicily. Once we drop anchor at Stromboli, I suspect it won't take long to determine whether this voyage in the twilight of humanity's dominion on this ailing planet has been a fool's errand or, as we hope, an inspired roll of the dice.

17

10151 A.U.C.T. +/- 18.583 years (estimated)

The most significant artifact he finds digging around in the soil stratum containing the Lab compound is a miniature bronze bust of Albert Einstein. As he clears away the grit using a pine bough as a makeshift hand brush, he's ambushed by the memory of the day he bought it for Natalie at a Charles Street antique shop. They were still graduate students at the time, strolling to their favorite breakfast place and having an unusually bitter argument. He can't remember the exact subject, but he does remember glimpsing the bust in the shop window as they walked by and, after they'd put in their orders at the breakfast place, making up some excuse to go back and buy it as a peace offering.

It's not the best likeness. The iconic features are somewhat cartoonishly rendered, with that enormous forehead and the moustache and the exaggerated sweep of hair. But Natalie was always particularly fond of Einstein, and the heavy little bust he now holds in his hand was once among the most prized of her limited material possessions. She kept it on her bureau, first in Cambridge and then at the Round Barn, for all the years they were together.

He installs it in a natural niche in the granite mountainside overlooking the ledge, decorating it with a bouquet of her favorite wildflower, late-blooming *Symphyotrichum novae-angliae*.

It's later in the year than he'd realized. The fiery reds and oranges of autumn, beginning in the high country, creep down into the lowlands day by day. Great vees of migrating geese fill the air with their throaty honking, and the eerie calls of loons reach his ears from the lakes down in the valley. He has no idea what winter will bring. According to projections, atmospheric carbon should have declined to the point where average temperatures at this latitude would now be cooler than peak greenhouse, though not quite as cool as in preindustrial times. This scenario seems to accord with his own observations thus far, and if the winter is indeed relatively mild, survival will be that much easier. But he's not counting on it.

He stacks the inner ledge and part of the entrance to the grotto with firewood and expands his makeshift root cellar to accommodate a good supply of nonperishable nutrition. There are cattail roots to dig and pollen powder to collect; fish and other small prey to brine and smoke; herbs to bundle and hang; mushrooms, rose hips, and wild berries to dry in the sun. He gathers acorns and hickory nuts and chips out a mortar and pestle to pound them into flour; boils water by dropping red-hot cobbles into a pot made of clay; strains off the oily scrim and fills a makeshift wood-fired clay jug with several months' supply of nut milk, as sweet and rich as fresh cream and an excellent source of preserved protein for long winter days.

One night, after a long day of hunting and gathering, he reclines on the ledge in the warmth of his small fire, staring up at the bright multitude of stars enlivening the velvet blackness of a moonless autumn sky. No ambient light pollution, no airplanes, no satellites. Somewhere out there the human-built space probes are still speeding outward, bringing the now-defunct global culture of H. sapiens out to the neighboring galaxies. *Voyagers I* and *II*, *Pioneers 10* and *11*, *New Horizons*, whatever craft the Chinese, Russians, and Indians managed to launch while they still had a chance. Perhaps someday one will be netted by an alien intelligence. Perhaps that intelligence will examine this strange work of primitive technology with puzzlement and release it back into the void with the equivalent of a shrug.

He retains a childhood memory of a car trip through western Colorado and eastern Utah with his father, a geologist for a big energy corporation.

The purpose of the drive was to visit natural gas facilities, but Jerry Hindman was not the sort of man to let a good opportunity go to waste, and he brought ten-year-old Nicholas along for a little father-son summer vacation. They took a detour up into the San Juan highlands, twenty degrees cooler and so refreshing after the blazing heat at home in the foothills above Denver. They set up a tent in a wildflower meadow with a view of jagged peaks streaked with snow. He remembers a yellow haze in the air from the forest fires burning all over the west, the aspen leaves making a sound like rainfall, a shimmering lake, and the sun filtering down through the trees to bathe the meadow in a mottled golden-green light. He can even remember their picnic dinner: cold fried chicken and huge blueberries in a clear plastic clamshell, before single-use plastics had been legislated out of the waste stream.

His father was a fossil enthusiast, and the next day, back down in the pounding heat of the high desert, they stopped at the site of an early Cretaceous seashore. Just a crumbling ridgeline, dry sagebrush, and big breakaway tiles of mud-colored slate heated to scorching by the unforgiving sun. But Jerry Hindman was good with words and he brought the place alive for his son, calling forth an ancient tidal flat preserved in stone with ripples so perfect you could almost feel your toes sinking into the mud, and using several fossils with the flawless impressions of leaves and fronds to evoke a riotous, long-extinct forest.

They visited the quarry at Dinosaur National Monument, a kind of air-conditioned hangar built over a half-excavated hillside. The site was terrifying and at the same time irresistible to young Nicholas: a steeply slanted plane of rock studded with the petrified bones and skulls of dinosaurs: Diplodocus, Camptosaurus, five or six other species whose names he can no longer recall. His dad told the story of a river that had once flowed swiftly across a fertile plain. Of a drought that had killed many of the dinosaurs, and a flood that had killed the rest. Massive corpses carried downstream in the current, rolling and grinding along the river bottom until they piled up like a logjam. Sand and silt deposited over them by the river, then the long process of petrification. The skull of one great predator caught his attention, jutting out of the rock at the end of a curving spine with vertebrae the size of paint cans, half-turned with its hollow eyes and teeth like knife blades leering down at him through the epochs.

On the cement ramp at the lower end of the quarry was a learning station where children were encouraged to reach up and touch some of the bones. He placed his hand on the curving length of an enormous femur, polished and cool to the touch, and felt suddenly disoriented, quaking, on the edge of panic. As if the act of touching this ancient thing could cause him to be swept up against his will and carried away to this entirely distant and alien time.

"One hundred fifty million years," his father murmured. "Just imagine it, Nick."

He hadn't been able to imagine it, not in any realistic way, and the truth is that he still can't. But that was his first encounter with the otherworldly vastness of geological time, and there was something so deeply moving in that moment that it's stayed with him ever since. Recalling it now makes him feel both reassured and profoundly sad.

From Dinosaur they drove west, into the heart of fossil gas extraction country, stopping for another picnic dinner at a highway pullout: cheddar cheese, summer sausage, and more of those improbably fat blueberries. Light and shadow; the golden-red dusk still hazy from the forest fires; the tall orange flames of the flaring wells like monumental torches arranged across the desert landscape. They could barely talk over the roar of the highway. Propane and cement trucks, eighteen-wheelers, and the locals' tricked-out pickups flying past Jerry Hindman's hybrid Toyota at ten or fifteen miles above the speed limit. Those unnecessarily profligate combustion engines. All that tire rubber thundering its staccato rhythms over the rumble strips.

Even then, as a ten-year-old child, he'd felt the sense of bleakness, or impending doom. No doubt some part of him had sensed what was coming. Not the end of the world—not of the 4.5 billion years of planetary history with which he'd come into intimate contact for the first time at those petrified mudflats—but the end of H. sapiens' dominion. The flameout of its fossil-fueled rise. And the end, in all probability, of the species itself, whose fate now seems to echo that of the creatures whose petrified bones had called out to him so evocatively from their resting place in that half-excavated hillside at Dinosaur.

He wakes full of anxiety, with a recent muscle memory tugging insistently at the edges of his consciousness. Something he'd scraped up against in the dirt at the bottom of one of his archaeology pits. The curved edge of a buried rock that had prevented him from digging farther down. He'd taken a break in favor of a different pit, where on the same morning he'd started to find artifacts and been so caught up in the excitement that he'd never returned to the first pit. But had there been something strange about that buried rock? It certainly hadn't seemed noteworthy at the time. But something about the way his homemade hand shovel had felt coming up against it, the slightly hollow sound that it might have made, keeps cycling back through his mind.

He finds the pit and drops down into it. He uses his hands to try to dig down around the offending rock and remove it, but he can't find the edges. It's immense, shallowly concave, not a rock at all but part of a large, very hard, very smooth piece of metal. And at a certain point he stops digging, because he knows that what he's found is a TDS—or, more likely, half of one, as they'd stored them in halves on the floor of what used to be the clean room, which is where he's apparently been digging.

He climbs up out of the pit and finds a place to sit on a mossy boulder among the wilting ferns. He's not sure why this new find fills him with such despair. He's known from the first—or at least since he went back down into the cave and found no other spheres—that the Centauri Project's efforts had failed. He supposes that a part of him had been holding on to some slight glimmer of hope. That the team had found another cave perhaps, or for some reason loaded the two remaining spheres on a flatbed to activate them at a distant site. Now, two of the three extant spheres are definitively accounted for, his own and this one; the third was in all likelihood buried somewhere in the soil nearby.

Which means that barring the existence of a population somehow hanging on somewhere else on the globe, he truly is the last human alive.

18

April 3, 2068 (12 A.U.C.T.)
Anchored off Stromboli

The island emerges from the hammered-steel surface of the Tyrrhenian Sea in a perfect storybook cone, white steam trailing sideways from its summit like an ostrich-feather plume across the indigo sky. It's nearly dusk, and we can make out a whitewashed village nestled at the base of the volcano, a shoreline of black lava cliffs, a sheltered beach of charcoal-colored sand. An idyllic vision straight out of Homer, or Sappho, or at least *Stromboli, Land of God* (Roberto Rossellini, 1950), the ancient digitized-celluloid film Dr. Q made us all watch back at the Lab to familiarize ourselves with the landscape of our destination. Over an ancient bottle of Nero d'Avola if I remember correctly, foraged from Cornelius Quist's depleted wine cellar. A wine so dark as to be nearly ink-colored, and tasty too, though none of us were accustomed to drinking wine except for Tollie, who'd polished off at least half the bottle himself before the credits rolled.

Anyway. From a distance, in this rapidly fading light, Stromboli looks to be almost as romantic a setting as it apparently turned out to be for Rossellini and his starlet, the gorgeous Ingrid Bergman. And if the rumors are to be believed—third-hand and out-of-date as they are—it's possible that the mythic appearance of the island might just indicate a certain underlying reality. Let's hope so. Because that jaunty feather-plume originating at the summit crater confirms that the island is subject to regular volcanic activity, which in turn points to the distinct possibility that it could indeed harbor a population with some lingering vestiges of human fertility. Excitement is not the right word to describe how this prospect makes us feel; Dr. Q especially, whose lifelong mission it has been to rescue our species from extinction. I'm cautiously excited too, on her behalf and on my own, though I am also filled with trepidation. Even if this *is* the opportunity we've been seeking for so long, will we be able to grasp hold of it? Or will our ambitions lead us into even worse trouble than we've already encountered?

We'll find out soon enough, though, given the difficulties we experienced in southern Spain, we're not in any rush to make a landing. For now the plan is to remain anchored offshore indefinitely—at least until we can figure out more about the situation on the ground, and whether making contact with the island's inhabitants is something we even want to try.

Meanwhile, as the sun sinks below the oceanic horizon on this pleasant evening, we're content to admire the flawless profile of the little Aeolian volcano that has been our destination from the first.

April 4, 2068 (12 A.U.C.T.)
Anchored off Stromboli

Above the village the island is steep and charred, yellow grass growing from charcoal-gray lava. The slope gets even blacker as it slants away toward the cone of the volcano's summit, hidden all day by shrouds of mist and steam. Over breakfast on the foredeck we witnessed a minor landslide just south of the village, a cascade of superheated rocks bounding downhill through the clouds, a sound ringing out across the water like breaking glass. Some of the lava made it all the way down to the sea, where it hissed and boiled up tendrils of steam from the crystalline Tyrrhenian. Later we heard the thunder of two additional minor eruptions, which seem to be quite a regular occurrence here.

I'm happy to report that our indecision about whether and when to make landfall seems to have been resolved. We received a surprise delegation from the island early this afternoon, a peaceful, seemingly civilized group of local residents whose visit has filled us with cautious optimism after the long and trying journey so far. They came in two double kayaks, embarking from a dock at the bottom of a long flight of stone stairs that led down from the village. We're anchored pretty far away, so I have to give them credit for their athleticism. Two men in their late forties or fifties, with long gray plaited hair and well-groomed salt-and-pepper beards, and two younger women, in their mid-thirties perhaps, around my age, one ash-blonde and one black-haired, with their hair pulled back just like the men, severely, in a single tight braid. Surprisingly and somewhat quaintly in my view, all of them put on cheap surgical masks as they approached the yacht, the kind people wore at the beginning of the hyperpandemic when it was still believed that the microbes spread person-to-person rather than through the atmosphere.

We put down the boarding ladder and all four of them scrambled up on deck. Men and women were all dressed the same, in simple, loose-fitting, knee-length white tunics made from high-thread-count cotton—repurposed linens from a pre-collapse resort hotel is our guess—with cobalt-blue embroidery around the collars and cuffs. Some tunics are more elaborate than others, which Dr. Q believes may be indicative of rank within some kind of hierarchy. But the main point is that beneath their surgical masks they looked fit—glowing with good health, really. And as I mentioned they were polite and civil, speaking to us in good if slightly formal English. It was initially surprising to us that while they have the deep tans of people who spend a lot of their time outdoors, none of them are naturally dark or olive-skinned as we would have expected given the island's proximity to Sicily. In the subsequent conversation we would discover the reason for this: they are northerners, Scandinavians, originally from Iceland to be specific.

As they explained it to us, they are players and coaches from an Icelandic women's youth soccer team, stranded in Rome where they'd come to compete in the European championships in the summer of 2056, right before the hyperpandemic hit. The news coverage that summer, indelible in my mind, was all about the volcanic obliteration of their home island. I still remember sitting in the breakroom of the original Centauri Project Lab in Cambridge watching the heart-wrenching aerial footage. It was an extremely unfortunate aftereffect, apparently, of the forced eruptions of the Pinatubo Solution—a massive secondary eruption that basically wiped the country right off the map, creating in its stead an entirely new volcanic landmass, smoking and steaming and barren of all life.

It made sense that an Icelandic sports team would have been stranded in Rome in the summer of 2056. These former youth soccer players and their older male coaches must be among the last surviving Icelanders—although this thought may seem a bit less staggering when you consider that they—and we—are also most likely among the last surviving members of the last surviving generation of humans on the planet.

Unless we can change the direction of that trend.

We invited them to sit on the cushions under the cockpit bimini. One of the women, very tall with beautiful clear skin and almost silver ash-blonde hair, whose embroidery was the most elaborate, seemed to be the leader or at least the spokesperson for this group of emissaries. She introduced herself as Edda Ingvarsdottir. Our guess is that she's the team's former goalkeeper. She certainly has the body for it: long, tall, strongly built, with an alert, athletic, loose-limbed manner.

"Rome was horrible that summer," she continued in her lightly accented English. "A city of chaos, and—what is the word? Mayhem. We had lost our homes and families, you know? And we had nowhere to go. So we found a boat and went south. To another island at first. Lipari. That is where we were staying when the hyperpandemic came. But then we heard about Stromboli, and we came here."

"What was it specifically you'd heard about Stromboli, dear?" Dr. Q asked.

Edda glanced quickly at her companions, who looked away with what seemed to be discomfort, though it was hard to tell because their mouths were hidden by the masks.

"We heard that it was safe."

"Yes? And how did the Strombolians fare during the pandemic?"

"Many left. Many died. Then and later."

"How many survivors remain, dear, in your estimation?"

A shadow passed over Edda's eyes then. I think she was taken aback by Dr. Q's pointed questions, which may have come as a bit of a surprise given the latter's unassuming, good-natured air of authority and her petite stature compared to the rest of us.

"Around thirty-five people live on Stromboli now," she said after a moment. "Including us."

I asked about their food supplies, and whether they had any trade with the mainland or Sicily.

Edda shook her head. "We are self-sufficient. Our gardens are on the far side of town. You can see them later if you wish to come ashore."

"And water?"

"Yes. We have freshwater springs."

She is a very attractive woman, Edda. Stately and noble of bearing, with striking pale eyes the color of tropical seawater over shallow white sand. And her beauty is not just superficial; you can feel her sensuous charisma even with her lower face hidden beneath the mask. Disconcertingly, I found myself drawn to her; I sensed that she might even be something of a kindred spirit. Even more disconcertingly, as she was speaking, I kept seeing those shockingly pale eyes stray to James, who was after all an imposing young man, and a good-looking one too in his unique way, despite the scarring. Perhaps it wasn't attraction on her part, but she, and all her companions too, seemed particularly interested in our youngest crew member.

In any case, the time had now come for her to ask us questions.

"You are Americans?"

We nodded.

"Scientists?"

"Remarkably perceptive, dear," Dr. Q observed in her good-natured way. "What tipped you off, if I may ask?"

"We have received other visitors over the years," Edda replied. "Always scientists."

I thought Dr. Q might use the opportunity to ask her about the rumors we'd heard regarding the possibility of fertility on the island, but she held off out of discretion, not wishing to put all our cards on the table at once. It was more than possible that these rumors were the reason other scientists had come calling, and Edda's voice hadn't sounded entirely positive.

She wanted to know about our areas of expertise. The purpose of our trip. Our observations about the rest of the world. She was curious about my medical training, but most of her questions were directed to Dr. Q, whom she appeared to have correctly identified as the expedition leader. I got the feeling from some of her reactions, however—a look of secretive doubt that crept into her eyes when we talked in general terms about our work—that she was utterly confident in her own beliefs, and perhaps also something of a skeptic about aspects of what used to be called "modern science."

"Why don't you come ashore?" she offered, once all her questions had been answered apparently to her satisfaction. "We will need to do some tests, and we will need to keep you in quarantine while we wait for the results—just a few days, several days at most—but after that I would be glad to continue this discussion. Does that sound okay?"

What could we say? We'd come for a reason. There seemed to be no better opportunity to explore what we'd come for than a formal invitation. So despite any misgivings—Granada was still fresh in our minds—we agreed to row over in the dinghy tomorrow morning.

When they'd gone, we all agreed that Tollie should stay with the *Solar Barque*. Not going ashore is obviously hard for him—he hates to miss any kind of excitement—but he's still recovering from his shoulder wound, and we need someone to stay aboard in case the need should arise for us to make some kind of quick exit. We also decided that his pistol and hunting rifle should remain aboard with him. Landing unarmed is a risk of course, and I myself have a few doubts about going ashore defenseless in such an unknown place—particularly, again, after what we experienced in Granada. But Dr. Q feels very strongly that we have no choice but to proceed boldly with our quest, and she is no doubt correct in her opinion that our best chance for success will be to approach the island's inhabitants with the same attitude of openness and goodwill they demonstrated by sending their own unarmed delegation out to greet us.

I guess we'll find out tomorrow. Wish us luck!

19

10151 A.U.C.T. +/- 18.583 years (estimated)

A week of rainstorms. He used to enjoy a good downpour, but this is different. There's a hysterical edge to it, a kind of demonic extravagance to the bucketing deluge and the ground-shaking thunder. Or maybe it's only his state of mind. It's one thing to appreciate an active weather system from inside a snug timber-frame building, and quite another from inside a cramped and leaking natural shelter made of rock and roots and soil that runs in muddy rivulets around your bed of pine boughs. Shivering, damp, and fretting about how you're going to need to find some way to seal this roof with winter coming, and no other being for company or consolation, nor any prospect of one, quite possibly forever.

Stop feeling sorry for yourself.

And then one morning the rain stops. The air is cool and fragrant with soaked conifer needles, leaf litter, and saturated dirt. A white nothingness of fog streams quickly past the ledge in a window-frame of dripping branches, as if the entire world he's been living in these last months was nothing but a dream. And from somewhere on the mountainside above the ledge, he hears a faint mewling that strikes him as familiar, a birdcall no doubt, from a catbird or a mimicking jay. But there it is again, that distinctive mewling, and it doesn't really sound like a bird.

Can it be possible, after all this time?

Standing on the outermost part of the ledge, he squints up into the shrouds of fog sifting through the trees. Nothing.

He walks the worn path to his latrine. When he returns, the creature is gazing down on him from a lichen-covered outcropping a few yards above the ledge. It's pure black, longer and leaner than the pets he remembers. He can see the shape of its spine and the hollow behind its ribs, and its face and muzzle seem narrower and more elongated, the way the animal used to be portrayed in ancient Egyptian iconography, but it's unquestionably a common house cat: *Felis silvestris catus.* He'd assumed the species had been lost, along with pugs and hamsters, in the evolutionary reshuffle following the decline of humanity, their main ally and protector. Apparently that is not the case.

The cat mewls plaintively and he takes a few slow steps toward it, holding out his hand. But it puts back its ears and hisses ferociously, backing away.

He goes to the grotto, pushes aside the rock lid to his pantry, and takes out the head and filleted carcass of a large yellow perch he'd been planning to use to make a broth. He sets it on a patch of bare granite in a little hollow at the base of a hemlock sapling and makes a show of leaving.

A few hundred yards above the camp is an exposed boulder with a view of the ledge where he can watch unobserved. After a few minutes the cat creeps in across the ledge, sniffs the day-old carcass, and eagerly tears into it. Nick tiptoes back down to the ledge, but when the cat sees him it freezes, then snatches up what's left of the carcass and disappears into the forest.

He leaves out a smoked fillet of perch; the cat comes and drags it off into the trees. He leaves out a handful of dried squirrel meat, which it consumes on the spot with gusto. It's a shame to waste his painstakingly hoarded protein, but the cat's shy craftiness is amusing. He finds himself looking forward to its morning raids, which soon become a predictable daily occurrence.

Gradually, the animal softens. It begins to linger in the vicinity of the ledge, careful to stay out of reach. It grooms itself incessantly.

It sleeps companionably on its own little outcropping of sun-warmed granite. One day it allows him to pet it briefly, sprawling on the stone and purring blissfully for a moment before bounding off. Nick remembers this hard-to-get coquettishness as a trait of the species—an evolutionary adaptation, possibly, to encourage its providers not to tire of it as one would a fawning lover.

As the weeks go on, and the air gets colder by degrees, the creature becomes more confident, sometimes visiting his bed of pine boughs in the middle of the night to purr and nuzzle. On colder nights it even curls up in the space made by his bent knees when he's lying on his side. The first time this happens, to his embarrassment, he finds himself wiping away tears, surprised by the extent to which he'd been craving physical affection, or interaction of any kind.

The shadows of clouds speed across the brilliantly hued valley with its lakes like little ovoid mirrors and then, overnight it seems, the hardwoods are bare. The tomcat makes itself a territory centering on the ledge, with an evident understanding that its strange but useful new ally will cherish it all the more if it keeps rodents and other would-be scavengers out of the food supplies.

It has been Nick's hope that the coming winter will be relatively mild, but as the air gets colder and a coating of frost begins to whiten the ground every morning, he wonders if his assumptions about the mildness of this climate might be mistaken. Admittedly, his worry about the comparative severity of the coming season is tinged with excitement. He has fond childhood memories of cold Rocky Mountain winters, and also remembers the snowstorms and frozen rivers of the winters after the launch of the so-called Pinatubo Solution. But for most of his life winter was a grim and disappointing season of dark nights, cold rains, and feverish spells of uncanny warmth. A true winter, while not without its challenges, could be a welcome distraction.

When the snow does begin to fall it fills him with both exhilaration and grim resolve. The more it accumulates on the mountainside the harder it will become to forage and hunt. He makes himself a warm hat of squirrel fur and prepares himself to be snowed in for days or even weeks at a time.

On some of those snowy days—the short, dark, blustery days of early winter—he does little but lounge under piled furs by his campfire with the purring cat for company. At times he feels himself slipping back into something like the semiconscious delirium of his time inside the TDS. The fire goes out; the furs, the cat, and his own body heat keep him warm enough. Days and nights lose their meaning, as do wakefulness and sleep, and he finds himself whirling backward through the darkness of deep time, haunted by half-realized visions of the world that came before. Electric vehicles and gated compounds, satellites and contrails, plant-based cheese and traffic jams. Centauri team dinners with garden vegetables and stockpiled pinot noir; bad news scrolling across flickering blue screens.

The dire events of the forties and fifties brought an urgent focus to the Centauri team's work, which was—unlike just about everything else on the planet during those years—going rather well. Under Natalie's visionary leadership, and with a well-funded physical infrastructure and an array of cutting-edge quantum computers, the team had created three functional prototypes of the TDS. The team and its partners at NASA, the European Space Agency, and other highly engaged governmental and private interests around the world came close to pulling the whole thing off, too. Humanity was within perhaps five years of launching its first interstellar colonizing mission when the hyperpandemic hit and threw everything into chaos. After the first surge, with most world governments entering various stages of dissolution, the surviving principals saw the writing on the wall and the Centauri Project was officially disbanded. Those humans still alive were preoccupied with their own survival in a world that had altered drastically overnight. There would be no more talk of interstellar colonization.

By this time the three prototype spheres and all the Lab's essential equipment had been moved up to Cornelius Quist's compound in remote New Hampshire, a place well-suited for the continuation of the team's now unofficial work: easy to quarantine and defend; invisible from any major public road; already gated off with a sophisticated, autonomous security system; and, with its large solar array, wind farm, deep water wells, and open pastureland suitable for both agriculture and grazing, completely off the grid.

In the weeks after their arrival half a dozen team members fell to the hyperpandemic, adding to a fast-growing tally of academic colleagues, old college friends, former professors, and members of everyone's extended families, especially children, amounting to somewhere within a standard deviation of thirty-five percent of the humans anyone in the world had ever loved or known.

He feels a hollow ache in his chest even now thinking about these staggering losses. And he generally does his best to not think about them, in part because it reminds him that in his own case the losses now stand at a solid one hundred percent.

Staring out into the white void of blowing snow, he wonders once again what happened to Natalie and the rest of the team in the end. He'll almost certainly never know.

He reaches down and tosses a few more sticks on the fire. The cat lets out an approving half-growl, stretching out on the stone to bask in the heat. He strokes its belly and it purrs loudly. Nick's made a friend, and he's grateful for the company. How could he not be? But it's really not the same.

20

April 5, 2068 (12 A.U.C.T.)
Stromboli

I pen this day's entry seated at a table in the roofed-in courtyard of our new "quarantining house," a rustic though spotless and actually quite lovely private cottage perched at the edge of a high lava cliff overlooking the Tyrrhenian sea.

After breakfast under the bimini, the three of us—Dr Q, James, and I—put on our expedition packs and lowered ourselves into the *Solar Barque*'s dinghy to row ourselves ashore. Somewhat inhospitably given the fact that we are supposedly honored guests, a loud warning siren echoed out over the glossy seawater, upon which a few dozen people—all wearing surgical masks—assembled at the base of the village above the waterfront.

The siren was only turned off as the nose of the dinghy bumped up against a well-built flotation dock attached to the flooded seawall that must once have been the island's main landing place. No one offered to help so we helped ourselves out onto the dock and stood at the base of the stone staircase with our packs, staring up at our new hosts. Our welcoming party was made up mostly of women, several older men, all Icelandic by the look of them, wearing the same knee-length white tunics with blue embroidery as the kayak delegation and similarly healthy-looking, though a certain percentage do have the tell-tale hyperpandemic scarring.

We climbed the stone staircase to a small piazza overlooking the sea. There we were directed to a team of three medical workers in white lab coats seated at a folding table. They took finger-prick blood samples and swabbed our mouths: the former for an antibody test and the latter, I assume, a buccal smear to extract genomic data. When it was James's turn the medical team gave him extra attention. They made him pull back his hoodie, and one woman even came out from behind the table to reach down into his pants and palpate his genitals. This was an awkward moment, one that I found infuriatingly unprofessional, but despite his basic shyness James handled it with aplomb. His severe hyperpandemic scarring is there for everyone to see, but it appears that they may believe, given his relative youth and obvious vigor, that he might somehow have maintained his ability to procreate.

I didn't like it. Not at all. And I must admit that it was a moment that made me question the wisdom of our having essentially surrendered ourselves to the presumed goodwill of our hosts.

Edda Ingvarsdottir was present too, towering over the others with her striking eyes and ash-blonde braid, but she did not in that moment deign to speak with us. Two women who appear to have been assigned to be our minders led us to the far side of the piazza and told us to wait, then walked back to stand in a circle that had formed around Edda, perhaps some kind of informal leadership council. They kept their voices low so we couldn't overhear them, though it was obvious from the way they glanced occasionally in our direction that we were the main topic of conversation.

"Where are the original inhabitants?" James said under his breath. "I mean, none of these people are locals. Are you guys as creeped out by this place as I am?"

Dr. Q and I nodded. "Don't forget why we're here though, dear," Dr. Q said quietly. "We need to keep our eyes open and find out what we can."

James and I murmured in agreement and the three of us stood there, observing as best we could as we waited to be told what to do.

What we hadn't counted on was being separated. Dr. Q and I were instructed to accompany the women north through the village, while

James was taken in the opposite direction by the bearded men from the coaching staff. As he was being led away he turned to meet our eyes one last time, shrugging helplessly and raising his brows with a humorous expression, as if to reassure us that he was going to be fine.

I really want to trust and believe this is the case.

Here are my impressions of the village so far: Doors of ancient wood, silvered and shrunken by the relentless sun. Streets narrow and winding, built not for cars but for pedestrians, not unlike those we walked in the old part of Granada, but with drifts of fine, charcoal-gray volcanic ash at the bases of the buildings. Whitewashed walls pitted and pocked as if they've been attacked by some huge stucco-eating bird—though of course this is only the impact scars of the lava bombs or scoria from the volcano, like the superheated rocks we saw yesterday cascading downhill into the sea. (Was it only yesterday? Feels like weeks ago.)

But my overwhelming impression so far is of the oppressive daytime heat. We're at a fairly low latitude here. The sun is high and hot, and the lava substrate seems to absorb it and radiate it back out in physical waves.

The older buildings, made of thick-walled masonry, are surprisingly cool inside, and the ocean breezes are a saving grace. Our pretty little cottage has a roofed courtyard and a broad window with wooden shutters that can be thrown open to receive them. Our minders are poker-faced and notably uncommunicative. We asked them numerous questions (not only in English but in French, German, and Norwegian, all languages Dr. Q has command of, though she has yet to master Icelandic), but to no avail, as they seem to be under strict instructions not to speak to us at all. After they'd shown us mutely around, using gestures and demonstrations to indicate the features of our temporary little home, they simply nodded politely and left us alone, locking the front door behind them as they went.

Interestingly enough, as these two women unlocked the iron gate that leads to the narrow alleyway connecting the cottage to the street, we did get a glimpse of a woman with a basket on her arm, dressed in the familiar blue-embroidered white tunic, with features that looked Strombolian. Seeing that we'd noticed her she cast her gaze down at the cobbles and hurried off—but we did get a good enough look to see that she was in her mid-forties perhaps, beyond childbearing age. So far we've had no indication that the rumors that brought us here are true—for that we would need to see at least one local woman of childbearing age, and eventually an infant, or at least a child younger than about twelve years old. But we haven't lost hope, far from it. We've come too far to give in so easily. So we will bide our time for now, observing patiently, unless and until more drastic action seems called for.

We've taken cool sponge baths in our vintage clawfoot tub, a great luxury after so many weeks at sea, and donned the clean high-thread-count tunics (no embroidery) that our minders left out for us. The cottage is simple and airy. We think it may have been part of a rustic bed-and-breakfast in the before times. We each have our own high-ceilinged bedroom, with whitewashed walls and no decoration at all other than a small mirror in an antique wood frame for each of us.

It's late afternoon as I write this. The blazing sun is a little lower outside, and in the shade of the courtyard with the wide-open shutters we're staying cool enough. We have a stunning view out over rugged lava cliffs to the sparkling sea. On the table where I'm sitting our hosts have left us candles for lighting, a heavy ceramic pitcher filled with cool, rosemary-flavored water, and a platter of food: half a loaf of dense brown bread, a sweet fruit preserve Dr. Q believes is made of prickly pear cactus, and two small ceramic bowls filled with a delicious creamy yogurt that originates, surely, from the herd of lean goats we glimpsed in a stone corral above the village. All in all it's quite the pleasant little hideaway. I wish we could relax and enjoy it, but there are far too many unanswered questions, such as why our hosts have found it necessary to separate us from James, and when we can expect to see him next.

In fact with every passing hour the situation we find ourselves in is more troubling to me. I'm afraid that our initial optimism may have been unwarranted, though Dr. Q does not appear to share my growing sense of dread. Then again, her ability to envision positive outcomes despite apparently intractable difficulties is one of the reasons she's achieved so much in her life. I should probably do my best to follow her example.

As for Tollie, we know the *Solar Barque* is still safely anchored off this island because we can see it clearly from our courtyard window. After spending the better part of three hours trying to get his attention with a mirror borrowed from one of the bedrooms, we have finally succeeded, so now he knows where to find us too. It's comforting to have established this sightline, and practically useful too. In the absence of an operational datacom network we've opted for a simple way of exchanging messages: a small folding whiteboard stowed in the bottom of Dr. Q's expedition pack. Tollie has its match, and with the help of an erasable marker and a small pair of binoculars, we now have an open line of communication should anything urgent come up.

The passageway leading to our cottage is closed off by that locked iron gate, and the heavy wooden door into the cottage is also locked from the outside. The courtyard window is big enough that we could easily climb through, but beyond it are lava cliffs plunging at least a few hundred feet to the jagged shoreline. Which is to say that we're *not* actually honored guests here on Stromboli. For the time being at least, while we remain in quarantine, our situation more closely resembles that of hostages or captives.

An uncomfortable thought. But as Dr. Q is at pains to point out, we must be patient. We must take whatever time is necessary to either confirm or disprove the rumors that have lured us all this way.

21

11th Millennium A.U.C.T. (estimated)

His first winter on the mountain is more snowed-in than he'd been expecting though fairly mild, with snowy weeks followed by balmy weeks and a few brief subzero stretches. As the days begin to lengthen again, he ventures down into the lowland forest more often, post-holing through the snow to look for winterberries and hawthorn apples. He even manages to spear a few fish through half-formed lake ice, rare morsels of fresh meat for himself and the tomcat. One morning he startles a flock of turkeys traveling across the slope, a group of unattached males, he believes, huge birds with intelligent eyes, bald blue heads, and little dinosaurian horns at the bases of their beaks. In their panic to get away several slip and fall on their bellies as their heavy claws break through the crust. He manages to catch and strangle two, nearly as big as ostriches. He plucks them and bastes one over the fire, then strips the meat from the other to brine and smoke for later use.

Another morning, during what he somewhat arbitrarily decides is the month of March, a second cat shows up at the ledge. It's smaller than the first, female, with a gray-and-black tiger stripe pelt and lynx-like tufts of black fur at the tips of its ears. The black male is unfazed by her arrival and it seems possible the two are already acquainted. That afternoon he returns to find them lounging on the stone in a patch of sun within a few feet of each other, ignoring and not-ignoring each other in that quintessentially feline way.

The spring rains come. The hardwoods blossom and bud, mushrooms poke their eager heads up out of the leaf litter, and down on the lowland lakes and streams the mayflies hatch in shimmering clouds. The new cat becomes a regular presence at the ledge, putting a bit more weight on her bony frame from regular feedings. She and the tom take to grooming each other, soon becoming an inseparable pair. Nick finds himself crediting them with a degree of intelligence that he might have been reluctant to assign to their species in the time before. The calm and intelligent way the pair seems to observe him, and the way he can make them understand things through gesture and tone of voice. They never talk back to him obviously, but their eyes and the flick of their tails are expressive enough, and they do seem capable of reading his emotions and his mood. It could be his own enhanced sensitivity; his loneliness simply making him pay closer attention than he used to. But these cats seem clever in a way he doesn't remember cats being.

Unlike the cats, he's pretty much lost hope that he will ever encounter another member of his own species. His biggest daily concern, other than not falling off a cliff or being surprised by a large predator as he forages, is that his life has lost much of its meaning. He's still following the protocol. Still gazing out over the lowlands in clear weather, looking for signs. But days will go by without him even thinking about it. And then he remembers and wonders if there's anything else he can do.

He remembers a public radio story about a dendrochronologist in Nevada who was drilling a core sample in an ancient bristlecone pine when the drill bit got stuck. Some other forest rangers came by to help him, but the expensive bit was so badly caught that they decided they had to cut down the tree to extract it. Counting the rings, the dendrochronologist was mortified to discover that he'd just killed the oldest non-cloning organism ever recorded on the planet. That bristlecone had been alive for more than 4,900 years.

The story feels especially poignant to him now, given that the oldest non-cloning organism living on the planet currently, in all likelihood, is himself.

One afternoon at the far edge of a beaver meadow he notices a huge flock of starlings gathered in an old oak. The volume of their chatter is surprisingly loud in his ears, even from several hundred yards away, and it seems to have some urgent purpose. He walks up into the shade of the spreading oak, where the birds perch like ornaments in an over-decorated Christmas tree. A few of the ornaments detach themselves, spilling out into the blue sky like blots of speckled ink, and suddenly there's an immense roar as the entire flock takes wing simultaneously. An uncanny stillness then descends over the meadow, as if the retreating birds have carried away with them all the other sounds of the forest.

He stands beneath the oak for a long time, trying to decipher the meaning of this new silence. But he can make no sense of it.

Awakening to a chorus of high-pitched mewling, he finds the female behind a stack of wood licking clean a litter of six kittens, all tiger-striped like herself except for one, a tuxedo, black with crisp patches of white on its neck, feet, and belly. The sight of these tiny creatures makes his throat ache, and not only because they're so cute. They feel like a direct link to human history, an unexpected reminder of a happy and mutually beneficial interspecies friendship.

The kittens grow stronger with remarkable speed. Soon they're chasing each other around the ledge and through the nearby trees. The boldest ones, hoping for an off-schedule morsel, come up to purr and rub against his shins and hands as he sits staring out over the lowlands, and on cooler nights, their warm little bodies press against him as he sleeps. The sometimes painful but always amusing interaction with the tiny creatures is a source of welcome distraction and joy. The fierce determination of their sparring and play. The way they stalk and lie in wait before bounding up to take an opportunistic swipe. He spars with them. They bite his fingers and hook their needle-like claws into the skin of his wrists and forearms. It's been so long since he's laughed aloud that it almost hurts.

As the weeks wear on, unfortunately, the kittens begin to vanish one by one. Snatched by predators most likely, or perhaps just striking off on their own into the forest. He doesn't remember enough about feline behavior to say how early this is supposed to happen. By mid-summer, however, he's left with just three: the original tom and two kittens, a tiger-striped female and a male, the tuxedo.

Among other things, these losses remind him that fleeting relationships with a commensal species, as pleasant as they may be, are probably not going to be sufficient to maintain his mental health. With the prospects of securing the companionship of any fellow Homo sapiens seeming less and less likely, he feels the need for something else.

One evening he catches himself blathering aloud as he sits crossed-legged in front of a little shrine that has taken shape in the natural granite alcove on the mountainside above the ledge. Over the months the shrine has become more and more elaborate, with the Einstein bust in a position of honor and various other meaningful objects arrayed around it: the coil of copper wire from the Atlantic beach; a piece of brick worn into a smooth round riverbed cobble; half a dozen bundles, dried now, of blue aster and other flowers that have at various times reminded him of Natalie; an interestingly shaped hickory bole he'd spent weeks whittling into something resembling a human face.

His blathering has to do with a new religion he's been toying with starting for himself. Nothing formal, just a little system of meaning suitable for a solitary hunter-gatherer. A practice of acknowledging the things he's grateful to see in the course of an average day: the sun, the moon, birds, plants, animals, rainclouds, certain special rocks and trees, and of course the cats—which do have the dignified and slightly mysterious character, he thinks, of miniature hearth gods.

But he can't really be sure whether this newfound spiritual pursuit is a harmless distraction—a way to satisfy his spirit's reflexive hunger for meaning—or if it's a sign of something more worrisome. An indicator of an increasing psychological imbalance. Because sometimes the sound of his own voice giving himself instructions or narrating his own walk through the forest will take him by surprise, and he'll freeze on the trail, or sit up with his heart pounding in the midnight darkness, and it will dawn on him that the voice he's hearing is nothing more than an artifact, an obsolete remnant of something elusive that humans used to call "culture" or "the self." And the thought that he might be losing touch with this will flood him with alarm.

Which is why one evening, sitting in front of his shrine, he cuts himself off mid-blather. He can no longer sustain the conviction that he's done everything possible to follow the protocol. He's pretty sure he can rule out the existence of any major population of humans. If there were one, even on this immense wilderness planet, ten thousand years would have given them plenty of time to expand, and he feels sure that he would have found some kind of evidence by now.

But perhaps there are small bands that persist. Groups of nomadic hunter-gatherers with a very light footprint that have somehow clung to life all these millennia. His instinct is still that no such bands exist—he's had a strong gut feeling about this almost from the beginning—but a feeling isn't the same as empirical evidence. Maybe it's time to take another shot in the dark.

It doesn't take him long to pack. Spear, deerskin bundle, dried foodstuffs, fur cloak, and the butcher's knife, for which he's carved a nice cherrywood handle to replace the original disintegrated plastic. The three remaining cats sense that he's about to abandon them, mewling pitifully for one last free meal. No doubt it's to their evolutionary advantage to make him believe they're helpless without him, but their pitiful remonstrances are a lie. They'll have the run of the camp while he's gone, or they can melt back into the forest. Their existence is proof enough that the species can survive perfectly well without human allies.

Having tried the coast, he aims to explore the sites of former population centers on the banks and shorelines of the major waterways to his west and north: Lake Champlain and the Saint Lawrence waterway; the sites of the former cities of Burlington, Montreal, and Quebec if he can make it that far. It's not physical ruins he's interested in, but places that might be perennially attractive to humans: river mouths, lake harbors, natural gathering points. If not permanent settlements then perhaps the nodes of far-flung fishing or hunting routes. If not the humans themselves then perhaps a few relics of their passage that might be awaiting discovery by an observant traveler.

He walks for weeks, purposefully if often lost in thought. He comes upon no sign of trails or footpaths, just mile after mile of fern-carpeted old-growth forest adorned occasionally by rocky streams, fast-moving rivers, and impenetrable swamps. He spots the crumbling abutments of old bridges and highway piers; at the mouth of a washed-out ravine he finds fragments of ceramic tile, decayed PVC plastic, an aluminum tap bolt still fused to its nut. Wolves howl at night, or perhaps some feral dog-hybrid that has reverted to wolf state.

He hears more howling than he's quite comfortable with, in fact, and becomes extra careful about choosing his sleeping arrangements, leaving time at the end of the day to find advantageously positioned tree branches and difficult-to-access rock ledges with good views. One morning as he's walking along a riverbank above a stretch of roaring whitewater, a lightning bolt of tawny fur strikes at him from the top of a fallen tree. The impact knocks him off his feet, sending him tumbling headlong over the riverbank. He lands on his knees among the stones at the edge of the rapid, recovering his wits quickly enough to splash out into the main current before his attacker, an immense puma, can launch another pounce. He bobs downstream through the whitewater, the big predatory cat twitching its black-tipped tail hungrily as it watches him escape.

On the far side of the river he hurries west for a few miles, hoping to avoid further contact with the lion. He climbs a tall white pine and finds a platform of branches in which to nurse his bruises and dry out the contents of his bundle, which by some miracle he has managed to keep. Near sunset he climbs to the pine's swaying top and spots a vast blue lake in the distance. This has to be Champlain.

In the morning he treks through an open forest of old-growth oak and hickory that grows right up to the lakeshore. He's disappointed but not surprised to find no obvious traces of humanity. If memory serves, the lake's elevation had been somewhere around a hundred feet, meaning that the ruins of Burlington and any other towns on the shore are now well beneath the waterline. Further, given the rise in sea levels, they may be under *salt* water—which proves, when he finds a cobbled beach and dips in a finger for a taste, to be precisely the case. It takes a moment to adjust to the thought that he's standing on the shore not of a large freshwater lake but of an inland sea connected to the Atlantic Ocean.

He follows the coastline north and then west, to a big river pouring into the sea. Seagulls and ospreys circle overhead, and a small pod of dolphins plays in the gentle wavelets. There are basking seals, diving gannets, shearwaters skimming the surface, and, wheeling over the water in the distance, the same bird resembling an albatross that he spotted on his previous trip to the sea.

Plenty of company, in other words, but none of it human. He wanders the area for several more weeks, living on mushrooms, speared fish, acorns, and the whole range of edible plants that have by now become so familiar. And he gradually makes his way back to the ledge.

Glimpsing the unmistakable rock summit of Mount Wingandicoa he feels his spirits rising in anticipation. And indeed, all three surviving cats are waiting for him at the ledge, their long period of suffering no longer possible to bear in silence as they yowl out their hunger and unrelenting annoyance at his wandering ways. He digs a piece of smoked fish out of his bundle, tears it in three, and holds out the pieces. The cats sniff cautiously, then seize the meat, retreating to separate corners of the ledge to dispatch it.

Nothing on this latest journey has given him the slightest cause for hope. If he dies tomorrow, no one but the cats will notice, and despite their protestations he's pretty sure that neither they nor their descendants will mourn him when he's dead.

Still, it's good to be home.

22

April 6, 2068 (12 A.U.C.T.)

Stromboli

Some time ago, in rationally composed sentences, I wrote that I was reconciled to the impossibility of forging any sort of lasting relationship with James Swamp. Now that I'm not seeing him multiple times a day, however, I feel compelled to reconsider. I can have no passing thought it seems, no idle daydream, without that familiar face appearing in my mind's eye. An objectively ugly and disfigured face, it's true. A face often half-hidden by that filthy, salt-stained hoodie, but a face nonetheless, that I've come to take quite a bit of solace in seeing throughout the day. One that I really can't seem to get out of my thoughts right now.

I must admit that after we dropped anchor a few days ago and I took a good first look at the island of Stromboli, it was such an idyllic sight that I allowed myself to fantasize a bit. What if there's a whole crop of children living here, I thought; the beginnings of a self-sustaining population? Maybe we would have no need to keep looking. No need to drag some unfortunate female captive back across the vast and dangerous Atlantic, very likely consigning her to a lonely, claustrophobic death. Or, if her luck is extremely good, to a hardscrabble, uncomfortable life as the founding matriarch of a tiny population of hunter-gatherers in some undetermined deep-future wilderness.

Maybe Stromboli will be as pleasant as it looks, I imagined. Its inhabitants so healthy and friendly and kind that the members of our little expeditionary team will choose to live out our lives here, telling stories of our silly voyage to entertain our new friends as we all get old together, with the laughter of children echoing in our ears. Dr. Q will repair happily to her books and equations. Tollie will cultivate killer strains of marijuana and use the yacht to take the locals on tours of the ancient ruins of the Mediterranean. James and I will finally let down our guards and become a loving couple. I'll take on the role of village doctor and he'll become a schoolteacher, freely sharing his knowledge of all those beautiful extinct birds with successive generations of new humans. Beautiful.

I regret to inform you, reader, that nothing resembling this wishful fantasy of mine is ever going to happen. The people here do not seem particularly hospitable or well-disposed toward strangers, and we have heard no laughing children in the distance. Of more immediate concern, we have yet to be allowed any further contact with James, and haven't caught a single glimpse of him since our separation. Thinking about that, and about him, gives me a sensation of almost physical pain, like some kind of restrictive mesh pulling tight around my heart. Dr. Q reassures me that there's no need to worry. Everything will be fine. We have no reason to suppose that he's not being treated with every courtesy during our period of quarantine, as are we. Still, I can't help worrying.

But I suppose I should tell you about our day.

We spent several hours this morning at the rustic table in our courtyard talking with Edda Ingvarsdottir, the tall and stately community leader whom Dr. Q and I have taken privately to calling the Witch Queen. She's fluent in English, though her accent has become more apparent now. I find her pale gray eyes distractingly beautiful, although her attractiveness is undermined by a lack of humor that's a little chilling, especially in close quarters.

She began by asking us about the *Solar Barque*, and its owner, the one member of our team who hasn't come ashore. We didn't tell her his name or clarify that he's Dr. Q's brother, referring to him simply as "our captain" (which he would no doubt get a kick out of) in the hopes that this would downplay his personal importance to us. She inquired about his age and we told her the truth, that he was in his mid-fifties. The fact is, however, that Tollie is not a person of primary interest to Edda.

We steered the conversation back to James. "He is well taken care of," she said. "We're just waiting for the test results to release all of you from quarantine."

I wish that I could accept these avowals at face value, but there's something about Edda that makes me nervous. A quick perceptiveness combined with an immediate self-confidence in those perceptions. A cool evasiveness that rubs me the wrong way, especially on the topic of James. Dr. Q is more optimistic, as she tends to be, though she agrees that it would be foolish to place all our trust in our hosts. At some point, after we're released from quarantine, we're going to have to figure out whether we have come all this way for a good reason.

And there remains the matter of our missing James, who dominates my thoughts as the minutes slowly tick by inside this pleasantly airy prison with a view.

April 8, 2068 (12 A.U.C.T.)
Stromboli

We read, we eat, we sleep. We do have the periodic visits of our minders to look forward to, Johanna and Berglind, who come at least three times a day to check in on us, replenish our food and water, and take our laundry. Both women's physiques, while coarser than Edda's, are still noticeably well-toned and athletic a dozen years on from playing soccer. Johanna's hair is dark, almost crow-black, while Berglind's is ash-blonde, like Edda's. Johanna is the more voluble of the two, while Berglind is shyer and more brooding. They both speak English, though they're clearly operating under strict instructions not to discuss anything with us beyond the most basic questions and answers about our needs and comfort.

But they don't seem to have noticed Dr. Q's uncanny ear for languages. Her comprehension of Icelandic improves by the hour, and with the help of this hidden advantage we've been able to gather a few potentially useful snippets. Edda is the unquestioned source of all major decisions. It is she who sets the tone. The roles of the male former coaches is less clear: they are helpers and laborers, ultimately subservient to Edda, though they do seem to have retained their status as authority figures to some degree. There appears to be a special emphasis on sanitation and cleanliness. Much of what Johanna and Berglind do while they're here involves scrubbing: the floors, the toilet, the double-basined sink in the bathroom. Certain things they've let slip have confirmed our impression of a generalized disdain for the niceties of modern science, although they do seem to possess a baseline medical competence and a large store of pre-collapse supplies such as syringes, antibiotic ointments, and various kinds of medical test kits.

With regard to our pressing need for more detailed and specific information about the island and its residents, Dr. Q thinks Berglind is more likely to be coopted and is focusing her considerable charm on accomplishing that. I'm less convinced. As the more confident and talkative minder, Johanna strikes me as the one whose tongue is more likely to slip, so I'm focusing my energies on her.

Mostly, however, we spend the hours alone in our charming prison. We have a running game of spades, very competitive, and I'm happy to report that despite Dr. Q's unfair advantages of generational brilliance and a near-photographic memory I currently hold a small lead.

Occasionally, especially early in the morning and around dusk, we'll hear murmured conversations and footsteps or the creaking of cart wheels on the cobblestone streets beyond our double-locked door. The wind often picks up at night, blowing in from the open water and howling through the lava cliffs and the cobbled alleyways of town, and every so often we hear volcanic eruptions from above, a loud thundering often followed by the glassy clatter of lava rocks careening down the mountainside. As far as we can tell it doesn't occur on a predictable schedule, but it's frequent enough that our ears are always pricked. It's a strange and unnerving way to pass the idle hours.

Also unnerving is to look out at the reach of ocean visible through our courtyard window and not see the *Solar Barque*. Dr. Q has given Tollie permission to circumnavigate the island, as it has become clear that our quarantine is likely to be relatively extended. Given the fact that we still haven't caught a glimpse of James, not being able to look out and see our trusty vessel resting at anchor fills me with unease. Tollie is under strict orders to be back within twenty-four hours. I'm hoping he doesn't smoke too much weed, or get so distracted by the electronica pumping in through his headphones that he loses track of time. It's true that we find ourselves in stasis, but who knows how long that will last?

Meanwhile, the sun inches its way down to the western horizon, painting the sky with glorious brush strokes of pink, orange, and violet as we gaze out through our cliff-top window at the rocks and surf and the dancing rose-faceted swells of the Tyrrhenian Sea. The view calls to mind that famous tuna slaughter scene in Rossellini's black-and-white movie. Even with sea-level rise, I'm sure if we watched it again we would recognize the specific shapes of these jagged cliffs and half-drowned lava boulders, and perhaps the specific little cove where Strombolian fishermen once consented to be filmed in their boats as they plied their ancient trade. Were they singing as they worked? Chanting? I can't remember exactly, but it's impossible to forget the cinematic images that came next. The slow drawing-in of that broad circular net. The surface of the ocean inside the net beginning to churn, then coming to a fast boil. The panicked fish splashing and leaping, and the fishermen with their gaffs and well-sharpened knives. The tuna with their scythe-like fins, their serrated tails and huge, saucer-like eyes—creatures of an alien, almost otherworldly beauty—wrestled into the boats and sacrificed, their blood flowing copiously, ink-black in the captured footage. A scene considered unique in the history of film, apparently. Now a reminder of the horrific truth that those magnificent predators, along with many thousands of other species, have disappeared from the Earth's oceans, never to be seen again.

Over a century has passed since *Stromboli: Land of God* was filmed. Apart from the rise in sea level, the backdrop hasn't changed much, but everything else has. It's hard to believe we're even living on the same planet.

Needless to say, I'm eager to get on with things. Find out what we need to, do what we need to about it, if anything, and be on our way as quickly and efficiently as possible.

23

April 10, 2068 (12 A.U.C.T.)
Stromboli

There are certain events in life that seem to freeze time in place, or preserve it in amber, so that a single moment may become fixed so clearly in your mind that it can be taken out at any later hour, held up to the light, and examined from every possible angle. Such an event unfolded for Dr. Q and me this morning. The dream has been living in our imaginations for more than a decade now, though we have hesitated to mention it aloud too often, because each of us has privately been expecting to be disappointed. It's the reason we've come all this way. Yet when it happened, I was unprepared for the emotional fallout.

Everything has suddenly come into focus. The game we are playing is now stomach-churningly, nail-bitingly, heartbreakingly *real.*

We have witnessed the miracle of our times.

At the break of dawn Johanna and Berglind unlocked our door and brought in our breakfast. They weren't wearing masks, and it made them look younger, friendlier, and more innocent than the tight-lipped, forbidding minders that had been looming in our imaginations. They told us that our medical tests had come back negative, though we still had to remain in quarantine for several more days, and gave us new, custom-fitted tunics, these with just a touch of blue embroidery on the collars and sleeves.

Thus properly attired, we followed them outside and down through the cobbled streets to the stone piazza where we'd been processed upon our arrival. The community had already gathered, though no males were present, including James. In addition to the fair-skinned Icelanders, there were perhaps half a dozen women who looked to be locals, given their darker hair and complexions. They wore the same tunics as everyone else but stood a little apart, looking sad-faced and old beyond their years. No one was wearing masks, so apparently the word had gotten around about our negative test results. These people have a noticeable confidence in their own medical expertise, though it has been clear to us from the beginning that this is ill-founded.

Apparently the soccer team had included some budding chamber musicians, because there was a string trio of Icelandic women—a cellist, a violinist, and violist—warming up at what seemed to be a considerable level of skill. Edda stood near them on a raised dais. When she saw that we'd taken our places in the crowd she nodded, and the trio began playing Vivaldi's "La Primavera." The crowd shifted expectantly, pushing closer to the dais, and from a narrow alley at the top of the piazza there emerged a small procession: four white-tunicked former soccer players bearing a litter decorated with an elaborate arrangement of basketry, dried grasses, and fresh flowers. Sitting cross-legged on that litter, clutching a little stuffed tiger and gazing solemnly down at the women who had gathered to welcome her, was a human child of perhaps seven or eight years old. (*Transcriber's note*: eight years, three months, and two and a half weeks on the day in question, as we were later to find out.)

The child is a rare beauty, with a clear olive complexion and deep-set, observant eyes. She was dressed in a pretty white gown, sewn from the same material as the tunics but more elaborately made, with ornate embroidery in both blue and purple, and her shining mahogany hair tied back in white ribbons and crowned with a wreath of fresh white roses. One of her litter-bearers gently took the stuffed tiger from her hands and helped her stand. Edda, beaming, reached out with both hands to swing her up onto the dais. As the trio reached a crescendo she held up a large basket and the child reached in to throw handfuls of rose petals out over the enraptured onlookers, many of whom reached for them or tilted their beaming faces up as if trying to catch raindrops.

Most of the onlookers, at least, appeared enraptured. The small group of Strombolians seemed to be looking on with a kind of aching resignation, and one of them—a grandmother or aunt, perhaps—used the shoulder of her tunic to discreetly wipe tears from her eyes.

When the basket was empty the little girl raised her hands in a kind of self-conscious benediction, holding the posture for a moment or two while Edda looked on approvingly. Then she became bored and started fiddling with her crown of flowers. The litter-bearer holding the stuffed tiger held it up to her, and she took it gratefully and pressed it to her cheek.

As the trio played the final notes of the Vivaldi concerto, the crowd began to disperse. Edda took the girl by the hand and led her out across the plaza to where Dr. Q and I stood with our minders. She greeted us with nearly unbearable sweetness, bowing slightly and saying good morning in perfect English as Edda looked on with a proud smile.

"Who is that?" I said, pointing to the stuffed tiger.

"Tigrotto," she said shyly. "He is very tired."

"He must be. Maybe you should give him a nap."

"Yes. He adores sleeping."

Gazing into those dark, innocent little-girl eyes, I felt my field of vision blur with tears. In the next moment her attendants were leading her back to her litter.

Edda stayed behind, gazing at us expectantly, as if eager to drink in our astonishment at the miraculous thing she'd just made it possible for us to witness. "Rosaria," she said, by way of prompting us out of our awed silence. "Her name is Rosaria."

"Are there others?" Dr. Q asked.

"No. Not yet, anyway."

"And her mother?"

Edda shook her head sadly. "Passed away."

"I'm so sorry to hear that, dear. How did she die, if I may ask?"

"We don't know. A fever. Something in the air. It happened quickly."

Dr. Q nodded, and we were silent for a moment.

"What about the father?" I asked.

"Also dead."

"Fever?"

"Accident." She glanced quickly at Johanna and Berglind as she said this and they both looked away uncomfortably, giving us the distinct impression that there had been something untoward about the way he'd died.

"Would it be possible for us to visit with Rosaria in private, dear? Dr. Morgan-Ochoa and I would treasure the opportunity to get to know her, and to conduct a basic physical exam."

"I'm afraid that would *not* be possible," Edda replied, shaking her head sadly. "We must take every precaution to keep her safe, as I'm sure you will understand. Even members of our community are not allowed private visits."

It strikes me that there is something off about Edda, especially now that we've seen her without the mask. Something about her mouth, which is narrower than I'd imagined, and set in what appears to be an expression of permanent censure. It is the mouth of an unhappy person, of a person accustomed to being obeyed, and perhaps—though I'm not sure why I have this impression—it's also the mouth of a *volatile* person, one whose mood could at any moment flip into anger or violence. In any case, judging that this was not the right moment to press our case, we let it go.

Back at our cottage, after Johanna and Berglind had fetched us fresh food and water and bolted the door firmly behind them, Dr. Q and I shared an unusually emotional moment, collapsing into each other's arms and sobbing.

All these years of work and speculation. The constant effort to maintain an optimistic outlook in the face of almost certain failure. Now, suddenly, the goal that has for so long been the defining purpose of our lives appears almost within grasp.

It was obvious from this morning's assembly that Rosaria is viewed with profound reverence here, reverence that may be verging on worship as a living goddess. And why not? Her existence is indeed a miracle. A small, bright spark of hope in the dim twilight of the human species, with the cave-black night rapidly closing in.

And yet what these white-clad former Icelandic athletes, these beautiful marooned orphans living out their strange utopian daydream don't seem to understand—or are perhaps choosing to ignore—is that despite any precautions they may think they're taking, that small, bright spark of hope is likely to be extinguished sooner or later. True, Rosaria's ancestors' prolonged exposure to whatever volcanic anomalies are present in the air and/or water of this place has given her immunity to the particular microbe that caused the hyperpandemic, and that led the rest of humanity to the dire situation we now find ourselves facing. But there are too many other novel pathogens still in circulation throughout the planet's atmosphere. And they will continue to circulate far beyond Rosaria's natural lifespan.

All of which is to say: the task before us now could not be any clearer.

What we saw this morning is interesting from a number of perspectives. There are fascinating questions to consider about this improvised religion of theirs, and how healthy they all seem, and exactly how they have succeeded in establishing what seems to be a self-sustaining community in the midst of the ongoing global disaster that continues to unfold all around them. But as Dr. Q is quick to point out, these questions are secondary now, and they may need to remain unanswered. We need to focus on our goal.

"What about if we ask for a meeting of the whole community and explain our pressing concerns for Rosaria, along with something about the nature of our project?" I suggested.

"We could try, but I very much doubt that something like that would persuade them. You saw how they feel about her. And if you think about it, any explanation of our work is bound to seem impossibly far-fetched to them."

"Right. So what's our strategy?"

"Well, first of all we have to establish communication with James. Then we have to formulate a plan, and for that we'll need a good deal more information—such as where Rosaria is being kept, who's guarding her, and so on."

Capturing Rosaria and/or persuading her to come away with us is far from the only challenge, of course. To begin with, we'll have to free ourselves from this prison-with-a-view. We've discussed using tied-together bedsheets to lower ourselves in stages down to the sea and signaling Tollie to swoop into shore to pick us up, but this doesn't seem very promising. And it also doesn't address the matter of James.

I keep thinking back to the way Edda looked at him when she first met him as part of that initial delegation out on the *Solar Barque*. I fear that she may have developed unrealistic and perhaps even dangerous misconceptions because of his age and what she might believe him physically capable of doing, despite his pronounced scarring. It could be that they're holding him separately in order to perform further tests, which I find extremely worrisome. Because if they think there's any chance that his reproductive system has remained viable or is somehow possible to restore, then they're even more ignorant of the underlying science than we've given them credit for.

24

11th Millennium A.U.C.T. (estimated)

It occurs to him that mushrooms might help in his quest to find meaning in a solitary existence. Not the ones that make up such an important part of his foraging diet—oysters, chanterelles, white-fleshed puffballs—but hallucinogenics. He's seen plenty of them on the forest floor, the characteristic bright red cap with raised white dots of *Amanita muscaria*, fly agaric.

Sure enough, in half a day of hunting he's able to gather several dozen. To be on the safe side, he begins with just a nibble, his taste buds revolting against the rubbery, foul-tasting flesh. But he forces himself to chew and swallow it, then sits cross-legged on his accustomed granite seat looking out over the lowlands. The last week has been rainy but the sky has cleared now and it's a warm morning, mid-September perhaps, with shrouds of mist rising from a canopy already spattered with the first bright dashes of red and yellow. After an hour or so, feeling nothing, he chews and swallows three mushrooms in their entirety, and sets off downslope on his well-worn footpath.

Beside a small stream on the lower flanks of the mountain he pauses to rest on a familiar boulder, checks in with himself, still feels nothing unusual. It's the right kind of mushroom, he's pretty sure, but maybe over the centuries its fundamental properties have changed?

Still, it's a pleasant morning, balmy for the season, with the sun slanting in through gently swaying boughs to pick out objects on the forest floor: boulders, mossy logs, gnarled roots. Getting up, he feels kind of woozy. His eyes have begun to water and he's slightly nauseated, but not enough to throw up.

He walks farther down the slope into a stand of tall hemlocks, their furrowed trunks arranged like sentinels along the banks of the gently murmuring stream, their upper branches making a pleasant, cathedral-like room within the canopy. In his time the hemlock woolly adelgid had ravaged the species, nearly extirpating it from the Smoky Mountains up into Canada. It's gratifying to see that they've made a comeback. They add much to this forest, he thinks, with their stolid trunks and elegantly spreading branches and the open understory they make for themselves: the rich springy duff of accumulated needles among the moss-covered roots, boulders, and deadwood. The arrangement of shadows and clear dappled golden-green sunlight that covers this ground feels pregnant somehow, waiting to be animated with meaningful movement, like a film set just before the actors arrive.

In the next moment he sees or rather senses a streaking shadow overhead, quicker and sharper than the shadows of the swaying boughs. He stops to stare up into the canopy, but he can make out nothing unusual. He dismisses it as his mind playing tricks and resumes his walk. He's only half-aware that his gait has become more expansive, freewheeling, a rolling march down the path. There's a buzzing sensation in the back of his throat. A hollow space opening up behind his eyes.

He comes to a stream crossing, above which the unobstructed blue sky appears in a wavering S-curve that echoes the meandering stream through a corridor of immense white pines, the crowns of which are swaying in a manner that seems exaggerated given the mild breezes down on the forest floor. He glimpses that hurtling shadow again, and in the next moment he finally sees what's casting it. One of those unexpectedly diurnal flying squirrels flares down through the gap between the treetops, the sun shining through its golden-red webbing like an x-ray picking out the skeletal outlines of the little creature's spread-eagle limbs. It seems impossible how far it's flying, how long it remains airborne. Finally it disappears into the canopy downstream, but he's left with a distinct impression of the creature staring intently down at him as it flew over. Considering him with the same wary, curious intelligence he's noticed in a number of the species he's seen here. Keeping track of his progress down the mountainside.

It reminds him of an essay he once read on the topic of evolution. The author affixed a tin baffle to the bottom of a bird feeder to keep squirrels from getting into his seed, then watched five squirrels in a row try their wits on it and fail. But the sixth squirrel paused for a moment, staring speculatively up at the baffle. It seemed to the author that the animal was turning things over in its mind, and in the next moment it leapt, catching the edge of the tin with its forepaw and flicking itself up and into the feeder, where it proceeded to dine with gusto. The author hurried over, waving his arms trying to scare the little creature away, but it stayed where it was, fixing him in a shrewd and insolent gaze for a long moment before it scurried away. The author felt a terrible sense of destiny closing in on him, and on the entire human species.

Now that humanity is pretty much out of the picture, has the torch of sentience been passed on to some other being? The flying squirrel, perhaps, or those big black hawks?

Clearly, the *Amanita muscaria* is messing with his mind.

He does have a destination, though. A giant beech whose far-spreading branches have shaded out a fern-carpeted hollow for itself in the forest. The tree is a splendid behemoth, with smooth gray bark that displays the underlying musculature of the wood, like the foreleg of a dinosaur browsing the canopy. He stands on a root that is like a colossal finger sunk to the knuckles in the soil and allows the callused soles of his feet to absorb the ancient being's slowly pulsating energy. He leans forward, resting first his hands, then his chest and forehead against the trunk, attuned to the faint vibration flowing out through the living bark and into his own body and brain. It's as if this familiar tree, always available to him for shade or contemplation, has decided to offer something new. Life. Solace. A new form of companionship to ease the ache of his loneliness.

After a time he steps back, feeling slightly sheepish to discover himself hugging what is after all just a plant. Or is it?

He follows the trail down to a section of the stream where it crosses a broad angled slab of granite. Over the millennia the water has worn a kind of sluiceway into the stone, terminating in a pool where he often bathes. The day has become muggy, so he sheds his makeshift clothing and lowers himself into the cool water. A fountain of bubbles blossoms continuously from the clear depths of the pool, fizzing pleasantly on his skin. There is a low waterfall where the stream comes off the slab, a membrane of falling water that glints in the sun like liquid glass. He swims upstream to it, finds a foothold, and pushes himself up through the sheeting water to find a comfortable resting place with his back against the slippery stone.

The rush of falling water mutes his thoughts. Pleasantly cooled off, he lounges in a state of simple awareness, gazing out through the transparent screen to where bright patches of sunlight glint amid the gently swaying shadows of the forest.

Suddenly he sees an animal: sunlit, paler than the vegetation, upright and slender. A deer he thinks at first, calmly browsing the understory along the streambank. He slips out under the falls and swims underwater, bobbing his head up in the middle of the pool to get a closer look, but his sudden appearance startles the creature, and it disappears into the forest.

He treads water, disbelieving. Unless he's terribly mistaken, the creature he glimpsed for a split second was not a deer, but a female human. Which would have been astonishing enough if the figure hadn't been wearing faded denim jeans, a Lab-issued hoodie, and the distinctive round-lensed glasses of a woman he knows without doubt *cannot possibly be alive.*

He splashes up out of the pool and runs, dripping and naked, after the apparition. And he does catch one more fleeting glimpse of her through the undergrowth before she completely disappears.

Even as it's happening a part of him is aware that it's a hallucination. That it's not real. But it's a hallucination too close to his heart for him not to pursue it again, and the next morning he ingests a generous handful of fly agarics, chewing and choking them down at his morning campfire. When he feels his eyes begin to water he sets off down the mountain toward the crystalline pool with its sheeting waterfall and fizzing, eternally replenished bubbles.

It's earlier this time and the morning is cooler, but he shrugs off his filthy skins and lowers himself in anyway, swimming up to the waterfall to take a seat with his back to the drenched rock behind the lens of falling water.

He stays that way, staring out into the blurred shadows at the edge of the forest until his teeth begin to chatter. The rational part of his mind warns that he's courting hypothermia, but he's reluctant to give up. Eventually he succumbs to the chill and swims down through the pool to the slippery rocks below. Shivering and discouraged, he staggers over to a slab of granite angled to face the sun and stretches out on the warm stone. He closes his eyes.

"Hallucinogens, Nick? Is this really the best use of your time?"

"I've looked and looked, Nat," he says. "There's no one else here."

"Yes. We were afraid that would be the case."

"You *were* going to send someone," he prompts.

"We did our best, dear." She's crouching beside him on the boulder, the bright sun refracting strangely through the round lenses. "In the end, for various reasons, it was simply not possible."

"So you decided to come yourself."

"Don't be ridiculous. I'm just a construct of your fly agaric–addled imagination."

"But you *are* talking."

She stands up, wiping her hands on her jeans. "This is you talking to *yourself*, dear."

"But it really does seem to be you."

"Well, it's not."

"What if I choose to believe that it is?"

She shrugs, holding up her hands in a familiar gesture of good-humored resignation. But he can no longer sustain the illusion, and he suddenly feels crushed by the weight of the planet's gravitational field pressing in on his body, grinding his buttocks and shoulder blades into the warm granite. The weight is making it difficult to breathe, and he opens his eyes again, but the sun through the gap in the canopy is unbearably bright, and he closes them.

It occurs to him that the more often he tries to play these kinds of mental tricks on himself, the more likely it is that he's actually going to lose his mind.

25

April 11, 2068 (12 A.U.C.T.)
Stromboli

We did catch a glimpse of James today on the daily walk allowed to us under the watch of Johanna and Berglind. We were on a trail above the village that winds through the community's well-kept gardens and paddocks on the lower slopes of the volcano. He was participating in a kind of work crew with three of the frosty-bearded former coaches, using hoes and shovels to mix mortar or cement for a repair job on the stone steps leading down to the dock and the submerged seawall. We started yelling his name as soon as we saw him. Johanna and Berglind, taken by surprise, stepped forward quickly to hush us. But James had heard our voices and, looking up, gave us a friendly wave. We don't know if he's volunteered to work for the community or if they are somehow coercing him, but it was a great relief to see him looking healthy and in relatively good spirits, at least so far as we could tell from a distance.

We also touched base with Tollie, who sailed the yacht to perhaps five hundred yards offshore of our quarters, close enough so that we could hear the popping of the breeze in the *Solar Barque*'s loosened sails. Dr. Q took out her folding whiteboard, wrote *ALL OK?* in big block letters with the erasable marker, and held it up for him to read through his binoculars. I took out my pocket-sized pair to read his response while she erased her first message, and there ensued a fairly lengthy conversation, during which he relayed to us that the town of Ginostra, on the far side of the island, appeared to be completely abandoned.

GHOST TOWN? Dr. Q asked.

INTENTIONALLY DESTROYED BY THE LOOK OF IT. BURNED TO THE GROUND.

PLEASE FIND EXACTLY WHERE JAMES IS SPENDING NIGHTS. WE'RE PREPARING TO IMPLEMENT.

ROGER THAT, he wrote.

We heard the sound of the door being unlocked and quickly stowed the whiteboard and the binoculars.

Half an hour later, as our minders were wrapping up their assigned tasks, we finally got the breakthrough we'd been hoping for. The source, just as Dr. Q had predicted, was Berglind, and what we learned from her was enlightening, though also, I must say, profoundly disturbing. We were sitting at the table in the courtyard. Dr. Q "accidentally" knocked over our pitcher of rosemary water, sending it pouring out onto the stone floor.

"Oh, hell," she exclaimed. "I'm such a klutz! Johanna dear, would you mind refilling this before you go?"

Johanna frowned annoyedly from the other side of the courtyard. "We will bring a new one first thing in the morning."

"I don't think either of us have enough left in our bedside water glasses to make it through the night in this dry climate, dear. Are you sure you couldn't run out quickly and bring us a refill?"

The dark-haired Icelander stood indecisively for a moment.

"You've been so kind," Dr. Q remarked. "So very thorough and welcoming. I've been meaning to tell Edda how impressed we are with both of you."

Johanna took out her key and picked up the empty pitcher. Saying something in Icelandic to Berglind, she stepped out, carefully locking the heavy door behind her.

As soon as she was gone, we both got up to corner Berglind, who was, for at least the second time today, mopping the floor of my bedroom. There was no time to beat around the bush, so we just kind of cheerfully if somewhat aggressively accosted her and began firing off questions. She hesitated, flushing deeply and shrinking away from us, but her back was literally up against a wall, and there was nowhere for her to go. We promised that we would never ever repeat to Johanna or Edda or anyone else anything she might say. After a moment she decided to share a secret with us that appears, as Dr. Q had somehow intuited, to have been bothering her for some time.

It seems that Edda, because she grew up in relatively close proximity to a volcano in northwestern Iceland and spent much of her childhood immersed in geothermal hot springs, believes that she is one of the small percentage of humans who have retained their ability to procreate. It's a belief that she can offer no evidence to support, but has apparently subscribed to for quite a long time, having tried to prove it a few years after the community's arrival on Stromboli with the man who fathered Rosaria—though, in Berglind's words, "it didn't work."

"She wasn't able to get pregnant?"

"No."

"What about Rosaria's mother? Was *she* able to get pregnant again after giving birth?"

"Yes. She was pregnant when she died."

"Oh, that's terrible. We're so very, very sorry to hear that. She died of a fever, we understand. How about the father?"

"Dead too. After Edda . . . "

"After Edda what, dear?"

"After Edda tried to . . . get pregnant by him."

"Tried and failed, you mean?"

"Yes. Tried and failed."

"And how long after Rosaria's mother died did Edda make this attempt?"

"Well, actually she began trying before."

"Before," I put in. "You mean while Rosaria's mother was still alive."

Berglind nodded miserably, resting the mop handle against the wall.

"And how did *that* go over with the remaining Strombolians?"

Dr. Q shot me a cautionary glance, and she was right. This question was a distraction from the line of inquiry that we actually needed to pursue.

"I'm so sorry, dear," she said to Berglind, who looked stricken and was now resting her weight, as if for support, against the wall beside the mop. "I know this is difficult for you, and we do very much appreciate you sharing it with us. Just a few more questions. Is it your belief that there is any woman alive on this island who is capable of getting pregnant?"

"There is Edda."

"According to her," I said. "But do you believe it? Given that she failed to become pregnant by Rosaria's father within months of him impregnating Rosaria's mother for the second time?"

"No." She darted a sheepish glance at me. "What I believe doesn't matter, though. What matters is what *Edda* believes."

"And Edda believes that she can still get pregnant."

"Yes." And then she added, very intentionally looking into both Dr. Q's and my eyes: "If she can find the right man."

"A man who himself somehow retains the extremely rare capability of fathering a child."

"No." Berglind shook her head. "This is what I've been trying to warn you about. If the man is young enough, Edda believes that the volcano can restore him."

Dr. Q and I looked at each other, wide-eyed.

"What exactly did Rosaria's father die of, dear?"

Just then we heard the key turning in the door. Berglind picked up the mop and set about finishing her work, and Johanna strode in. The conversation was over, though there was one last development. Along with the refreshed pitcher, Johanna had come bearing two freshly sewn tunics, custom-fitted to our measurements, a little longer than our other ones and more formal looking, with three-quarter sleeves and a few rows of cobalt-blue embroidery on the collars and hems.

"Wear these tomorrow, please," she instructed. "In the morning will be another ceremony."

"With Rosaria?"

"With Rosaria."

"And will we see our shipmate there too, dear? The young man?"

"You can be sure of it," the raven-haired Icelander replied.

Berglind, meanwhile, stared at the floor, no longer willing to meet our eyes.

When they'd gone, we placed a small inflatable solar-powered camping lantern in the window and set it to blinking mode, an emergency signal we'd pre-arranged with Tollie. Fortunately he was still anchored within easy view. Given the disturbing nature of what Berglind has told us and how quickly events now seem to be unfolding, Dr. Q and I have made the decision to proceed. The execution of this plan will be complicated by certain on-the-ground realities we face at the moment, in particular the unexpected separation from James. But we spent many hours aboard the *Solar Barque* and back at the Lab gaming out contingencies, and we are cautiously optimistic that, with a bit of luck, we can pull it off.

The plan hinges on two specialized pharmaceutical substances. One is Kolokol-3, developed by the Russians more than six decades ago, a fentanyl derivative "aerosolizable incapacitant"—essentially, a sleeping gas. It took a great deal of effort to get our hands on this, including a harrowing pre-voyage trip down to a heavily armed compound in New Jersey owned by an old school chum of Tollie's. But that's a story for another time. For now, it's enough to say that Kolokol-3 is highly effective even at low concentrations. There are risks associated with it. We don't expect that we'll end up killing anyone, though it is possible, but given the existential goals of our mission, this is a chance that we must be and are willing to take.

The second substance was developed as part of the suite of pharmaceuticals integrated into the TDS system. Its main ingredients are epinephrine, naloxone, and mescaline, a compound derived from peyote, a psychedelic plant. It's a powerful sympathomimetic, and incidentally a highly effective antidote to the incapacitant—though emergency resuscitation and resistance to the sleeping gas aren't its only applications. It also happens to change the user's perception of time, in effect shifting the world into something resembling a film playing in very slow motion. I should emphasize that the user's experience of this latter substance is likely to be highly subjective and limited in duration. We remain in the dark about any long-term side effects, though possibilities include permanent damage to the heart and the central nervous system, depression, dissociation, and psychosis. Given these and other hazards, I've been reluctant to actually inject anyone with the drug, which is to say that it remains largely untested. But if the proper dosage were to be injected into a subject's bloodstream, as in the case of a TDS malfunction, the user's subjective perception of slowed-down time would theoretically allow them to get a lot done in a brief period. Which is exactly why it may be useful to us in the execution of our plan.

Tollie will anchor the *Solar Barque* just out of sight beyond a bend in the island's coast and hike into town during the night with a backpack containing a dozen canisters of the incapacitant, which he will place strategically, then conceal himself with a good view of the ceremony. When he judges that the right moment has arrived, he will use a remote trigger to release the gas, causing everyone within a sixty-yard radius (unless it's windy) to temporarily lose consciousness. Before releasing the gas he will give an auditory signal in the form of a distinctive birdcall he knows—a shrill, bad-tempered crow—giving Dr. Q and me a chance to inject ourselves with the second substance before inhaling the gas. If necessary we'll use another injection to resuscitate James, while Tollie runs back to the yacht and brings it around in time to meet the three of us, with Rosaria, at the bottom of the stairs to the inundated seawall.

It's not an ideal plan, to be sure. James had been a key player in almost all the scenarios we gamed out, and as Tollie has not been able to zero in on his sleeping location or otherwise make contact with him, we are one crew member down. Typically it was James who was supposed to fire off the gas canisters. Most often he would have helped in retrieving the unconscious subject and carrying her down to the water while Tollie stayed in the yacht with the emergency motor idling. Given the present situation, not only can we not count on James to help us, we're probably going to have to figure out a way to resuscitate and/or free him as well.

In short, there are a dangerous number of variables. Given our inability to communicate with our youngest colleague, however, and everything Berglind has told us—the most salient point being that

Edda has a delusional and quite possibly dangerous mindset—we judge that the time has come. Both James and Rosaria will apparently be present at tomorrow morning's ceremony, which seems like the best opportunity we're ever going to get.

Fingers crossed that all goes well.

26

11th Millennium A.U.C.T. (estimated)

He's doing his best to hold on to memories of the time before. He was never much good at retaining details. Not nearly as good as Natalie, for example, who could recite back something she'd once read or heard verbatim, months or years later. But it feels like the more time passes, the more quickly he's forgetting, even on subjects that used to be of major personal interest: biology, literature, cultural and natural history. He dreads these steadily accumulating losses and what they might portend.

He spends his days and nights trying to reconstruct what he remembers of humanity's masterworks: the *Iliad*, the *Odyssey*, the King James Bible, *Don Quixote*, Shakespeare and Lao Tzu, Hemingway and Austen, *War and Peace* and *Black Elk Speaks*, Tolkien and Baldwin and Ishiguro and Le Guin and García Márquez. Far too many great books to name, though he was once an avid reader, and scenes from classic movies too: Lawrence of Arabia materializing at the top of a Sahara dune; Bogart and Bergman puffing cigarettes and falling in love in a chiaroscuro vision of wartime Morocco; a huge red sun rising over a birch forest in an uncannily beautiful Russian film whose title he can no longer remember. Music too of course, some of which he can still play out in his head. Not whole pieces, just fragments of rhythm and melody, and a few lyrics here and there. A few stanzas of poetry.

But the truth is, although it does kill time, attempting to breathe life back into these dying embers of human culture is a deeply unsatisfying exercise, making him crave the real thing all the more. To read, to listen to music, to appreciate great art, to spend days and weeks living inside great novels in all their diverse and flawed glory—none of these things he once took for granted, and whose existence once seemed boundless, infinite, will ever be available to him again. The creative bonfire of human genius, that inconceivably valuable treasure trove of a species gone missing. Kept alive now, apparently, only in the dwindling memory of one pitifully inadequate mind.

He considers suicide. He could eat a poison mushroom, jump off a cliff, dive into a swollen river, let the cold current's strong arms drag him under. Why not? It's not as if there's anyone left to disappoint.

In the end he decides against it. Natalie's voice is distant in his head, but from wherever in the star-speckled firmament she now resides he can still sometimes hear it. *Keep plugging away, dear. Stay alive and healthy. You never know what destiny will bring.*

And she's right. However unlikely it may seem, there is always still a possibility. A statistical chance at least, however tiny, that in some remote corner of this immense wilderness planet a remnant band of humans might still be at large.

So he keeps his daily vigil, sitting cross-legged on his high ledge, gazing out over the forest as the sun goes down, reflexively scanning the terrain for that elusive column of smoke. Sometimes he'll stay there after sundown too, and well into the night, staring out at the star-ceilinged darkness in the hope of glimpsing the tiny orange spark of a fire.

But he never sees it. And the months go by.

The months go by, and the years. He lives mostly on the ledge, though to avoid having to trudge up and down the mountain in deep snow he spends the coldest months in the Lab cave. At first he feared that sleeping in the shadow of that split magnesium-alloy seedpod would invite nightmares of death, loss, and inescapable claustrophobia. But the virtues of a dry floor and the cave's natural climate-control outweigh the grim associations of that changeless ink-black darkness. He stockpiles wood and keeps a fire burning at the front edge of the high-ceilinged chamber, with the narrow passageway out serving as a natural chimney.

Much of his time is spent thinking about his new religion. It's a psychological coping mechanism, he fully understands, and yet there are moments when he feels that he's discovering it in the world around him rather than simply making it up out of whole cloth. Its center of gravity seems to be the forest itself, which he's come to see as a light-filled sanctuary with rooms, corridors, and a soaring, cathedral-like dimensionality of space. Its floor is supple and alive under his bare feet; the trunks of its ancient trees are like stone-gray columns; its canopy is something akin to an elevated coral reef, where the light-worshipping trees thrust their branches skyward to be blessed by the sun. And the sun itself. The way it warms the stone and nourishes the plants. The way it filters down through the moving boughs, bathing the ferns and boulders in splendid green-gold light, throwing evocative shadows that sweep rhythmically over a forest floor that sometimes feels like the bottom of the ocean.

The element of stone also figures strongly in his new religion, especially the local granite. He doesn't really think of it as worshipping, but he does periodically climb up to the treeless summit of Wingandicoa to meditate. More often he'll simply pause during one of his foraging circuits to rest a hand on a boulder or an interesting ledge formation jutting up through the moss. He no longer remembers the geological epoch responsible for the formation of this granite, but he's certain that it's the oldest material substance he will ever actually touch, and it reminds him of his father, the geologist, and of the thing he'd felt that day at the dinosaur quarry all those millennia ago. The sudden, vertiginous sense of connection to the unimaginable vastness of planetary time.

He remembers himself and Natalie climbing the mountain one afternoon shortly before the death of her father. They'd smoked a joint and spent an hour or two wandering around awestruck by the expanse of granite, the cold permanence of its ancient weathered facets, the way the lichen seemed to have been spattered across it in harmonious compositions of abstract art. They'd laughed at themselves for being so easily entertained—it was just inanimate rock—and yet there had been something undeniably sublime about that afternoon, and the memory was lodged in his mind with an unusual vividness.

He's thankful for the clean little brook chattering down the mountainside a short walk from his ledge that is his drinking water supply, and for the larger stream it joins, that flows down onto the lowlands with its bathing pool and lens-like waterfall. He's thankful for the moon and its mysterious energies, and for the plants and animals that nourish him, and for all the other living beings as well, including of course the cats. In their seventh or eighth generation by now—he's lost track of the litters—the great majority disappear into the forest, snatched by predators or setting out to make their own way. But there are always a few that stay behind with him. Providing for them adds to the work of foraging, cutting into his free time, but he doesn't mind. They're his tribe. His adopted family. And he has plenty of free time to spare.

27

April 12, 2068 (12 A.U.C.T.)
The Tyrrhenian Sea

So much has transpired over the last twenty-four hours. I don't really know where to begin. What I wrote last night about Edda—about her delusional and possibly dangerous mindset—well, that was an understatement. But I guess the easiest thing will be just to lay out a straight chronology of what occurred.

First thing in the morning, Johanna and Berglind came in with our breakfast. The freshness of the simple food we'd been eating on Stromboli already felt like the greatest of luxuries, but this breakfast went above and beyond. Scrambled eggs, deliciously grilled and salted cactus leaves, rosemary tea, and community-made goat yogurt, cool and sour. We now suspect that this bounteous spread, like our new blue-embroidered tunics, might have been intended to soften us up in advance of the disturbing spectacle we were about to witness, and also, possibly, as a kind of overture attempting to usher us into the inner circle of the community's true believers. It's hard to be sure. In any case, given that we already knew it was going to be a day of extreme exertion, we helped ourselves to generous helpings at breakfast and did our best to savor it.

The sound of many footsteps and murmured conversations reached us from the street. It seemed that the whole community was heading down to the piazza. Before we joined them, in the chipped mirror over the double sink of our shared bathroom, Dr. Q and I had a chance for one last conversation.

"Should be an interesting ceremony," I remarked.

"Let's just hope it doesn't take some kind of apocalyptic turn before we get a chance to do our thing," she replied, shaking the water off her hands before wiping them dry on the luxuriant hand towels our attendants had left folded beside the sink. "Are you ready, dear?"

I grimaced, the direct question sparking a new flood of the nervous uneasiness that had kept me awake most of the night. "Yes. I'm ready."

Johanna and Berglind escorted us through the cobbled streets to the piazza, where an old, badly scarred Strombolian woman pounded out a mournful rhythm on a large bass drum. The entire community was there, milling around in the piazza—minus the men and Rosaria, worrisome absences for us—and there was a palpable mood of excitement in the air. With Rosaria and James missing, our action plan was on hold for the moment, driving my own anxiety levels even higher. We glanced around covertly to see if we could spot the canisters Tollie must have placed, but they were nowhere in sight, which was in fact, we hoped, a good sign. There was a large rusted-iron drain a few yards from the dais that looked like an optimal hiding place. I hoped that he hadn't had any trouble lifting that heavy grate to fit them all inside. I caught Dr. Q's eye, and she gave me a barely perceptible nod.

The litter-bearers came in with Rosaria and Edda helped her up onto the dais, where the beautiful little Strombolian girl waved distractedly to the gathered community. Her mahogany hair was dressed more elaborately today, coiled braids upon which she wore a fresh wreath of the same small cream-white roses. Despite my worries it was a thrill to see her again, this miraculous human child, and for a moment the whole piazza blurred with tears. I wondered what her life would be like if we allowed her to stay on Stromboli, lonely captive to a group of eerily worshipful outlanders. Who knows what kind of pressures she would have to face, assuming she'd even survive into adulthood.

Maybe I'm just rationalizing. It's every bit as valid to ask whether our designs for her are any better. I hope so, but there's no denying that the risks are exceedingly high. There are two inactivated spheres remaining. The fusion reactor of one can be calibrated to open within the approximate timeframe when Nicholas Hindman will (in the best-case scenario) be living out the rest of his life. There is of course the matter of the potential age disparity, though the fusion reactors have a margin of error of plus or minus eighteen and a half years, so there's no predicting what their chronological ages will be when they meet. *If* they meet. If either one of them even emerges from their respective sphere alive. In any event, Dr. Q is confident that we can tweak the cryo-hibernation system in order to add as many additional years of physiological aging as are optimal for the subject's viability, assuming she does make it all the way to the deep future.

As you have no doubt gathered, this entire operation depends on optimistic assumptions and some fairly enormous leaps of faith.

I managed to catch Rosaria's eye, and her face brightened for a moment before she glanced away. Dr. Q noticed and nodded approvingly. Apparently I'd succeeded in making an impression in that brief first meeting.

Then, almost before we had time to think, the community formed itself into a line and began filing into an alleyway at the upper end of the piazza. Dr. Q frowned at me. We seemed to have no choice but to obey as Johanna and Berglind hurried us into the line. Suddenly, instead of standing in a close-packed crowd in the contained space of the piazza, we were part of a mobile procession. One destined to continue, as we would soon learn, all the way up to the crater of the island's periodically active volcano.

This was obviously a development of the utmost concern to us. We hadn't had a chance to prepare for it. Neither had Tollie, presumably looking on helplessly from somewhere nearby. As to the gas canisters, they were also presumably still hidden under that heavy iron drainage gate at the lowest-lying point of the now-deserted piazza.

Edda held Rosaria's hand at the front of the procession uphill through the village. We formed a single-file line to climb a steep staircase to an ancient stone archway, beyond which a foot trail slanted up toward the mist-shrouded peak of the volcano. We followed a series of steep switch-backs up through goat corrals enclosed by lava-stone walls and tall stands of prickly pear cactus. As the hillside steepened, the procession slowed to a turtle's pace, those in front pausing frequently to place fresh flowers at half a dozen trailside shrines: whitewashed masonry niches placed among the lava boulders and yellow-grass tussocks. Each shrine contained identical copies of a ceramic statue around three feet tall, like an oversized doll depicting a dark-haired girl with her hands folded protectively over her belly. Each freshly wreathed statue wore a miniature version of Rosaria's elaborately embroidered tunic, with a standardized glazed-ceramic face that struck me as creepily sexualized: big doe eyes, blushing cheeks, swollen red lips.

It ended up taking this accordion-like procession around two hours to reach the crater, during which time we were completely hemmed in by our Viking shield maidens, Johanna in front of Dr. Q, and Berglind, tight-lipped and apparently regretful of her previous lack of discretion, behind me. I kept glancing around for some sign of Tollie but there was none, and we hadn't caught a glimpse of James or the male coaches either, which was obviously a source of extreme anxiety. After the final wreath-crowning there was one last arduous stretch of steep climbing.

We were well up into the cloud layer now. Visibility was limited, and it had become noticeably harder to breathe because of the high sulfur-dioxide content of the volcanic fog. The plodding rhythm of our march matched the slow tattoo of the drumbeats traveling back to us from the front. The reality had begun to sink in that as far as our action plan went, Dr. Q and I were pretty much on our own.

Finally, we arrived at the crater, a steep inverted cone from whose deepest bowels issued a whistling jet of steam that billowed out as it rose to join the astringent fog we were breathing. Edda, holding Rosaria's hand, let her halfway around the crater rim to where a wooden platform jutted partway out over the steaming cavity.

This is the moment we first noticed James, and finally understood the nature of the ceremony we'd been marched all the way up here to witness. Though perhaps *ceremony* is the wrong word. *Cruel and misinformed experiment* would be more accurate. From our conversations with Edda and our attendants, we'd already gathered that the community's grasp of modern scientific principles was shaky. Now it was impossible to ignore the fact that they—under Edda's charismatic leadership—were guided by a different belief system entirely, underpinned by some extremely dangerous assumptions.

Up on the platform James was seated on a folding chair with his hands and ankles bound. Around his neck hung what appeared to be a repurposed medical respirator, connected to a length of green plastic tubing that looked like it might have been salvaged from an old garden hose. Below him, twenty or thirty yards downhill on the steep interior slope of the crater, a team of four of the coaching staff pulled on the edges of an immense sail-like canopy of sewn-together plastic tarps. It extended partially out over the crater by a makeshift scaffold of aluminum tentpoles. The top of this canopy had been sewn into an inverted funnel, clearly designed to capture some of the steam issuing from the crater—and from there, via the garden-hose tubing, directly into the respiratory system of our bound shipmate.

It was utterly insane.

When James saw us, he gestured with his chin down at the collecting system the coaches were installing over the crater, shaking his head in grim wonderment.

"Edda! Edda Ingvarsdottir!" Dr. Q waved both arms to get the tall woman's attention across the crater. Having handed a miserable-looking Rosaria over to some attendants, the Witch Queen had climbed up onto the platform to confer with the man who seemed to be the senior coach or chief centurion of the community, a big, pot-bellied Icelander with a high forehead and a long white beard.

"We see what you're trying to do, dear!" Dr. Q continued in a polite but ringing voice. "It will not be effective! And you are putting our colleague at great risk!"

Edda flushed deeply; we could see the clear skin of her cheeks darkening even from a distance. "You don't understand the process, Dr. Quist! Later I will explain it to you in detail!"

"What you're trying to do is not supported by medical science," I yelled, "and could easily prove fatal! We demand in the strongest possible terms that you put a stop to it right this instant!"

She drew herself up, her countenance darkening even further. Clearly she was unaccustomed to having her authority challenged, especially in so public a situation, and it filled her with rage. She signaled our minders, a quick cutting gesture. Johanna and Berglind stepped forward to encircle us tightly in their strong arms, placing their hands over our mouths to shut us up. She said something to the white-bearded coach, who stood behind James to pull the respirator up over his mouth and nose. James shook his head violently, dislodging the mask and craning around to address the man. Whatever he said apparently struck a nerve. The white-bearded face went a livid shade of crimson. James, meanwhile, had managed to shake the mask entirely loose. It fell to the platform, and the weight of its hose dragged it off clattering down onto the slope of the crater.

This really set the head coach off. He drew a heavy-looking truncheon from his belt and smacked James hard on the side of his head. James went limp. Dr. Q and I gasped in shock and disbelief. We were both struggling mightily to free ourselves from the grips of Johanna and Berglind, who had, in the process of securing our arms and shoulders, been forced to take their hands off our mouths.

"This is *unacceptable*, Edda!" Dr. Q yelled across the crater, her usually unassuming tone now angry, resonant, and steely.

I wanted to add something, but I was so furious that I was unable to choke out the words. Instead I focused on trying to free myself from the vise of Johanna's arms pinning my own less muscular arms to my abdomen. The head coach had bent down to retrieve James's mask, using a loop of hose that had been stopped by his chair to pull it back up to the platform. That accomplished, he placed it over our unconscious shipmate's face and pulled the straps tight.

I glanced helplessly at Dr. Q, who looked more confident than I felt. She gave a little surreptitious flick of her eyes, calling my attention to a low ridge of lava boulders to our left, half hidden among the wandering shrouds of astringent fog. I glimpsed a little swatch of bright-orange fabric disappearing behind a rock. It was a color that in one of our pre-arrival briefings Tollie had called "safety orange" in reference to the old sun-faded, travel-stained Osprey expedition backpack that was presumably still loaded with the gas canisters.

Just then we heard, or rather felt, an ominous rumble beneath our feet, coming from deep in the mountain. Edda felt it too, taking Rosaria's hand to lead her back from the crater rim, and signaling the rest of the community to follow. The men working down in the crater scrambled quickly up the slope, kicking landslides of tinkling lava pebbles back down into the steaming depths. James, meanwhile, still unconscious and apparently considered expendable, was left strapped to the folding chair on the overhanging platform to breathe in the miraculous fumes through his respirator—and quite possibly, if the threatened eruption was severe enough, to be cooked alive where he sat.

We registered all this in a single crowded instant, as one does at such times, even as Johanna and Berglind wrestled us back away from the crater. I myself was nearly paralyzed by fury and indecision, but Dr. Q caught my gaze, and there was a meaningful gleam in her eye as she brought a free hand to her mouth as if to repress a cough, then raised and lowered her thumb, mimicking the act of injection. Sure enough, in the next moment I heard the unmistakable call of Tollie's bad-tempered crow.

I'm sorry, but I must interrupt this narrative here for the moment. I'll do my best to finish up tomorrow. Then we can all turn our eyes to the future, with all the risks and uncertainties and brightly shining hopes it may contain.

28

April 13, 2068 (12 A.U.C.T.)

Somewhere in the Mediterranean

With Tollie's unmistakable crow caw, the deep rumble of the volcano, and the high-pitched whistle of pressurized steam coming up out of the crater all in my ears, I reached down into my hip pocket and felt a sting as I injected myself in the thigh through the fine cloth of my tunic. Still working blind, I pushed the syringe back through the stopper, drew the plunger to refill it, and gripped it securely in my fist. Groaning dramatically, I fake-collapsed, falling backward into Johanna and successfully knocking her off her feet. Dr. Q lunged forward to my aid, and I managed to inject her in the shoulder as she and Berglind helped me to my feet.

"You okay, dear?" she asked. Then, switching to Spanish, a language we were pretty sure our minders didn't speak: "You attend to James. I'll get the girl."

A voluminous rope of steam poured up out of the crater, and in the next moment a shower of superheated lava gravel was pelting down out of the billowing gray fog above our heads. Everyone was crouching for cover now and I no longer had a good view of James on the platform.

Johanna, after my stumble, seemed to discern that something was afoot. She kept her arms wrapped tightly around my shoulders as we crouched, maintaining an iron grip on my wrists with her strong hands.

Having taken off the expedition pack and donned a gas mask, Tollie was setting off the canisters and rolling them down into the midst of the crouching crowd. Some of them must have seen this, but the incapacitant is very effective, even in small concentrations. The fact that everyone was huddled together made it even more so, and after a few more seconds it was too late for anyone to say or do anything.

The injections, thankfully, were also fast-acting. A kind of hyper-alertness flooded my brain and nervous system, accompanied by a speeding pulse, nausea, and the sensation, almost imperceptible at first but rapidly gaining force, of subjective time slowing down—as evidenced by the hiss and roar of the eruption shifting to a slightly deeper and grainier sound, like an audio file played at half speed. The most salient effect, of course, was that Dr. Q and I were not affected by the incapacitant, while everyone else present, except Tollie with his gas mask, was soon laid out unconscious on the hardened lava field. Weirdly, Johanna's fingers remained locked around my wrists, but it wasn't too hard to pry them off, and I ran over to the platform, picking my way through the splayed bodies. James still had his respirator on, which most likely kept him from breathing in too much of the sleeping gas, but he was still unconscious from the blow of the coach's truncheon. I injected him, then tore the respirator off, worried about the permanent damage breathing the volcanic fumes might cause.

Looking his body over as I untied the cords around his wrists and ankles, I saw that dozens of the super-heated pebbles had landed on him, raising ugly blisters on his hairless scalp, burning holes through his tunic, and charring the skin of his shoulders and thighs. The sympathomimetic took effect almost immediately. He came back to consciousness, coughing violently, his expression quickly changing from blank surprise to excruciating pain. Explaining the basic situation, I helped him up and off the platform. I may have mentioned that James is a big man. He was weakened by the fumes and the blow to his head and in severe pain from the lava burns, but the injection gave him a boost of adrenaline and he was able to move on his own. Which is a good thing, because if he'd had to rely on me to support him we probably wouldn't have made it very far.

At the head of the down-mountain trail we found Dr. Q protectively cradling the still-unconscious Rosaria. She told us that she'd already sent Tollie down to bring the yacht around. We briefly considered going back for Edda—it was possible, after all, if unlikely, that she too was a fertile human subject—but in the end we opted against it. She was a tall, heavy-boned woman and was, once she regained consciousness, not likely to be cooperative. With Rosaria still unconscious and James weakened, it was really all we could hope to get the four of us down to the floating dock in one piece.

We set off down the trail at a half-jog behind James, who insisted on carrying the little girl across his shoulder like a sleeping baby. It was difficult going: our perception of time seemed to oscillate with disorienting side effects. My footsteps skipped and stalled on the steep gravel trail, making me stumble. The shrouds of mist swirling across the mountainside seemed to move faster, pause altogether, and start moving again. The sound of the wind scouring the rocks was like the strange wavering howl of some agonized giant conjured from the depths of ancient mythology.

Fortunately, going down the trail was a lot faster than going up it. Once Rosaria regained consciousness, James gently put her down so that she could walk. I asked him if he was okay and he said he was fine, though it was easy to see that he was in a great deal of pain from his burns. There was no time to stop now, however. Dr. Q and I held the little girl by the hands and she skipped along between us, dazed and disoriented but offering no resistance. I think it helped that we'd made a friendly impression on her in advance. Though if she'd known then what she knows now—that our plans included stealing her away from the only home she's ever known—she might have been less easygoing. In any case, the fact that she'd regained consciousness so quickly was in itself a reason to hurry on, as it meant that Edda and her followers would not be far behind.

We made it down to the stone arch and through the village. We were standing at the top of the staircase to the floating dock when we caught sight of a line of white dots running down the switchbacks out of the fog. But Tollie was still nowhere in view. We continued on to stand on the dock and finally we heard the emergency motor. Then the *Solar Barque* itself appeared, never more welcome and beautiful than it was now, plowing steadfastly toward us over the glassy seawater.

The hull scraped alarmingly on the top of the drowned seawall and for a moment we worried that Tollie might have grounded it, but after we'd handed Rosaria up and James had staggered aboard as well—barely able to stand now because of the burn shock, dehydration, and the after-effects of extended toxic gas inhalation—our captain gunned the motor backward and we slipped free. As we chugged slowly out into the harbor the fastest runners from the community appeared at the top of the stairs, gasping for breath as they screamed for us to stop. I took James below, gave him water and several hydrocodone pain capsules, and made him undress so I could cover his burns with antibiotic cream.

Up on deck Dr. Q was kneeling beside Rosaria, doing her best to be soothing. The little girl was half-turned away from her, gripping the rail, with tears streaming down her rosy cheeks as she watched the shores of Stromboli slowly recede. Meanwhile, our white-tunicked hosts were making furious preparations to come after us, on the floating dock and a narrow beach south of the village where they kept various watercraft. Those who weren't busy with this were screaming and wailing and shaking their fists at us, raging and lamenting the loss of their beautiful little fertility goddess.

Poor Rosaria. I can only imagine how she must feel. It's true that she's an orphan, and from what we saw doesn't seem to feel any particular fondness for her main guardian, Edda. Still, a few of the surviving Strombolians are undoubtedly her relatives, and it's difficult to rationalize the fact that we've stolen her away from the only home she's ever known. We've given her the *Solar Barque*'s master cabin (Dr. Q and Tollie were previously sharing it), which has a comfortable bed and a small, niche-like berth. She went straight to the latter when we brought her in, burrowing in under the sheets like a frightened kitten.

Tollie had all the sails out and the emergency motor at full throttle. A fleet of kayaks and rowing skiffs followed in our wake with desperate energy, but they were of little concern. What *was* concerning was that the community also turned out to have a motorboat and, apparently, the fossil-fuel reserves to power it. This was now speeding after us, overloaded with heavily armed passengers. Given its speed across the gentle swells, it looked—and *was*, as it turned out, with tragic results—all too capable of overtaking us.

Ten minutes on, the kayaks and rowboats had dwindled to distant toys on the water. The island too had receded, that picture-perfect cone with its white feather-plume still swollen and soot-stained by the recent eruption. But the drone of the motorboat kept growing louder as it slowly closed the gap. Through my binoculars I could now make out the faces of its passengers, four men, including the white-bearded chief steering the boat, three female acolytes including Johanna but not Berglind, and Edda Ingvarsdottir herself, looking every inch the Witch Queen, ash-blonde hair flying in the wind, an expression of pale tight-lipped fury, and what appeared to be a high-powered rifle strapped over her shoulder. Johanna and two of the men had rifles as well.

"Better fetch Tollie's rifle, dear," Dr. Q remarked, and I knew how much it must have cost her even to make such a suggestion, this mild-tempered woman who has dedicated her life to saving the human race. She was only being realistic, however. The mission was all, especially now that we had Rosaria with us. And that motorboat was already dangerously close.

Tollie stood at the wheel with his headphones on, his unruly gray curls gathered back in a loose ponytail and his gaze glued to the horizon. He was focused on getting every last millimeter of speed from the wind and the emergency engine and seemed oblivious to our inevitable clash with the occupants of the speeding motorboat. I waved my hands in front of his eyes to get his attention, then mimed the act of shooting a rifle. He gestured with his grizzled chin to a cupboard built into the teak housing of the cockpit.

The rifle felt surprisingly heavy in my hands, as if made of something considerably more dense than simple wood and metal. Dr. Q is near-sighted, unable to aim through a rifle scope with those thick lenses, and with James and Tollie indisposed, it fell to me. I knelt on the deck, rested the heavy barrel on the rail, and squinted through the scope.

It was surprisingly hard to bring anything into focus. Finally I was able to find the white seam of the motorboat's wake expanding across the glassy ocean. Slowly, I moved the barrel to the left until I finally got the boat itself in the crosshairs. A shifting closeup of intent and furious faces; then a glancing view of Edda, standing in the prow like an avenging angel. But I couldn't seem to hold the rifle steady. I think the white-bearded coach driving the boat might have been subtly swerving the boat left and right as he gained on us, but for whatever reason the crosshairs kept jumping around and I couldn't keep them in one place long enough to aim.

Dr. Q knelt beside me at the rail, murmuring words of encouragement as the drone of the outboard grew ever louder. I took a few deep breaths and squinted again through the scope, but it was no good. My hands were shaking, and I was gripped by a growing sense of panic. Every time I tried to zero in on a specific target I would lose the boat entirely and find myself staring at a magnified circle of green seawater. The boat was almost even with us now. The community members with rifles had the barrels raised and were themselves starting to take aim.

"Can I?"

It was James, pale and quaking and gritting his teeth through the pain, naked except for a faded red beach towel wrapped around his waist, his left eye swollen nearly shut from the truncheon blow and his burned scalp and shoulders glistening with antibiotic ointment.

"James, sweetie, what are you *doing*? You're dehydrated and in shock. You need to be lying down."

"Al, please." He held out both hands. "Just give me the rifle."

Dr. Q squeezed my forearm, nodding, and she was right. This was no time for medical protocol. Even in his current state, James almost certainly had a better chance of hitting something than I did, given what we'd seen him do in Spain. I stood up from the rail and handed him the gun.

When the motorboat had closed to within about a hundred yards of us, they started firing. Most of the bullets hit the water nearby, but we could hear some slicing the air above us, and a few made little pops as they perforated the sails. One bullet put a hole in a stanchion inches from where Dr. Q had been resting her chin. I grabbed her, pulling us both down as flat as possible on the teak. I screamed for James to lie down too but he ignored me, pressing his cheek to the rifle stock as he took aim.

The automatic rifles produced a brisk chain of explosions that sounded almost celebratory, like firecrackers in the wind. From his place at the wheel, Tollie let out a surprised yelp, followed by a long and bitter string of curses. I crawled back to the cockpit, where he'd slid down behind the wheel with legs crossed, keeping the *Solar Barque* on a steady course with one arm. The other arm had been hit.

"You okay?"

He held out his left forearm, the same side as his previous shoulder wound. Fortunately the bullet had passed cleanly through the flesh without shattering any bones. There was surprisingly little bleeding, and it was actually not a worrisome injury, though of course it must have been quite painful.

"I'll be right back," I said.

"Stay low, Al. Beneath the rail so they can't see you as you move."

I hurried below for iodine, gauze, scissors, and medical tape. Back up in the cockpit I sterilized and wrapped the wound, suddenly noticing that the gunfire had paused. They were probably trying to conserve precious ammunition. In any case the motorboat's engine had changed pitch. Nearly beside us now, the driver swerved to avoid giving James a clear target and Edda screamed out orders. One of the men had a coil of rope in his hand, with a small anchor tied to the end of it. Three others were aiming their rifles, and the remainder had taken out hunting knives, except one who'd picked up an intimidatingly long spearfishing gun. It seemed they were preparing to board.

The automatic rifle shots started up again, earsplittingly close now, and in the next moment Edda Ingvarsdottir, our formidable hostess and Witch Queen, collapsed from her position in the prow of the motorboat like a marionette whose strings had been cut, plunging head-first into the sea. The motorboat's engine cut out. Edda floated in the water behind it, face down, loose-limbed, and motionless, her embroidered tunic billowing rhythmically in the swells. As the *Solar Barque* put more distance between ourselves and the motorboat, I watched through binoculars the faces of its passengers change from determination to shock, disbelief, and extreme dismay.

After a moment the white-bearded chief coach revved the motor again, circling back to retrieve the body. I'm nearly certain it *was* already just a body, because in the split-second before Edda had fallen, a small purple dot had appeared suddenly at the center of her flawless forehead. Our wounded rifleman's aim had been perfect.

It was a sickening, hollow-feeling victory.

For a few moments it looked as if we were going to come away relatively unscathed, with the exception of James's burns, Tollie's uncomplicated bullet wound, and some nonstructural perforations in our sails and decking. Alas, such luck was not ours for the taking.

Tollie kept the sails out and the emergency motor running, putting as much distance as possible between ourselves and the bobbing motorboat, where Edda's shocked acolytes were hauling her lifeless body up out of the sea.

"Nice shot," I said, putting my hand carefully on unburned skin on the back of James's neck as he rested his forehead on the rail. "Let's get you back down to the infirmary."

When he didn't respond or glance up, I got on my knees beside him, discovering that he'd completely lost consciousness again. It was only when Dr. Q helped me ease him back from the rail and onto the deck that we saw the bullet-hole in his upper chest, just below the left clavicle. We have no idea when the bullet passed through the teak of the rail and buried itself in his flesh—whether it was before or after he fired off his own decisive shot—but it doesn't matter.

I stanched the bleeding, sterilized and bandaged the wound, and, when he stirred and started to moan in pain, gave him an injection from the *Solar Barque*'s nearly depleted supply of morphine. When it was clear that the motorboat no longer had any hope of catching us, Tollie turned off the emergency engine and put the yacht on auto-steer. The three of us managed to lift James onto one of the cushioned benches in the shade of the bimini, where he continues to rest—peacefully, for now—as I write this.

His vital signs are good, but the bullet didn't exit, meaning that it's still lodged somewhere in the chest cavity. Not in the heart or lungs—if that were the case, it's very unlikely that he would still be breathing—but maybe in one of the bones or muscles of the upper back.

It's maddening, especially in a case involving a loved one, to be a physician at a time when we no longer have access to MRI scanners or even a simple x-ray machine. Once the swelling goes down, and the regular injections of antibiotic I'm giving him have a chance to do their work, I will have to try to extract the bullet. In the meantime, the best I can do is to keep him hydrated and let him rest. He has a tough constitution, as he's proved not only in the course of this voyage but also by the simple act of recovering from a case of the hyperpandemic so severe it would have killed anyone else.

I write this sitting in the shade of the bimini across the low table from him, watching the steady rise and fall of his breath under the clean sheet we've covered him with. I will accept nothing less than a full recovery. If there's one thing I've learned on this voyage it's that no one is irreplaceable. Everyone on the team has a role to play, and our success depends on our sticking together. Besides, there are a number of outstanding issues I would like to address with Mr. James Swamp once he's recovered. Some of them, preferably, in private.

Rosaria is sleeping soundly, snuggled up with the old stuffed tiger Dr. Q had been quick-witted enough to scoop up off the ground as we fled. Soon we'll have to begin to explain our intentions.

29

11th Millennium A.U.C.T. (estimated)

One blustery summer afternoon, Nick is stretched out in the sun on the ledge after eating a handful of fly agarics. He imagines what would happen if he were to get to his feet and simply launch his body out into the gusting wind. As it turns out the air seems capable of holding his weight perfectly, and he finds himself floating downhill over the canopy. Down in the lowlands he circles the nearest lake, hazed in summertime humidity, admiring its shape from above and the novel perspective on its reed-grown shoreline. Then he gets nervous. Hurrying back up the mountainside he's relieved to find his body still reclining in the sun on the ledge where he left it. He feels the warmth of the stone at his back and judges it safe to open his eyes.

The next day he eats another large handful of the ill-tasting fungus and repeats the experiment, imagining himself leaping off the ledge, buoyed up in the wind. This time he concentrates on going farther out, making a circuit around some of the more distant lakes. In the following weeks he repeats the experiment often enough to realize that he doesn't really need the mushrooms to pull off the trick—and also that his range of travel isn't limited to terrain that he's actually seen with his physical eyes.

He understands, of course, that these are merely controlled hallucinations or visions, a kind of lucid daydreaming. Yet everything he sees is so vivid and convincing, and it does seem to correspond with physical reality in surprising ways. One morning, for example, he watches a bull moose splash up out of the shallows onto the shore of the nearest lake. Later he goes down to the same shore to forage and discovers fresh moose tracks in the mud exactly where he would have expected—and in the next day's bird's-eye view he spots his own tracks intersecting the moose's.

In subsequent days he ventures westward, to the glinting ribbon of the Connecticut River, where he gets the idea to follow it south toward its eventual meeting with the sea. A brazen kitten leaps onto his physical chest and he startles, the vision fading. This makes him realize that he doesn't need to go through the laborious process of imagining himself back to the ledge to reenter his body, which frees him up to range even farther. But in the course of all this uncannily realistic lucid daydreaming, he encounters no hint of a human presence.

Once, on a sudden thrilling hunch, he attempts to fly backward through time, but unfortunately this proves impossible except in memory. And honestly he can no longer be one hundred percent confident that what he thinks of as memories aren't themselves hallucinations. Just more delusions swirling through the addled mind of a human castaway who is clearly losing his mind.

30

April 16, 2068 (12 A.U.C.T.)
The Western Mediterranean

The bullet that had entered James's upper chest wasn't as hard to extract as I'd feared. It had passed through the scapula and embedded itself in the infraspinatus muscle, thank the gods, not somewhere in the thoracic cavity where it would have done untold damage to his heart and lungs. With Dr. Q acting as my surgical nurse, I managed to dig the bullet out cleanly with minimal extra damage before suturing and sterilizing the wound. Given his condition and the difficulty of moving him, we have left James laid out on the cushions in the shade of the foredeck bimini. He remains weak, slipping in and out of consciousness, and when his senses do return I find him in great agony. The burns are apparently even more painful than the bullet wound, and my heart aches to see him suffering so. I'm running low on medicines, especially morphine, and in fact gave him one of the last remaining injections a few minutes ago after changing the dressings on his burns, topping it off with several big breaths of Tollie's homegrown indica smoke, which I blew directly into his mouth from my own. He's quiet now, but I fear what the coming days will be like for him.

As for Rosaria, it's a little difficult to gauge her state of mind. In a rare burst of talkativeness, she told Dr. Q that she has no memory of her birth mother, whom we figure must have died before she was three or four years old. She is not aware of having a grandmother or any other blood relatives on Stromboli; if the older woman we saw crying at the first ceremony was indeed her grandmother or aunt, that information was kept hidden from her. Edda, apparently, had considered herself the child's adoptive mother, but Rosaria never thought of her that way, and in fact doesn't seem to harbor any lingering warm feelings for her. There are a few of the Icelandic attendants she was fond of and misses, but overall she seems to have lived out her early childhood in a state of lonely permanent quarantine. In the time we have, we're determined to give her a better experience.

Not that any of this reduces our culpability in abducting her (or *rescuing*, to use a more generous verb), but we do have our mission. It's not something we've taken on idly, and it is our intention to do absolutely everything in our power to make it work. If we succeed, Rosaria will be able to live out her life in peace on a healthy planet beginning to recover from the terrible damage we've done to it, free of the microbes that appear to have doomed our species to extinction. A planet where she may have the honor of becoming—again, we're talking best-case scenarios here—the founding matriarch of a new human tribe. One with a chance to get the future right.

In any case, her tears now seem to have run their course, and she is adjusting to her changed circumstances as well as can be expected. Mostly she keeps to the small berth inside the cabin, where in addition to the comforting old stuffed tiger we have left drawing materials and a stack of James's obsolete bird guides for her to leaf through. For the last few days we've been coaxing her out into the air for short periods, keeping a close eye in case she falls overboard, although that does seem unlikely. She seems to have an abiding fear of the sea, and ventures out of the cabin only reluctantly, staying well back from the rail and keeping her eyes downcast so she doesn't have to look at it.

For now we're tacking west into a steady wind, making frustratingly slow progress toward the open Atlantic. Our final destination, of course, is the Centauri Lab, the closest thing any of us has to a home, where stockpiles of food and medical supplies await us, along with many months of urgent work. Rosaria's well-being is our foremost concern now. We intend to tell her the whole truth gradually, when the time is right, doing everything possible to ease her mind.

April 19, 2068 (12 A.U.C.T.)
The Atlantic Ocean

Yesterday we passed through the Pillars of Hercules and out into the open Atlantic. The wind has mostly died out, and as a result from the events on Stromboli our fossil fuel supply is gone. So we drift. Thankfully, we still have Lab jerky and Tollie was able to fill our water tanks from a spring he found on a hidden stretch of the Strombolian shoreline. But the heat is intense. The humidity too, dangerously close to the dreaded "wet bulb." Our sails hang slack, shifting weakly with the air's minimal stirrings. No one has the energy to converse. Dr. Q and I do our chores and care for the needs of our charges: James, Rosaria, Tollie. Most of our waking hours are spent staring out at the glassy, acidified ocean, hoping for the alchemy of a rising wind.

Both injured parties seem to be recovering well, though in James's case the progress is slow. I change his dressings and clean the burned areas twice daily. His pain has subsided to manageable levels, which is a good thing as I have completely run out of morphine. Tollie's marijuana supply is also dwindling, which has put him in a bad mood, though in his case the healing is uncomplicated and I suspect that he doesn't actually need much pain relief. We exchanged words yesterday, and after some resistance, to his credit, he handed over most of his stash, keeping just a handful of joints for himself. More worrisome is that my supply of antibiotics is nearly gone. That is not a circumstance I would wish on any physician, but there's nothing that can be done about it except to get back to the Lab as expeditiously as possible—which of course is what we're trying to do.

James was half-lucid for a brief interval this morning. "It's great to have you back," I said.

"We'll be seeing a lot of each other," he said. "You. Me. Dr. Quist. Tollie."

"Of course we will," I said.

"No, I don't mean *now*," he said. "I mean *always*. Everything we've shared. Love, friendship. Those things can never be taken away."

"Let's just focus on getting you healed," I said, uneasily. "When that's accomplished, you'll be seeing as much of all three of us as you can possibly tolerate."

He shook his head. "That's not what I'm saying. Time is—it's not what we think it is, Al. It doesn't move exactly the way we think it does."

"Now you're sounding like Dr. Q."

"Well, she's right. Before, I didn't . . . I guess it seemed abstract. Now I see that she's been right all along."

I was in no mood to contradict him. He was half-delirious, and clearly quite stoned, and I didn't think either of us had the energy to engage in philosophical argumentation. Before I left him though, acting on a pressing intuition that it needed to be said without further delay, I told him that I was in love with him. He gazed up at me, his bloodshot eyes suddenly swimming with tears. "I love you too, Al. And I don't want you to worry if I—if we—what I was saying before. We'll always have what we've had. It never goes away. Just because we see it as already . . . having happened . . ." he trailed off.

"Now you're talking nonsense, James Swamp. Just focus your mind on getting better, okay?"

I leaned down to give him a lingering kiss on the lips. He closed his eyes, and I used a scrap of gauze to wipe away the tears that were streaming down his scarred cheeks.

Rosaria seems okay, though we have no doubt that she's suffering from PTSD. We're no longer worried about her falling overboard, though we do of course continue to keep a very close eye on her. We're experimenting with different ways to keep her entertained: guessing games, songs, picture books, a few special treats we've kept squirreled away, including hard candy, dehydrated apples and blueberries, even a few Mylar-wrapped Snickers bars from Cornelius Quist's old survivalist stash. I've added her to our daily rounds of preventives—probiotics, vitamins, prophylactic antivirals—and it goes without saying that we treat her with the utmost kindness. She has a long journey ahead of her. Far longer, it is to be hoped, than any one of us.

Dr. Q feels a renewed sense of urgency regarding the project we've been referring to as "The Afterlife Handbook." Something in human nature seems to crave religion, or at least a belief system that can bestow a sense of larger meaning. Perhaps the Handbook is a chance for us to exert some influence in this regard, and she's eager to get started on producing it in some highly durable format when we get back to the Lab. Our highest priorities, however, will naturally be to make sure the TDS tech is still in good working order, and to prepare Rosaria for her journey into the unknown but presumably much more livable realm of Earth's deep future.

31

11th Millennium A.U.C.T. (estimated)

Flying. Is it reality, hallucination, or the harbinger of approaching insanity? For the moment he's too exhilarated to care. Ridge upon ridge the wilderness unfolds below him on his westward trajectory, miles of uninhabited old-growth forest until the land flattens out and he's chasing his own shadow as it speeds across a tree-covered plain. Clearings begin to appear, and the trees space themselves out into the open glades and grassy meadows of something like a savannah. Farther west the trees disappear entirely except in the old riverbeds, and he's crossing a yellow-green prairie teeming with megafauna: elk, antelope, wild horses, endless herds of an animal he can't identify, like shaggy cattle with extraordinarily broad upcurving horns and long, elegant bodies, slim-hipped and broad-chested like the aurochs of the old cave paintings at Lascaux or Altamira.

He comes to the ruins of a city half-submerged in an immense lake; Rochester or Buffalo maybe, even Cleveland or Chicago, though he can't say for sure because there are no buildings standing, just geometrical patterns buried long ago by wind-blown silt and accumulating organic soil from the annual growth cycles of the forbs and grasses. But he can make out street grids, the curves and figure eights of former interstates, rectangular parking lots and warehouses, even a large circular depression in the grass that might once have belonged to a football stadium. The lake's shoreline teems with the tiny white flecks of waterfowl, nesting, floating, and wheeling over the turquoise water, and suddenly he starts to feel worried. This is much farther than he's ever imagined going.

On the opposite shoreline there are dunes, from which rise a range of gentle hillsides covered in meadows and great spreading oaks. The landscape is alluring and he zooms in for a closer look. The area has a pleasant park-like feeling, with golden sunlight filtering down through the rustling leaves. It seems a perfect place for a meditative stroll through the grass—or sedge, actually, the species name echoing back to him through the fog of distant memory: *Carex pensylvanica*, Pennsylvania sedge. At the edge of a meadow a white-tailed doe raises her head from grazing to peer meaningfully over her shoulder at him. At least that's how he interprets the look she gives him—meaningful—but this is no doubt wishful thinking, rooted in his hunger for interaction with some kind of sentient being. He raises his hand in greeting and she bounds away, her long white tail flashing like a signal flag. He watches her go, then follows her trail uphill through the oaks. Suddenly, he detects the scent of woodsmoke. His pulse quickens.

In the next clearing he comes to a crackling campfire, with a large, robed figure sitting cross-legged behind it. The figure is human, in form at least, wavering and flickering in the vapors of the fire. Its head is bent, in sleep, perhaps, or in contemplation, its face hidden by a monk-like hood.

"Greetings," Nick says. It's the first time he's spoken aloud in months, possibly years, and the word issues from his physical throat in a hoarse, half-strangled croak, to the alarm of several cats dozing on the ledge near where his body lies.

The figure raises its head. Its hooded face remains in shadow, difficult to make out in any detail, but he gets a vague impression of hyperpandemic scarring, of a careworn cragginess hinting of great age. The eyes glint with the orange reflection of the firelight, and he can't be sure, but he thinks he detects a flash of humor in them.

He starts to say something else, but before he can get the words out the figure raises its hand as if to silence him, and then makes a quick gesture with its gnarled fingers—a slight upward swirl. The fire erupts in a cascade of flame and in the next instant he's barreling skyward, spiraling up through a column of smoke and sparks, faster and faster up into a sky that's blue then violet then a midnight black dotted with the brightest stars he's ever seen. Floating now, his consciousness drifts in the lonely vacuum of geospace.

The vision evaporates. Opening his eyes, he finds himself sitting cross-legged beside the smoking cinders of his breakfast fire, with three lean cats eyeing him cautiously from strategic positions around the ledge.

32

April 24, 2068 (12 A.U.C.T.)
The Atlantic Ocean

It is my sad duty to report that as of early this morning, six days after passing through the Straights of Gibraltar, our valued Centauri Project colleague and beloved friend James Littlerose Swamp has departed from this world. His condition had been declining for at least three days. We haven't quite run out of antibiotics, but for whatever reason their efficacy decreased. With his own weakened immune system unable to protect his body from infection, he was gripped by fever, delirium, and pain. As the infection inevitably spread to the blood he presented with sepsis, followed by respiratory distress and ultimately multiple-organ failure. For James himself this passing was undoubtedly a relief. For the rest of us it is an unspeakable loss.

Say what you will about Tollie Quist, he has a flair for extemporaneous speaking. In our little deckside ceremony he had us all laughing through our tears about James. Then Dr. Q, from memory, recited the Haudenosaunee Thanksgiving Address, the Mohawk prayer of gratitude James had introduced during those early brainstorming sessions for "The Afterlife Handbook." This really got the tears flowing, though I think it made us all feel marginally better about losing James, given what we are all part of in the long term. Due to my emotional state and the private nature of my thoughts regarding James, I didn't dare say anything original or spontaneous. Instead, I read some of the passages he'd marked in those old bird guides with the ranges, habitats, and descriptions of several of his favorite extinct species: the puffin, the bobolink, the northern Goshawk, the snowy owl.

It would be disingenuous to pretend surprise. To feign shock that such a thing could happen. That such dreams could prove illusory, like so many of the gifts that we once took for granted: the electrical grid, reliable food networks, a habitable planet. The assumption that generation after generation of humans would keep renewing themselves forever, like oak leaves budding in the spring.

I miss him terribly. It feels as if something vital, unexpected, and astonishingly beautiful has been ripped from the core of my being. But I see no point in going on about my own emotional state. The mission is all. From here on all my efforts must be focused on helping Dr. Q get Rosaria safely back to the Lab. On preparing her physically and emotionally for the day we place her inside that fully prepped TDS. Her egg. Our egg. And, we believe, almost certainly the last shot for humanity's survival.

We stitched the body up in a tattered canvas sail cover, weighing it down at the feet with Tollie's old diving belt. Rosaria looked on in silence from the shaded benches under the bimini as the three of us—two and a half, really, considering Tollie's injured arm—managed to hoist the impossibly heavy package up onto the rail. Our eyes met briefly. We took a breath, then rolled it over the side.

I leaned on the rail to watch it spiral like a leaf or a feather down through the clear green water column. Soon it was nothing more than a rhythmically flickering point of white.

And then James was gone.

33

11th Millennium A.U.C.T. (estimated)

As much as he tries to interpret the vision of the deer and the robed figure, he can never quite make sense of it, and with the passage of time the controlled hallucinations—or lucid daydreams, whatever they are—begin to lose their appeal. He once imagined using them methodically to scour the globe for human survivors, but he can no longer sustain the belief that what he's seeing truly corresponds to reality—or, for that matter, that any such survivors exist. So he practices the technique less and less, and eventually it ends up like any other discarded plaything, consigned to a forgotten corner of his mind, gathering dust.

He's lived too long without human company. The tribe of cats; the invented religion; the pleasure of simply being a living part of a functioning, biodiverse ecosystem—none of it is enough. Nor are his fading memories of the time before, which, when they do return, are often distorted and ghostlike, mental souvenirs from an extinct reality whose persistence is more torture than consolation. His loneliness feels incurable. It feels terminal.

On a day in late autumn he climbs to the rock summit and perches with his toes gripping the edge of the highest cliff. He begins to count his breaths, with the intention that on the tenth exhalation he will jump. And he nearly follows through with it too, though in the end he finds that he still can't quite summon the willpower.

Moving firewood down into the cavern, he gets the notion of making himself a pair of skis. One of the most unpleasant and potentially life-threatening problems he faces in the coldest months of winter is having to trudge through the deep snow, which tends to accumulate in heavy bouts, drastically limiting his movement for days and even weeks at a time between thaws. Skis would allow him to forage more efficiently during these periods, and to get up to the ledge to check in on the resident cats. It might be a nice distraction too: first the challenge of making them, then the fun of using them. He was an avid skier in his youth, chasing the dwindling snowpack up into the high Rockies and later, during college, striding cross-country through the remaining conifer forests of northern Quebec. He still remembers the sensation of it—like flying in real life, as opposed to in a hallucination.

He sets to work methodically, splitting staves out of straight-grained young hickory, boiling water in a clay vessel for steam to bend the tips, sanding smooth the flexible slats with pumice, and rubbing them with goose fat to cure. When he has a dozen plausible prototypes he selects the best-matched pair, crawls up out of the cave onto the snow, and straps them to his fur-wrapped feet.

It's a sparkling blue-sky day in what is perhaps late January, not overly cold, with just a breath of thaw in the air. The snow on the mountainside is deep, but it has a crust that's melted and refrozen often enough to hold his distributed weight. He uses a stick to push off and glide downhill into the lowlands. He trudges out onto the ice on his favorite lake, where the tracks of birds and small animals are like perfect etchings on a pane of frosted glass. He laughs, striding fast across the lake, the skis gliding even better than he'd dared to hope.

The next day he cuts two long sticks to use as poles and ties strips of squirrel fur to the bottoms of the skis so he can make his way up to the ledge. It's the first time he's been back in a month or so and the cats are lethargic and irritable, mewling their displeasure at his long absence. He builds them a fire and spends the afternoon petting and sparring with them, and leaves behind a supply of dried meat to ease their way. He's so enthralled by the sensation of plummeting down through the forest that he only half-notices a thick fog that has descended over the lower mountainside. It's only when he finally glides to a stop that he realizes he has no idea where he is. Without the snow he might be able to find one of the trails his own feet have worn through the forest, but all such traces are covered up now, and for the moment he's as disoriented as he would have been in any remote forest.

A family of white-tailed deer making its way across the frozen slope pauses to watch him with their tall ears cocked in alarm. Odd that his sudden arrival on the scene hasn't sent them fleeing, but a moment later he discovers the reason for their hesitation. They're waiting for a straggler, a fawn with a badly broken leg. The poor creature is doing its best to make forward progress through the snow but its front limb dangles uselessly, swinging as it hobbles like a length of half-frozen rope. The family group lingers, clearly resisting their strong instinct to flee. He knows this is the way nature works, but it still guts him. In the end he decides to put the young creature down himself.

When he moves, the other deer take their cue, leaping powerfully over the snow and away into the forest. He approaches the wide-eyed fawn slowly on his skis, cooing softly. The young creature seems to understand what's coming. Resignedly, it lowers its belly down on the snow-crust. He slips his spear out from under a leather strap on his back, lifts it high with two hands, and plunges it like a matador's sword into the flesh between the animal's shoulder blades, through its heart, and down into the snow with a rush of rapidly pooling crimson blood.

He stares down at the bloody tableau for a moment, panting for breath. Suddenly he feels a presence in the trees above his head; looking up he sees one of the raven-black hawks watching him from the lower branches of an oak, huge and hulking. Its intelligent black eyes take in the bloody snow, the newly killed deer, Nick himself. Its expression is coldly inquiring, as if it would like to ask a question of him. "What do you want?" he asks it. "Is it the deer? Could you carry it?"

It cocks its head, as if considering the question, and then flaps away quietly through the winter-bare trees, an immense winged presence soon disappearing as completely as if it had never been there at all.

He field dresses the carcass and drapes it across his shoulders to carry it back to the cave. But he's still lost and has to wander for hours more. With dusk casting ominous blue shadows through the forest, he breaks one of the skis trying to bridge a frozen gully; from then on he has to posthole through the deep snow, sticky and reeking from the young deer's blood and entrails, stiff-bodied and shivering from the intensifying chill as darkness falls.

In the moonlight, his fingers and toes numb from the cold, he finally crosses his own climbing ski trail and follows it downhill back to the cave. Stowing the carcass in the arched hollow at the foot of a buttress-like oak root, he squeezes through the tiny entrance and worms his way down to the relative warmth of the main chamber.

The relief of having avoided freezing to death is quickly overtaken by an intense bout of self-pity. Something about being lost, cold, and hungry, and then finding his way back, not to any kind of home, but to this place of darkness and claustrophobic memory, where nothing but ghosts await him. No lover, no friends, no children or grandchildren. No weddings, no birthdays, not even, eventually, the prospect of a lightly attended funeral.

He lies in the darkness with his forehead resting on the cool limestone floor of the cave, his outer extremities stinging as they slowly come back to life. He would settle for a few lesser comforts, like the aroma of coffee or fresh-baked bread or bacon simmering in a cast iron skillet with the *Morning Edition* theme song in the background, or that feeling of core relaxation under a showerhead blasting steaming hot water. Or a good novel to lose himself in, a distraction for which he would gladly sacrifice a painfully thawing finger or two.

He gets up, fumbles around for some twigs, a roll of birchbark, arranges it in his usual fire ring near the chamber entrance. It's as he's striking the flint that it registers. The sense-memory of his forehead resting on the stone. Had it felt slightly harder, slightly smoother, than he might have expected?

The fire crackles up. He throws a few bigger sticks on it and takes a burning brand back to the spot, or as close to it as he can approximate, where his forehead had rested on the stone. Seeing nothing unusual, he's about to go back to tend the fire when the brand flames out suddenly, catching on the merest hint of something before it dies. A kind of dull semi-gloss under the surface of the limestone. He gets a new brand and takes it back to the spot, holding it right down to the floor. Sure enough, he can make out a straight line where the texture of the stone changes. Getting on his hands and knees to investigate, he discovers an ancient metal plate in the floor, covered up over the millennia by a scrim of accumulated limestone grit. It's extremely hard to see unless the light picks it up in exactly the right way—*In my defense*, he thinks—his heart pounding wildly as he spits and uses his fingertips to rub away some of the accumulated grit.

His torches keep going out, but after several more trips back and forth to the fire and a good deal of scrubbing and polishing with his fingertips, he can see it with stunning clarity. A metal rectangle, solid gold by the look and feel of it, mortared into the cave floor. Etched into the plate is an arrow, and a few words of instruction: 50 PACES. LOOSE STONE IN FLOOR, EDGE OF WALL.

He gets to his feet, struggling to control his breathing. Fifty steps in the flickering firelight, along a straight line following the direction of the arrow, past the hulking cracked-open shell of the TDS, right up to the back wall of the cave. There's an overhang in the rock. He has to crouch down to reach the actual corner. He claws at the floor with his fingers. Nothing but grit and slightly damp limestone.

Then, his fingers find a very faint, almost imperceptible straight line. He digs with his fingernails, eventually tracing out the four edges of a neatly cut rectangle in the limestone.

Mother of god. How have I been such a fool?

PART III

It is like what we imagine knowledge to be:
dark, salt, clear, moving, utterly free,
drawn from the cold hard mouth
of the world, derived from the rocky breasts
forever, flowing and drawn, and since
our knowledge is historical, flowing, and flown.

—Elizabeth Bishop, "At the Fishhouses"

34

April 30, 2068 (12 A.U.C.T.)
The Atlantic Ocean

We sailed through a violent hailstorm yesterday, stones the size of ping-pong balls bounding and exploding on the deck. Like giants making popcorn, the shattering of a whole city's worth of windows—

Reader, forgive me. I thought I was ready to resume this narrative, but my heart is broken. The pen just feels too heavy to push across the page.

May 22, 2068 (12 A.U.C.T.)
The Atlantic Ocean

Tollie says we're only two or three days from the coast of Newfoundland. This would be an encouraging development for the successful completion of our mission, except.

Except this morning, when I went into the cabin to bring Rosaria her breakfast, she seemed unusually listless. Her forehead was burning hot. I went below to get the thermometer: 104.2 degrees Fahrenheit. This is not a good sign.

Dr. Q and I take turns sitting in the chair beside her berth. On my last shift her temperature had come down to a less alarming 101 degrees. She ate a few spoonfuls of miso broth. With luck, she'll be back to her normal self in a day or two. Dear gods—whatever protective deities may still be lingering out there—please make it so. We know that it was our own kind's willful and blind disruption of the natural order on this planet that caused you to loose these scourges upon us. Just please don't let this be one of the deadly ones.

May 23, 2068 (12 A.U.C.T.)
The Atlantic Ocean

Today Rosaria's fever is back up to 103, and we have found a small crimson lesion at the corner of her lips. We fear the worst.

May 26, 2068 (12 A.U.C.T.)
Within sight of the North American continent

We have buried Rosaria at sea. After all these years of preparation, all the trials and losses we've experienced on this voyage—well, you can imagine our feelings. And what of that beautiful, innocent little girl? How long would she have lived if we'd left her undisturbed? Perhaps we can console ourselves with the thought that she could just as easily have been struck down there as here—but we don't know for sure if that's true. We *can't* know. And the terrible fact is, she has died in our care. What we're trying to do is important, yes. There's nothing more important from the perspective of humanity itself. But telling ourselves that doesn't make us feel any better.

Dr. Q refuses to abandon hope. We can start over again, surely. It's not impossible that another little pocket of fertility persists somewhere on this planet. Given everything we've just been through, the ultimate success of the mission we've dedicated our lives to seems unlikely to say the least. Time is running out.

Including mine, I fear. I write this bundled up in my threadbare and much-patched down sleeping bag that I've brought up to my favorite spot behind the bowsprit. It's a beautiful day on the ocean, cloudless and warm, but I can't seem to shake this chill. I have no idea regarding the precise identity of the airborne microbe that so quickly infected and carried away our poor little miracle girl. I'm pretty sure my immune system has the antibodies to fight off any of the familiar ones, so I'll have to assume this is something novel. Hooray.

In the distance I can make out the hazy khaki-green line that is the coast of North America: Nova Scotia, Tollie says. Dr. Q brings me miso broth and one of her wonderful mushroom elixirs, along with some optimistic words about a very quick recovery. The sight of her lovely wrinkled, determined face, and the love, strength, and affection in the eyes behind those big flashing lenses fills me with peace. I am among friends. James is on my mind too, and especially that last conversation we had. It's a strange thought to have, but he feels every bit as real to me now as he did before he died.

ACCOUNT ENDS

Transcriber's note: Three days after the last entry, the two surviving crewmembers of the *Solar Barque* buried the author of this account on land and in a place that she would have appreciated: beneath a healthy young oak perched on a bluff overlooking the Atlantic in what used to be the state of Maine. It was a sorrowful day, one of many such days we have experienced, and one that was for the transcriber especially sad given that Dr. Alejandra Morgan-Ochoa was a close friend and confidant. I have transcribed this account exactly as written, and typeset it in its current format as a kind of prologue to the accompanying pictorial guide so that readers of the future (extremely hypothetical as I admit you are) may understand what the world was like in the twilight of human history as we knew it.

If you can't read these words, I presume that your attention will be drawn to the graphic representations in the accompanying codex. If you *can* read these words, then it is my hope that you now understand that we have tried our best. And perhaps we're not quite done trying yet.

Approximately seven decades before I completed these pages a scientist by the name of James E. Lovelock proposed the idea of the last book on Earth, a user's guide to living sustainably on this planet after the fall of human civilization. Our version of Dr. Lovelock's idea—the codex that accompanies this one—begins with illustrations detailing the factors that led to this fall and continues with some of the most important discoveries made by the species during our first flourishing on this planet. Continuing in graphic form, we include detailed instructions intended to provide a future population—you, my futuristic friends, whom I address across the gap of however much time may have passed—with knowledge that should help to avoid making the same mistakes we did. With humble affection and great hope for our mutual success, I am yours,

Natalie Quist

Written and inscribed by the former at the Centauri Project Lab Complex, in what was formerly the state of New Hampshire, the United States of America, October 2068 (12 A.U.C.T.)

35

11th Millennium A.U.C.T. (estimated)

The cache, a rectangular cavity long ago jackhammered out of the stone floor, is packed with an array of useful tools: knife blades, machete blades, spear points, axe heads, a whole box of fishhooks in a range of sizes, a compass, a sextant. Everything cast in the same corrosion-proof magnesium alloy, dusty, gritty, with the patina of the ancient objects they are, but otherwise good as new. He should have known, given the time and resources, that Natalie would have assembled such a useful collection and left it somewhere obvious for him to find. Perhaps not as obvious a place as she'd hoped—there may have been more obscuring limestone deposition on the cave floor than she'd banked on—but it's his own fault for not having conducted a much more methodical search.

At the bottom of the cache are the codices: two flat rectangles the size of an artist's sketchbooks, well fitted to the excavated box and heavy enough that it takes a bit of effort to lift them out. They're durably made and quite beautiful as objects, solid gold, pressed from Cornelius Quist's stockpiled ingots no doubt, with durable covers identical to the marker plate mortared into the cavern floor, and pages as thin as card stock. Gold makes sense as a material of course, a noble metal, durable enough to resist corrosion but soft enough to receive a fine impression. Such as the subtle patterns covering the pages. Patterns that he can't make out in the subterranean darkness but that feel very much—he realizes with a rush of excitement—like *writing*.

And so he throws more sticks on the fire and worms his way up again into the exterior air. It's nearly dawn by now, with a deep winter chill still covering everything, but there is just enough light to see by, and in his excitement he barely notices the cold. When his fingers get so numb that he can no longer turn the pages of Alejandra Morgan-Ochoa's account, he retreats back into the cave, builds the fire high, and keeps reading. He forgets to eat. At one point he dozes off and the fire goes out. Waking in the darkness he lugs both codices outside again, clears the snow from a flat boulder and sits down to finish them.

As promised in the transcriber's note, the pages of the second volume are filled not with words but with graphic representations, finely engraved and densely pictorial, the Lab's clean room having of course contained exactly the kind of specialized instruments that could easily have been adapted to do such fine work. Diagrams of DNA and the solar system; the basics of physics and mathematics, chemistry and biology. A stylized chart of the planet's geological history, with all the major eras symbolized by representative life forms and the six mass extinctions marked by deeply engraved flatlines. Schematic illustrations of plate tectonics, a clever explanation of evolution. Several densely illustrated pages detailing major waypoints in the human species' trajectory, including a piquant summary of all the ways that species doomed itself: the poisoning of the air and the water, carbon emissions leading to climate destabilization, relentless habitat destruction, biodiversity loss.

The graphics in the second half of the codex are more forward-looking: instructions for sustainable practices such as bio-char and no-till agriculture; rudimentary systems for capturing solar and wind energy; a stirring graphic on the Native American concepts of the honorable harvest and the seven generations. And on virtually every page, the same unmistakable message: Tread lightly. Think ahead. Respect the reality that despite your intelligence you are inseparable from the great web of life, a species to whom much has been given and of whom much is expected in return, namely a firm commitment to stewardship as opposed to thoughtless exploitation.

All very nicely imagined and executed. And all, he's afraid, completely useless, bound as it is for eternal obscurity as soon as he dies.

He sighs, finishing the written account with a heavy heart. He's long been craving more definitive news. A better idea of what happened, and what went wrong. The written codex fits that bill, in some ways, but in others it feels worse than not knowing at all.

From the first page it was obvious that the nameless transcriber was Natalie. He reads the last few passages again, hearing the distant echo of her voice ringing out in his head. He supposes one could think of it as a kind of direct line of communication across the expanse of time. Her brilliance, her idealism and optimism, her actual personality captured in words, inscribed in gold and sent down through the millennia directly into his hands and mind and heart. A connection to Alejandra too, and to the last remnants of the Centauri team, their admirable final effort, and through them, in a sense, a connection to the entirety of the beautiful, problematic, defunct human race.

But the sense of connection to these spirits of the distant past gives him no joy. To the contrary, it makes him feel worse. He holds in his hands the record of an ancient failure. The inconsequential words of a few people who'd died so long ago that it's unlikely even their bones persist as microscopic fragments in the soil.

He traces the pages with his fingertips, resolves to commit all the best lines to memory, looks in vain for some personal message. Some indication of what might have happened to Natalie and Tollie upon their return from that ill-fated voyage. Finding no such indication, he puts the second codex on top of the first and gets to his feet, intending to take them down into the cave and stow them safely back in the bottom of their cache.

But just as he's standing up, something flutters out onto the snow. It's a paper-thin strip of gold, like a handmade bookmark. Picking it up he sees that it has writing on it, and that unlike the machine-printed text and graphics in the actual pages of the codices, this writing appears to have been etched by hand, perhaps using some kind of electronic engraving tool. The handwriting is shaky, as if hurried, but it's unmistakably Natalie's. Heart pounding, he puts the codices down and sits on the freezing boulder.

SPECIAL NOTE FOR DR. NICHOLAS HINDMAN

Dear Nick,

As you will have read for yourself, after your departure rumors did reach us of potentially viable populations in a few remote corners of the globe. You will also have read of our recent visit to one of these locations, and its ultimately discouraging results. Considering the distances involved and the rapidly declining state of human affairs, I must say that it is a distinct possibility that we won't be sending you any company. Not that I'm giving up, dear. Far from it! Nor should you.

Regarding the two codices you now have in your hands: Alejandra Morgan-Ochoa's account has been transcribed for posterity, and also to satisfy your curiosity. We're very much hoping that you will have the opportunity to pass the pictorial guide on to a human population if one has managed to hang on, and specifically to get it into the hands of potentially enlightened leadership and/or other people who are likely to appreciate and disseminate its contents. It's possible that you will have encountered evidence of such a population already. Even if you haven't, I urge you not to stop looking.

In any event I must now turn my focus back to the many tasks at hand. But I do want to take this opportunity, my darling Nick, to remind you that I will always love you. And I mean that *always* not just as emotional or spiritual boilerplate but also as a reflection of the underlying reality. As you will no doubt remember from our recurring debates, I've always been skeptical of our human fixation on time as an arrow, as an unvarying one-way progression. But perhaps your own experience has brought you closer to my way of thinking on that?

Anyway. With love, affection, and deep respect, I remain forever yours,

Natalie

Tears blur his vision, and with shaking hands he puts the bookmark back where he found it. He takes both codices down into the cave and places them, the compass, the sextant, and certain other tools he has no immediate use for back into the excavated cache.

He squeezes back up through the passage and out into the cold air. Using a magnesium-alloy knife to butcher the frozen deer, he's amazed at how quick and precise the machine-honed blade makes the work of skinning it, cutting out the inner loins, detaching the shoulder joints, the back straps, and hind quarters. He wraps the venison in deerskin along with several other new tools, ties squirrel skins to a new pair of skis, and sets off up the mountainside, greatly desirous of the warmth and company of his cats.

He will spend the rest of the winter on the mountain. There may be some harsh weather, a few more big snowstorms to make life complicated, but suddenly the idea of sleeping even one more night with the ghost-memories inside that lightless cave has become unbearable.

36

2068 (12 A.U.C.T.)

The Lab was shabby and bleak. Gardens and pastures overgrown with weeds, paint cracked and peeling, many windows boarded up, others dulled by accumulated grime. The Round Barn, the repurposed airplane hangar and Quonset huts, the entire compound really showing signs of accelerating decay. But perhaps these impressions were exaggerated in Natalie's mind by the bitter aftertaste of so much loss, so much tragedy and thwarted hope. One had to find a way to look on the bright side; otherwise it would be impossible to keep moving forward. Which was exactly what she needed to do.

Apart from the plainly demoralized couple who'd remained behind as caretakers, the Centauri Project team was no more. Thank the gods she still had Tollie, and a fully restored Tollie by all appearances too, lean and brown and wrinkled as a walnut shell from the sun and sea wind, his gunshot wounds commemorated by purple knots of well-healed scar tissue on his forearm and in the hollow above his left clavicle. He looked like an old man now with that wreath of wild gray curls and the full gray beard he'd recently grown out—*was* an old man, actually, and she was an old woman, though she didn't really feel like one. All the more reason to redouble their efforts.

Just the two of them now, sister and brother. Like those summers long ago when their globe-trotting parents had essentially left them to go feral at the family compound off the coast of Massachusetts. Jumping off high dunes, wandering the tidelines in search of sea glass and interestingly shaped pieces of driftwood for the elaborate beach sculptures they used to make, zipping around in Tollie's sixteen-foot Prindle catamaran. They'd had a lot of fun on that boat, though sometimes the fun had been tinged with other emotions too, like terror. One especially windy day he'd insisted on taking her out through the mouth of the island's protected harbor into the open ocean. She'd argued against it, but her protestations had only delighted him, and he'd kept going. Once they were out of the harbor the wind had picked up to the extent that they'd had to strap themselves into the trapezes and lean way back out over the water to keep the little sailboat from capsizing. Tollie had hauled on the rudder, laughing in his Tollie-ish way as he'd steered them up and over swells the size of small houses, greatly amused to see his older sister so frightened. In fact after the first few moments she *hadn't* actually been that frightened—thirteen or fourteen by then and quite an experienced sailor herself, she'd known that her younger brother was far too smart to put them in any real danger. But she'd made a show of being terrified so as not to spoil his fun.

They'd had a happy childhood, though an unusual one. Cornelius and Emi Quist, back when they were healthy and walking the earth, had been a brilliant and glamorous power couple, often busy attending professional and social obligations, but they'd been good parents too. They'd always had interesting people in their orbit—actors, writers, artists, scientists, and philosophers from all over the world. Most of the time it had been a lively and joyous household, full of games and laughter and delicious home-cooked meals provided by a small staff of beloved live-in servants—

But gods, Natalie, why do you insist on torturing yourself with these memories?

Because love is one of the things that happens to a person in their life, she thought. You can't just ignore happy memories of people you once loved, or let conjuring them up make you sad. If you conjure them up, you might as well allow them to make you happy. Because they *do* belong to you: Mommy and Daddy, James and Alejandra, little Rosaria, all the great hearts she'd known over the years, not to mention Tollie and her own dear Nick. Looked at from a certain angle, memories of the past were every bit as real as plans for the future. And yes, even as real as one's moment-to-moment experience in the present.

It wouldn't be long now before she'd be joining all those loved ones in the afterlife, or the *inframundo*, or Valhalla, or just some vaguely defined chemical dance out into the universe, choose your metaphor for whatever happens to the human spirit after the body expires. Yes, she would be with them all before too long. Except for Nick of course, who still had around ten millennia to wait if the TDS worked as designed.

Meanwhile, it was time to turn her attention back to the present moment. What was it that old incarnation of the Dalai Lama used to say? *Participate joyfully in the sorrows of the world.* One really had no choice but to carry on.

They'd left the *Solar Barque* well hidden in a riverside cove overhung by weeping willows half-strangled by invasive vines just south of what used to be Hadley, Massachusetts. It was a good mooring place and Tollie had felt reasonably confident that it would remain undisturbed—though if it didn't, well, never mind. They almost certainly wouldn't be needing it again anyway. The hull had sprung multiple leaks, the sails were threadbare, the teak decks cracked and splintered from the sun. The old girl had performed her duties admirably, though with the advantage of hindsight it was hard to see the entire voyage as anything but an extended fool's errand. At least they knew more about the true state of the planet now and had confirmed certain gloomy suppositions related to humanity's tenuous hold on life.

They'd walked the rest of the way back to the Lab, a grueling overland trek that had taken them more than two weeks. The situation appeared to have deteriorated even more in the intervening months. With high mortality and a birth rate of zero, the number of survivors was obviously dwindling, and the faces of those humans they did glimpse from a distance were desperate-looking and often unfriendly. Many bridges and large sections of roads and highways had been washed out by flooding from seasons of torrential rainfall. Those thoroughfares that were still intact were overgrown jungles of fallen trees and brambles, perfectly suited for an ambush. Mostly they'd stuck to the footpaths that led north along the river, where it was easy to hear any approaching parties and crouch in the undergrowth to avoid being seen.

The access road was still passable, though at the entry gate they'd been greeted by three rifle shots fired just above their heads. Waving their arms and screaming into the video surveillance camera, they'd finally succeeded in getting the suspicious caretakers to take a good look at their faces, but the gate's electronic opening mechanism had stopped functioning in their absence, and they had to climb over it like burglars.

The caretakers were veteran Centauri scientists: Dae-Ho, a mechanical engineer, and Petra, a nutritional chemist specializing in food preservation and manufacturing vitamin supplements for the TDS's elaborate life support system. Like most other surviving humans, they'd pretty much abandoned these previous careers for the all-consuming work of survival: growing potatoes, soy, and vegetables; taking care of the Lab's small remaining herd of goats; doing their best to keep up with the maintenance and repair of the Lab's quickly disintegrating physical infrastructure. It was understandable that they would have been leery of unannounced visitors after so many months in isolation. Even if those visitors did have the unmistakable features of old friends and colleagues and were, after all, the hereditary owners of the entire compound.

Considering the desperation and lawlessness that had descended upon the exterior world, Natalie was just relieved to see the Lab still standing, though despite the couple's efforts much of it had fallen into disrepair. The roofs leaked. Some of the brackets and wires in the solar arrays were beginning to corrode. The banks of old carbon nanotube batteries were rapidly losing their capacity. The lights tended to flicker. Most of the cooking had to be done over an open fire. Things were reverting, as was inevitable, to a state of unmediated nature.

Tollie enlisted Dae-Ho to help him bring the infrastructure systems back to life as best they could, while Natalie spent the first several days down in Cavern A, running system checks. The activated TDS hummed along on its fusion reactor, a maintenance-free, self-sufficient, self-depleting closed system designed to keep functioning on its own over the very long term. It was uncanny, and strangely moving, to stand alone in the subterranean chamber only a few yards from the man who for decades had been her best friend, her lover, and the person she cared about most in the world, but whose beloved face she could now scarcely reconstruct from memory. Yet here was his physical body, technically still very much alive inside the deep darkness of that gently vibrating sphere, its magnesium-alloy surface already slightly tarnished after just over a decade, reflecting back her own ghostly image in the cave's LED work lights.

Petra helped her transplant a dozen new oak saplings into the weedy patch of ground over the excavation where the chamber had been capped and backfilled, and when they were done with that they transplanted a few dozen camouflaging shrubs around the cave entrance on a rocky hillside at the lower end of the pasture. This was the original opening and it had the advantage of being geologically stable, small, and naturally well hidden. Natalie was fairly confident that no human being who wasn't specifically seeking it out would find it. And with each passing month, it was less and less likely that anyone would ever go looking.

She was less confident about the newer excavation, which the engineering team had imaginatively dubbed "Cavern B," about half a mile's walk over the rolling pasturelands at the foot of Mount Wingandicoa. After the activation of the first TDS, the risk of destabilizing the original cave system had been deemed serious enough to make further excavation there inadvisable. Instead, the engineers had chosen this spot to design and quarry out a second chamber capacious enough to house the two as-yet inactivated spheres. They'd brought in a construction crane to lower them down into the pit, then capped it off with immense slabs of granite, covering the entire excavation with many tons of topsoil. That had been eight years ago. In the absence of viable test subjects, no further work had been done on Cavern B. Perhaps with time, she thought, the forest would creep back and the excavation would blend into the landscape. For now though, it remained an eyesore, impossible to miss, the entrance a black chasm of squared-off rock halfway down the side of what was unmistakably a machine-made hill.

She turned on her headlamp and made her way down the steep staircase hewn into the granite to the main chamber, where the two inactivated spheres sat lifeless and cracked open like giant metallic Easter eggs waiting to be filled with jelly beans and chocolate bunnies. Unlike the naturally formed Cavern A, this chamber had an echoing, artificial feel to it, an atmosphere of cold-blooded silence that reminded her uncomfortably of a barrow tomb or a pyramid, the grandiose final resting place of some megalomaniacal ancient ruler. After a brief equipment check she was happy to be back out under the open sky.

And so the months went on. When the most pressing repairs to the compound were done, they dusted off some of the precision instruments in the old clean room and began the project they'd brainstormed aboard the *Solar Barque*. Tollie and Dae-Ho figured out how to press gold ingots from Cornelius Quist's remaining stockpile into nine-by-twelve–inch rectangles, each about three-quarters of a millimeter thick. Natalie used an old laptop with a graphic design program to create the pictorial aspects and transcribed Alejandra's journal into a word processing file. Due to the degraded state of the batteries they could only use the machines on sunny days, but eventually Dae-Ho connected the laptop to a laser engraver to apply the words and images to the pages, and the project was complete: two codices of solid gold, one a kind of cautionary greeting card to a new human culture of the deep future and the other a detailed encyclopedia and instruction manual, their pages bound with ingenious little magnesium-alloy hinges salvaged from a supply cupboard in the clean room.

Tollie and the newly energized Dae-Ho took a jackhammer and a stone saw down into Cavern A to hollow out a cache in an out-of-the-way corner of the chamber floor for which they made a close-fitting limestone lid. This was to house the codices and a selection of ingeniously designed magnesium-alloy survival tools the two of them had fashioned in the clean room. The final touch was a solid-gold panel imprinted with simple directions to the cache, which the men mortared flush to the floor a few yards from where Nick, gods willing, would eventually emerge from his spent TDS.

It did all of them good, she could see, to be useful again. To be taking steps toward a larger goal, however unlikely it now seemed that the Centauri mission could ever achieve what they'd once envisioned for it: the phoenix-like revival of a new human society in some idyllic version of deep-future Earth. And she could see it did them all good, after the trauma and tragedy of loss they'd all experienced, even as the world continued to crash down around their ears, simply to be in the company of other human beings. Not only working, but taking time to relax. She felt it in her own body and spirit, and she saw it in Tollie, and in Dae-Ho and Petra too, now that the arrival of others had awakened them from their reclusive stupor. Playing bridge and chess and dominoes, grilling goat meat under the stars, drinking up what was left of Cornelius Quist's precious wine cellar—it was almost like the old days, in a sense. Of course things could never be the same, but the human spirit did possess a remarkable resiliency as long as its basic needs were met: food, shelter, the miracle of ongoing good health. It possessed a default instinct to squeeze all the juice from one's brief life while such a thing was still possible.

With each passing day, however, she couldn't help feeling the window for positive action narrowing. The truth was they were running out of time. The pre-collapse infrastructure both within and outside the perimeter of the Lab compound was entering a stage of accelerated decline, and as they'd seen, you couldn't predict when one of them might be taken without warning. With the idea of mounting another globe-ranging expedition in search of a viable female test subject seemingly out of reach, the entire weight of humanity's survival as a species hung on a tenuous thread of accident. That somewhere on the planet, somehow, there might exist a small, anomalous population capable of delivering its heirs to a remote, healthy future Earth. Given everything Natalie knew and had seen, this seemed a tenuous thread indeed. But in order to keep moving forward with their work, they almost had to take it as a given.

It was with these grim and determined thoughts echoing in her mind that she had the unaccustomed experience of having to stop herself from flying into an almost murderous rage when, after more than three months of mind-boggling forgetfulness, Dae-Ho and Petra finally remembered to give her the vintage plasticized Priority Mail envelope with her name on it that they'd found rolled up and jammed into the ironwork of the entry gate while the expeditionary team had been sailing across the Atlantic.

Inside the old envelope, further protected by a vintage, wrinkled, slightly brittle ziplock bag, was a hand-written note from a former colleague at MIT, who'd been serving for a few years prior to the collapse as a professor of physics at the Rensselaer Polytechnic Institute. The man had gotten wind of something that seemed important enough to rouse him from the daily work of sheer survival to have this message hand-delivered to the gates of the former Centauri Lab on the off chance that Natalie or members of the team might yet be alive and working on their famous project.

It was dated March, seven months earlier, and once the initial rage at her delay in receiving it had subsided, Natalie read it over multiple times with a dawning excitement. It described a report passed on to the professor by sources he considered highly credible, about a miracle pregnancy observed in a subject in her late teens living in the Adirondack region of what was once upstate New York. Even if the rumor proved false, the location of this unexpected lead—the note included an actual street address in Lake Placid—meant that it could be investigated without the need to mount another fully outfitted expedition to some distant part of the globe.

Destiny, it seemed, was granting them one final shot.

37

11th Millennium A.U.C.T. (estimated)

One rain-soaked morning in late spring, attempting to spear a smallmouth bass, he loses his footing on a slick log and splashes into the lake, throwing out his back. The pain is intense. It takes him the rest of the day to hobble back up to the ledge, where he's effectively immobilized for weeks. His food supplies dwindle. The cats mewl at him with increasing irritation. Eventually he regains the range of motion to forage again, but the distance he can cover on any given day is limited. But even if it weren't, he wouldn't go far, because he's lost the desire to cover any more ground than the bare minimum required for survival. He can no longer imagine, for example, visiting the relatively nearby Connecticut River, much less anything akin to the long-distance treks he once undertook to the Atlantic Coast or Lake Champlain. Mostly, out of long habit, he sits on the ledge, gazing out over the lowlands.

Then one moonless, brilliantly star-speckled night, everything changes. He's leaning his back against a familiar yellow birch, stroking his current favorite midnight-black cat and staring out over the dark forest, when for the first time in all the accumulated months and years of vigilance he suddenly sees exactly what he's been looking for: a little pinpoint of bright orange light. He closes his eyes, massages his eyelids with his fingertips, shakes his head to clear it, and opens his eyes again.

It's still there. A tiny orange spark, not far from the base of the mountain, flickering hesitantly but not going out. It's partially obscured by the canopy—if he moves his head back and forth he momentarily loses sight of it—but there's no mistaking what it is.

He gets stiffly to his feet. He hesitates a moment, a hand to his sore back. On a moonless night like this, the broken contours of the forest floor will be drowned in shadow and nearly impossible to see. On the other hand, it was his own feet that made all the trails, and he knows them well enough not to get lost. He finds his best spear leaning against a granite boulder and sets off down the mountainside.

38

2068 (12 A.U.C.T.)

Natalie had been an odd kid. They'd both been odd, Tollie supposed, though in different ways. She'd had amazing powers of concentration and could speed-read a hefty tome in a single afternoon. He'd needed to be constantly in motion, like a shark that had to keep swimming or it would drown. She'd blown through entire grades in school, memorizing textbooks on advanced calculus and linear algebra, while he'd been stuck trying to figure out what the hell a hypotenuse was. By the time she was ten she could defeat all comers in chess—grown men and women, intellectuals, friends of their parents who considered themselves masters of the game—while he'd barely had the patience to finish a quick round of checkers.

She'd always seemed to *care* more than he did, about ideas, people, animals. As a child she'd spent a lot of time rescuing injured creatures and releasing them back into the wild. He remembered an elaborate clinic she'd set up on the dunes behind their family's island property for wounded crabs and seagulls. She'd been the sort of kid who gravitated less to her peers—whom she'd mostly found baffling—than toward whatever adults happened to be kicking around, especially the cleverest ones. Weekend guests, the film producers, artists, Nobel Prize–winning academics, and eccentric computer geniuses she'd find reading by the pool or sitting in one of the many comfortable chairs their parents had placed strategically on the sprawling compound's various decks and porches.

These figures had returned Natalie's attention too. They'd been drawn to her, as people always had. She had a way of changing the weather in a room when she walked in. It wasn't just her famous brilliance, or the fact that if things had maybe gone a bit differently she might have been the savior of the entire species. It was that they sensed that her interest was sincere. That she truly *cared.* Just being near her lifted you up. Something in her eyes, her voice, her laugh, her smile—it helped you see your potential as a human being, and you felt a sense of gratitude for that. Tollie hadn't participated in too many of those high-level conversations around the compound. He'd never really considered himself part of the brilliant set; he'd preferred to be out sailing, road-tripping, or getting into various kinds of trouble with his friends. But Natalie had managed to find time for him anyway, seeming to genuinely enjoy his company. They'd gone on a lot of adventures together over the decades. In fact, going on adventures together was pretty much the essence of their relationship.

He'd never said so directly, but it had been the privilege of his life to have her as a sister, and when she told him about this new potential test subject in the Adirondacks, he said immediately that he would accompany her. Petra and Dae-Ho offered to come along too, but it was obvious that the couple needed to stay on at the Lab compound, keeping it occupied and maintained for as long as possible.

Before they left, Natalie spent half a day down in Cavern B starting the pre-activation protocol for one of the unoccupied spheres. The systems took time to gain momentum, and she wanted to minimize the delay once they got back from the Adirondacks. This meant they now faced a hard deadline, she explained. If the TDS weren't activated within the prescribed window—around sixty days—the self-contained cold fusion reactor would disable itself, and the shutdown would be permanent. After that, if they ever wanted to activate the third and final sphere they would have to find more palladium and zirconium-oxide for its reactor, which, given the state of things, would be a very difficult if not impossible task. Still, she felt it was worth the risk to reduce the time during which anything might go wrong with this hypothetical new test subject.

Air travel was of course a thing of the past, and due to the sorry state of the highways and bridges, driving to the Adirondacks was also out of the question. Without municipal road crews to maintain them, most of the backroads had stayed viable for only a few years after the collapse, and things had gotten worse since then. The changes entailed both shrinkage and expansion: shrinkage in the average person's expected travel radius, and expansion of the planet itself to a size resembling the way it must have felt before the industrial revolution. Almost all travel was by foot now, or by water for the lucky few who still had access to sailboats, rowboats, kayaks, or canoes. Humanity had in effect rediscovered the meaning of distance. The trip from the Lab compound in what had once been northern New Hampshire to Lake Placid, while no transatlantic voyage, was therefore a good deal more of a commitment than the pleasant four- or five-hour drive it had once been. The rivers in this part of the continent generally flowed north to south, so boats were out of the question. The Lab did have a fleet of vintage e-bikes equal to degraded roads and foot trails, but there was the problem of spare parts and inner tubes, not to mention finding functioning PV panels or wind turbines to charge them up on the road. So the plan was to go by foot.

With friendly goodbyes and a few pointed instructions for Petra and Dae-Ho, Natalie and Tollie climbed the rusted entry gate and set off down the access road. Despite the grim state of the exterior world they were venturing into, Tollie felt more cheerful than he had since they'd made that ill-fated stopover in Spain. Something about him and Natalie setting off together with backpacks. It just felt right.

The years immediately following the hyperpandemic had brought about a surprising resurgence in the use of the internal combustion engine, but by now the vast majority of fuel stockpiles were depleted. The highway leading westward from the half-collapsed bridge over the Connecticut River was littered with the corpses of old cars and pickups rusting in the breakdown lanes, their bodies, now half-swallowed by encroaching vines and saplings, like distinctive visual echoes of the consumer society that had once held sway over an entire world. They followed this road for as long as it made sense, walking mostly in silence to avoid attracting undue attention and giving every occupied property a wide berth. Tollie had his hunting rifle and in their packs was a good supply of Lab jerky. Every so often they would stop to forage in the overgrown gardens and orchards surrounding the many abandoned houses and farmsteads.

Generally they avoided going inside any of these buildings, though in a small ghost village they did find an old general store that had by some miracle not been completely looted. Loading cans of peaches and green beans into his pack put Tollie in an oddly nostalgic mood. Natalie found a deck of playing cards and they spent the next few evenings around the campfire immersed in a running game of cribbage, using toothpicks for markers and the top of an old Styrofoam cooler for a game board. Occasionally they would glance up from the game, peering nervously into the shadows to assure themselves they had no silent spectators.

The bridge over the southern reach of Lake Champlain looked like it had at some point been deliberately sabotaged with explosives, and it was in no way passable. They didn't feel like swimming with their packs, so they made a long detour south and west before turning north, and four days later, without meaningful incident, they finally made it to Lake Placid. The old tourist town looked completely abandoned, most of the buildings burned-out shells. They spent the night in a beetle-infested pine forest above what used to be a community skating rink, and the next morning, on Tollie's insistence, visited the Winter Olympics sporting complex. A surprising number of the old facilities remained intact: a rusting chairlift; the bramble-choked bobsled run; the massive cement trellises of two side-by-side ski jumps profiled against the dull white sky, like monuments to some long-forgotten god.

The address in the former professor's note belonged to a house on the main road a few miles north of town, a decrepit old faux-Austrian ski chalet at the top of a steep driveway with the Adirondack peaks as a backdrop. Much of the siding had been ripped away by windstorms, and the roof was partly covered by several tattered blue tarps, having been damaged, it appeared, by a fallen tree that now lay rotting and covered in moss beside the house. The place was occupied, though. Dim candlelight flickered behind a grimy picture window.

They walked cautiously up the driveway to the front steps, Tollie cocking his rifle and transferring it to an unobtrusive one-handed grip with the barrel pointing at the ground. Standing on the stoop they met each other's eyes silently, and Natalie rapped on the door.

A disheveled man answered. He looked to be in his forties and in pretty grim shape: threadbare Jets sweatshirt, stained khaki shorts, sharp shoulders and sunken eyes suggesting malnutrition. A few wisps of pale red hair on a bare scalp flecked with scabs. When he opened his mouth they saw that several of his front teeth were missing.

"You're too late," he said, after Natalie had explained that they were looking for a young woman. "She died six months ago." He glanced quickly back over his shoulder at the candlelit emptiness of the house, as if half-expecting to be contradicted by some other person who lived there. But there was clearly no one else.

Tollie watched with sympathetic chagrin as the bitter disappointment crashed across his sister's face, though she only allowed it to show for a moment.

The man beckoned them inside his filthy hovel. The smells of urine and mildew were overwhelming. Natalie dug into her pack for a brick of Lab jerky and a can of pilfered peaches. He wolfed down the jerky greedily, examined the can, and placed it reverently on the cluttered dining-room table.

"How old was your daughter when she died?"

"Girlfriend," the man said, wiping crumbs from his mouth with a filthy sleeve of the sweatshirt. "Early twenties, I'd guess. Don't know for sure. She came up from Guatemala, orphaned in the collapse. Never knew her birthday."

"What happened to the child?"

He shook his head. "There was never any child. She wasn't pregnant. That would have been something, eh? For some reason people spread around the idea that she was. She was a healthy-looking girl, heavy-set, not from around here. I guess if people really want to believe something, they make it happen in their own minds, you know what I mean? But no, she was never going to have a baby. You're scientists, I'm guessing?"

Natalie nodded, and he stared at her for a moment, then glanced at Tollie, as if considering.

"I tell you what, though," he said after a moment. "I do have something of hers that you might find interesting. Do you want to see?"

"Of course. What is it?"

"Don't move. I'll be right back." He picked up the can of peaches and slipped off into the shadows of an unlit hallway.

"You okay, Nat?"

"I'm fine." She smiled ruefully, but Tollie could see how hard the disappointment had hit her. Another wasted trip. No other possibilities in sight.

The homeowner edged back into the room with a shotgun pointed straight at Tollie. "Now put down that rifle."

Tollie glanced at Natalie. She gave him an exasperated look and nodded. He bent his knees and placed the rifle carefully on the floor in front of him.

"Kick it away."

Tollie pushed the rifle with the toe of his boot, and it slid three or four feet away from him on the floorboards.

"Good. Now take off your packs."

They both complied. Tollie lowered his onto the floorboards, leaving the path between himself and the rifle unobstructed.

"Where's home?" the man asked. He was having trouble keeping the barrel of the shotgun steady. Tollie could see the tremble of it.

"Far away," he assured him. "It took us two and a half weeks to walk."

"What's in the packs?"

"Nothing valuable," Natalie said. "Old sleeping bags. A little more food, which we're happy to give you."

"Bullets for that rifle?"

Tollie shook his head. "The only bullets I have left are in the chamber."

"You're lying. Asshole."

"I'm not lying." Tollie glanced at the rifle on the floor, calculating his moves. He could dive and roll. Though he was no longer a young man, he was still athletic enough, he thought, that he might be able to pull it off. But Natalie caught his eye and gave him a small shake of her head.

"Get the fuck out of here, both of you. Leave those packs and the rifle. Now!"

Tollie lifted his hands in what he hoped was a calming gesture and inched backward toward the door. Natalie, surprisingly, stepped not backward but forward, gently raising a hand to the shotgun barrel. The man's eyes widened, but he didn't pull the trigger. When she brought her other hand up and twisted the gun, he released it easily. She tossed it underhand across the room, where it came to a clattering rest against a far wall.

Tollie picked up the rifle.

"So this is pretty much the end, right?" the man asked. "The whole human race is done for, aren't we?"

Natalie gave him a sympathetic look as she squatted to take half a dozen wrapped packets of Lab jerky bricks and a few more cans out of her pack. "Not necessarily," she said, arranging the supplies on the table. "There may still be a glimmer of hope for the long term."

"Welp." The man shrugged and dropped his weight onto a filthy couch. "I certainly don't see any glimmer."

"How did you know the shotgun wasn't loaded?" Tollie asked as they strode down the driveway.

"Educated guess, Tollie, dear. That man is clearly starving to death, and his main interest was bullets. He probably used up the last of his shotgun shells years ago."

Reclining on his elbows beside their campfire that night, Tollie articulated Natalie's thoughts before she even had a chance to think them. "You're going to get into that pre-activated sphere yourself, aren't you?"

"Heavens no! What good would that do?"

"Well, Nat, it seems to me that you'd have a better chance of being of service to humanity where old Nick's going than here."

"You're assuming the survival of a viable remnant population somewhere on the planet. Which is a roll of the dice at best."

"Same dice roll you'd be making if you stay here. Except here you've basically run out of both resources and time. Am I wrong?"

She stared at him across the fire. "It's not my intention to leave you alone, dear brother."

"What if I told you that I *wanted* you to leave me alone?"

"I wouldn't believe you."

"What if I insisted it was the gods' honest truth?"

"I still wouldn't believe you. You're a notorious liar."

"And yet you're not completely dismissing the idea, are you?"

She held his gaze for a long moment, her noble features flickering ghost-like in the heat vapors. "No," she finally said. "I suppose I'm not."

39

2068 (12 A.U.C.T.)

Back at the Lab she walked him through the procedures. There was actually a physical manual, a doorstop ring-binder printed way back in the days when the Centauri Project had still been aiming for the stars. But they both knew that following complex written instructions was not Tollie's greatest strength. And she wanted him, not Dae-Ho or Petra, to be with her at the very end.

It was Tollie himself who'd clinched the argument on the long walk home from Lake Placid. "You've given your entire existence to saving humanity, Nat. I've given my entire existence to . . . what? Enjoying life? Taking unnecessary risks? Growing the best strains of homegrown weed? Yes, I'll miss you terribly. Yes, I'd much rather spend whatever months or years I have left playing cribbage and arguing with you, but this is my chance to finally make a contribution of my own. A sacrifice for the greater good. Let me do *that* at least, while you go off into the future to work your magic. We've had a good run of it, dear sister. Nothing can take that away."

She'd cried then, they both had, and a lot of the time since had been spent hugging and laughing and just enjoying each other's company. Of course she wouldn't even have considered leaving him if she thought there was any utility in staying. But as she reflected, she came to understand that all her hope had shifted to the deep future. The passage of coordinate time would have to be the test, the filter. Could humanity make it through on its own? Was there a population that had survived, and if so, would it be possible to find and help them? It was a thin thread of possibility, but it was all she had left.

And what of her feelings about Nick? This was the first time she'd given any serious thought to the idea that they might somehow be reunited, and she had to admit—though it could have no bearing whatsoever on her final decision—that the thought of seeing him again *did* make her happy, if also a little nervous.

While she focused on launching the final protocols for the pre-activated sphere, Tollie and Dae-Ho used an old fossil-fueled excavator to pile and arrange new boulders around the Cavern B entrance. The resulting jumble still stuck out like a sore thumb, but at least the passage was narrower now, and harder to find, no longer just a blatantly artificial-looking square hole in the hillside. With time, hopefully, its appearance would be softened by the colonization of vines, hardy shrubs, and eventually trees, though it hardly mattered. With every passing day there were fewer and fewer humans left to stumble onto it—and those who were left were too preoccupied with their own survival to wander aimlessly through the pastures of a fenced-off rural compound.

Eventually the appointed hour arrived, and with the rising wind heralding an impending storm, Natalie sat with Tollie at one of the old picnic tables behind the Round Barn's communal dining room. The table was weathered silver, covered with lichen and rotting from the ground up. Indicative of the whole compound really, which despite the recent uptick in maintenance seemed to be losing ground at an accelerated rate in the unrelentingly humid weather: peeling paint, decomposing shingles, turbine blades rusted nearly to a standstill. It remained a strikingly beautiful property however, built into gently sloping pastureland at the head of a broad valley dotted with ponds and lakes, with the distinctly shaped rock summit of Mount Wingandicoa as a backdrop, grand and impassive beneath gathering purple rain clouds.

Dae-Ho and Petra came out to say their goodbyes. Natalie thanked them warmly for their years of service to Centauri and reassured them that there was nothing further they could do now other than live out their lives in as much happiness and good health as they could muster. Dae-Ho offered to use the Lab's remaining reserves of fossil fuel to further naturalize the boulder arrangement at the Cavern B entrance, but she told him it was fine the way it was; he should hold on to the reserves in case they were needed for something more pressing. Petra vowed to continue transplanting shrubs and saplings for as long as she was able to use a shovel, and seeing how determined she was to help, Natalie didn't attempt to dissuade her—though she did remind her to get all her seasonal gardening done before she wasted time and energy on that. The conversation played itself out. An awkward silence descended over the picnic table, until Natalie stood up and told them to say goodbye and go about their business. They wished her well, and there were tears shed and lingering hugs exchanged before they made their way back inside.

"Well," Tollie said, sitting back down at the table across from her. "If you *do* run into Nick, tell him his old fishing buddy sends regards. I never did get the chance to say a proper goodbye."

"You were sailing around the Canadian Maritimes when we sealed his sphere, if I remember correctly. But yes, dear brother, I will certainly tell him."

"Do you want me to unseal the cache in Cavern A and update your message?"

"I don't think so. If my sphere opens first it won't matter. If not, I don't want him frittering away his time waiting for me. He really needs to focus on the search for survivors."

"Okay. We'll let it be a surprise, then."

She stared at him across the picnic table for a long moment. She wasn't sad or frightened for herself, but she *was* concerned for him. And despite his protests to the contrary, she still felt guilty for abandoning her little brother.

"Don't worry about *me*," he said. "I'm planning to make the most of the time I have left."

"And what exactly is that going to entail, Tollie?" she asked gently.

"Another sailing trip, maybe. Establish my own fiefdom, or simply live off the fat of the land. Who knows? Maybe I'll find a young lover to share my twilight years."

"I *like* that idea," she said.

They were quiet now, gazing into each other's eyes. Suddenly hers were glistening with tears again, and she reached a hand across the rotting pine boards to squeeze his forearm.

"Don't *worry*, Nat. You're the one who always said it was a mistake to think of time as a one-way arrow. We'll always be together, brother and sister. Those years can never be erased in a certain sense, right?"

"It's true. That doesn't mean it isn't hard to say goodbye."

The tears were flowing freely now for both of them. He stood from the table and held out his hands to help her up, and they strolled arm in arm over the rocky pastureland.

40

2068 (12 A.U.C.T.)

Tollie squeezed up out of the newly modified Cavern B entrance into a heavy downpour. Walking back down through the lukewarm rain to the compound, half-blinded by the sting of raindrops mixing with his own salty tears, he realized that he had little desire to prolong his time with Dae-Ho and Petra. Contrary to his usually sociable nature, all he really wanted now was to be on his own.

He found them sitting in silence at the Round Barn's kitchen table. Petra handed him a dishtowel, and he used it to dry off his face and ears. "Just dropping in to say goodbye myself, actually," he said. "And to thank you again for looking after things."

The couple expressed alarm at the unexpected news of his imminent departure. Where would he go? What would he do? Didn't he at least want to wait for the rain to stop? But with Nat gone he couldn't bear the idea of sticking around for even another minute. *It's best for all concerned*, he told himself. Lingering on in his present state would only alarm them further, or at least make them uncomfortable.

So he rolled his old sleeping bag into a tarp and stuffed it into his faded orange Osprey backpack along with a week's supply of Lab jerky. The rain eased up a bit as he climbed over the rusting entry gate and started down the access road. It occurred to him that he hadn't really thought about a destination, so he settled on the first interesting place that came to mind: an old stone bridge across the Connecticut River perhaps two days' walk south. Supposedly there was a group of ancient petroglyphs carved into the cliff below the bridge. He'd always been curious to see it and in fact he and Nat had passed it on their way north after their return from Stromboli, but she hadn't wanted to stop.

Avoiding the half-ruined paved roads, he followed the riverside trail southward. The rain stopped after a few hours, and he heard the rumble of a fossil-fueled motorboat coming upriver. As it rounded the nearest bend, he saw that it was a jury-rigged pontoon boat with a gun turret welded to a steel scaffold over the sunshade. It was good that he'd hidden himself in a tangle of driftwood on the muddy riverbank, because the boat was crowded with a rough-looking crew of men and a few women. They looked high on something, and the expressions on their gap-toothed faces as they scanned the shorelines were wild-eyed and notably bloodthirsty: a gang of nihilists out for an end-times joyride, it appeared. Crouching lower, he tried not to move a muscle until the boat was well out of sight upstream. Going down in a hail of hoarded machine-gun bullets was not his idea of a good exit strategy.

On the afternoon of the second day he came to the old stone bridge, slightly crumbled at the far end but still standing, with the high-volume thunder of falling water coming up from beneath it. After the demise of a nearby hydro plant, the river had smashed through the levees to reclaim its original course, so that its entire pressurized volume now shot through a narrow stone gorge, dropping twenty or thirty feet into a whitewater rapid that churned chaotically downstream through half a mile of scattered boulders and debris. The petroglyphs were carved into a steeply sloping granite wall beneath the bridge. He no longer owned a climbing harness or a rope, so he had to free-climb down what was essentially a slanting cliff to get a better look. The rain had been continuous, and the river's swollen brown torrent gave off a mineral fragrance as it roared through the narrow granite chute. All the rock was wet and slick. If he were to slip a handhold, there was nothing to break his fall. He would land in the torrent and be shot downriver and quite possibly pulverized in the cataract or in the boulder-strewn rapid below it. It had become profoundly important to him to see the petroglyphs, though, and he eased himself carefully down the slanting cliff.

Finally he was eye to eye with them, dozens of circular figures chiseled long ago into the granite, varied in size but identical in design. Simple human faces such as a child might draw, with pecked-out cavities for the eyes and mouths and pairs of lines sprouting up from the foreheads like the antennae of grasshoppers or cartoon aliens. The faces did have a comical aspect, but there was something deadly serious about them too. An aura of uncanny menace that grew more and more powerful the longer he was face to face with them.

Tollie clung to the wet black wall, awed by his intimate proximity to these strange ancient faces in the pounding roar of those millions of gallons of silt-laden whitewater surging through the gorge right below him. Rollicking tongues of the river licked up at him from below, as if making feints to demonstrate how easy it would be to dislodge him from the wall. And what would it matter if that happened? He had nowhere else he needed to be.

A big dollop of river water leapt up to slap him hard on the side of the face, dousing his beard and his threadbare t-shirt. A faint echo came back to him from the opposite wall of the gorge, as if from some distant remove, of his own delighted laughter. And if there had been a sentient observer looking down from the bridge that day, it might have heard a shred of that laughter before it was swallowed up by the whitewater roar. It might have watched a grizzled head disappear into the cataract and bob up as it tried to stay afloat amid the jagged black boulders and huge standing waves downstream—or it might have watched that same gray-haired being make its way back up the cliff to the bridge and set off on some other soon-to-be-forgotten adventure.

But there was no sentient observer. Only the faces that had been chiseled into the hard granite thousands of years before. Faces that would remain in place above the unceasing roar of that narrowly channeled river, unseen by human eyes for at least ten thousand years to come.

41

11th Millennium A.U.C.T. (estimated)

Standing in the ink-black night just beyond the reach of the flickering firelight, heart pounding, scarcely daring to breathe, the man who used to be called Dr. Nicholas Hindman braces himself for disappointment. A long time has gone by, but this feels exactly like the mind-trickery that nearly unmade him more than once in the past. Plausible yet somehow otherworldly. A highly improbable scenario that feels dangerously akin to the fulfillment of his deepest wishes. A small human female, or the illusion of one, dressed in a dirt-stained Centauri jumpsuit. Sitting cross-legged before a small campfire, head bowed, face indistinct, hands outstretched as if warming herself. He stays where he is, waiting for the hallucination to waver and evaporate. It does not.

He steps out of the shadows into the firelight. The woman jumps to her feet and grabs a flaming branch from the fire.

"I come in peace," he says, holding out his hands. The words are clumsy and alien-sounding in his unpracticed mouth; nothing like the smooth background narration that has continued to run through his mind all these years.

"Nick! Is that really you?"

"*Natalie?*" He staggers back in shock.

"Let me get a look at you, dear." She tosses the branch back on the fire and looks him up and down, shaking her head with a faint smile of affectionate disbelief. It *looks* like Natalie, certainly, and plausibly aged under the dirt smeared over her face and jumpsuit: lean, with pronounced wrinkles radiating out from her eyes and around her mouth, hair cut shorter, grayer, almost white. At least a decade older than when he last saw her, but then he must have aged at least that much himself, if not more. But the features are handsome in exactly the way he remembers, with that characteristic radiant optimism, and she's even wearing the same big round-lensed eye-glasses he remembers. *But she couldn't have worn those in the TDS*, he thinks, his heart plummeting.

"Yes, well, thankfully, we thought about the glasses in advance," she says, as if reading his mind. "We added an extra pocket to my jumpsuit, on the sleeve opposite the ferrocerium rod and striker. I would be lost without them, you know."

He nods, speechless. *Can this actually be a real thing he's experiencing?*

"Well, Nick, aren't you glad to see me?"

She holds out her arms, and in the next moment he's enfolded in the embrace of a real human body. And it's *her* body: soft, small-boned, familiar, smelling of earth and limestone, warmed by the fire. He attempts to say another sentence but his throat is too tight, the tears streaming down his cheeks. She laughs softly and in the next moment he's laughing too, and choking back sobs, and their faces are buried in each other's necks and hair.

He keeps bracing himself for the whole thing to evaporate. To find himself alone again on this dark night, in this endless solitary wilderness, hugging a tree perhaps, or a tree-stump softened by moss. But it doesn't evaporate. It's Natalie, solid and in the flesh. And the relief he feels to hold her in his arms is like nothing he's ever experienced.

He'd assumed that the lack of other spheres meant that they'd either gotten buried somewhere or been taken off the property. He hadn't even considered that they might have excavated a Cavern B. Perhaps it's not surprising that he never found it. Many generations of trees had grown and decayed on the artificial hill covering it, and there had apparently been enough soil deposition to completely bury the hurriedly arranged boulders camouflaging the entrance. After recovering her equilibrium in the darkness, Natalie had had to tunnel out through the soil and roots that had accumulated, nearly suffocating in the process. She'd made it out though and, very chilled, had used the ferrocerium rod and striker sewn into the sleeve of her jumpsuit to build a fire.

They stamp that fire out now, and he takes her hand and leads her away through the forest. A nearly full moon has come out and the night is lighter than it was. "You moved some earth here too," she remarks as they walk by the weed-choked mounds left over from his excavation of the Lab site.

"Years ago."

"Did you find anything?"

"Not much. There was a hot fire at some point—after your time, I guess?"

She nodded, glancing at the mounds. "I hope they got out before that."

"There must not have been many team members left, from what I read in the codex."

"You found our cache, then. I'm glad."

"Not right away, for which I blame myself. It would have been nice to know that you were coming, though."

"I didn't want you wasting your energy waiting for me," she explains, a little guiltily. "Or driving yourself crazy about it if something went wrong."

"And if I'd known you were coming I might not have been quite as focused on looking for survivors?"

"I have to admit, I did consider that."

"I forgive you."

"Thank you, my darling. I knew you would."

They stand in silence for a moment, looking around at the excavation mounds in the dully gleaming moonlight.

"And *have* you?" she asks.

"Have I what?"

"Found surviving humans? Or any sign of them?"

He glances at her face in the moonlight, trying to think of the best way to put it. He doesn't want to distress her so soon after she's regained consciousness, but he feels that he has to be honest. "I've had a chance to look around quite a bit, Nat," he finally says. "Maybe you'll feel it too once you've been here awhile. It's palpable. There's no one else."

She frowns and shakes her head noncommittally, and he can tell that she isn't ready to accept this conclusion. It's understandable. The survival of humanity has driven her entire professional life. But it seems to him that ten millennia would have been plenty of time for any hypothetical survivors to spread out, even if they'd originated in some distant part of the planet.

"I did recover your little bust," he says, by way of changing the subject.

"The Einstein? You're kidding."

"I still have it. Up at my—" He gestures vaguely at the dark profile of the mountain looming up ahead of them. "Where we're going. My permanent camp. The bust has been important for me, like a—" Language seems to be failing him now. It's been so long since he's spoken aloud.

"Like a talisman?"

"Exactly. Against forgetting."

She gives his hand a squeeze, and he leads her slowly up the trail.

His intention is to get her up to the ledge tonight so she can recover in greater comfort, but it soon becomes apparent that she's not strong enough to make it on her own. In the end he carries her piggyback most of the way. She's not that heavy, and they stop often at various places on the trail so she can rest.

By the time they reach the ledge, the first hint of dawn is lightening the eastern horizon. While she rests under furs on his bed of moss and pine needles in the grotto, he makes a fire and prepares her one of his favorite breakfasts: roasted mushrooms lightly stewed in hickory milk.

"My compliments on your accommodations," she says a little while later, looking around at the orderly stacks of firewood, the racks of drying meat and fish, the hanging bundles of dried herbs. A tiger-striped scion of the current generation of felines peers out at them from the shadows at the edge of the forest, early in the process of overcoming its shyness with the new human. "You've made a very nice home for yourself. No doubt we could both be comfortable here."

"Why do I get the feeling there's a 'but' at the beginning of your next sentence?"

She laughs, and in the strengthening sunlight he gets his first clear look at her. She's lost weight, he thinks, but aged well overall, as if time has boiled her down to her radiant essence. Despite all the years of subjective and coordinate time that have passed, she's still retained all the sweetness of the brilliant, awkward, idealistic young graduate student he once met in line at that MIT campus café.

"*But*, my dear Nick. As wonderful as it is to be reunited, it wasn't an easy decision for me to come here. I did not do it for romantic reasons. I came because every other avenue we tried ended in failure, and we simply ran out of time. I can't in good conscience really give up the search now, no matter how unlikely it might seem. If there are any human survivors on this planet, I need to do everything in my power to find them and help them thrive."

He knows better than to argue. As far as he's concerned, the only salient matter is that he's no longer alone. Natalie is his best friend and the love of his life. Now that she's here, he has no intention of ever letting her out of his sight. He will follow her unto death in other words, to the ends of this wilderness earth.

42

The first problem is where to begin. Nick has already been to the coast, and to the northern seaway, and for these reasons and others Natalie believes that the most fruitful direction for their search will be to the south. Quite far south in fact, and also to the west. Apart from Stromboli, the most plausible-sounding rumors about the persistence of human fertility had centered on the Juan Fernández Islands, off the coast of the land that had once been Chile. An expanding population originating on those highly volcanic islands would have had formidable barriers to surmount. Four hundred miles separated the archipelago from the mainland; then there is the Darien Gap, which is at this point likely to be drowned by a few hundred feet of sea level rise, meaning that the continents of North and South America—in addition to having barely recognizable coastlines—are separate land masses for the first time since the late Pliocene, more than three million years ago.

The problem is these formidable barriers to the diffusion of a theoretical surviving population are also formidable barriers to a pair of—let's face it—no longer youthful travelers from the distant past. Natalie has always been an optimist, however. She's confident they will find a way.

For now they're content to stay put, walking and foraging in a gradually ramped up, increasingly rigorous daily regimen designed to prepare them for a long overland trek. At the end of each day's labor, they stop to cool themselves off in one of Nick's favorite streamside pools before walking up to the ledge to process their takings and eat a hearty dinner by the fire. It's good to be with him. Time has altered him, of course—his hair and beard are long now, and silver-streaked—and he's been changed even more profoundly on the interior, she suspects, by the experience of being so long on his own. He smiles less easily than he used to, and his face is craggier and more care-worn. At certain moments she glimpses a look of fear in his eyes, as if he's being stalked even now by some long-lived inner demon—though mostly, she's happy to see, he's the same old Nick she's always known: laconic, competent, practical, steadfast.

Sleeping arrangements have improved in the grotto since her arrival, their bed expanded and made more comfortable with extra layers of freshly gathered moss and pine boughs. They sleep in a spooning position, his arm draped over her middle, her hand resting on his wrist or forearm. In the morning he resurrects the fire and she feeds the cats, who've readily welcomed her as the newest member of their everchanging tribe. Nick brews a breakfast drink of pine needle tea or some elixir of herbs and mushrooms, and the two of them share the day's first meal. Then they walk again.

One day dissolves into the next with what seems to be a gathering momentum. Weeks pass, a month, then two. It's a time of great happiness for them both. She's seeing this world through his eyes now as well as her own, the dual perspective of the brand new and the long familiar only enhancing her appreciation for these surroundings. For the thriving ecosystem of a pristine old-growth forest; for the beauty of the rocks and mosses and trees and birds; for the absolute clarity of the unpolluted night sky; for the cool delicious water they can drink just by cupping their hands in any bubbling spring or woodland brook. In the early mornings they recount their dreams to each other, dreams that often bring up memories of the people and places they once knew.

Sometimes in the evenings by the fire they'll take out the codices and linger over the pages. The beauty and durability of the pressed gold has come at a cost she hadn't considered before. The codices are heavy, adding a great deal of extra weight for an extended foot journey, though there's never a question of leaving them behind.

For his part, privately, Nick harbors a few doubts as to whether, in the unlikely event they do find a remnant population, the illustrated pages will have the impact Natalie hopes. Something about the human spirit seems to need systems of belief. During their time apart, in very different ways, Nick and Natalie both experienced this firsthand. And while the illustrated codex might well fill this need in a positive way, even the clearest truths can be twisted into lies that can be used to justify all manner of evil: tribalism, corruption, exploitation, violence. Maybe there's something inevitable about this whole process, like a glitch built into the very DNA of the species. Maybe a beautiful golden codex filled with clear explanations of thousands of years of accumulated wisdom would help keep a new culture of humans out of trouble. Then again, maybe it wouldn't. It's all beside the point anyway in his view, as he's fairly convinced that they're not going to find any survivors.

He keeps these thoughts to himself, however, not wanting to trouble Natalie with negative thinking. Her enthusiasm and can-do spirit are doing wonders to keep them both healthy and strong, and he feels better than he has in years, both physically and mentally. He's actually enjoying this new training regime of foraging and walking. And he has no problem with the prospect of embarking on what will undoubtedly be a long, one-way journey. As long as they're together.

At first he's too embarrassed to mention his own little private religion, the one that sort of developed organically for him over the years. Very little escapes Natalie's notice, however, and the shrine set into the niche in the granite hillside above the ledge would be hard to miss. She doesn't react with the skepticism he might have expected from one of their era's most eminent physicists. To the contrary, she grasps immediately how assigning some kind of spiritual meaning to objects and natural elements might have been essential to get him through his long years of solitude with his sanity more or less intact.

And when he confesses the strangest aspect of that practice—the controlled hallucinations or lucid daydreams that gave him the uncanny illusion of being able to cover vast distances outside his body—she doesn't judge him. In fact she's read quite a bit about intentional out-of-body-experience or astral projection, which was, after all, a key feature of the religious and shamanistic beliefs of many original human cultures. Her curiosity is piqued. He has no desire to revisit the hallucinations, which he's pretty sure were nothing more than vivid distractions generated by a mind desperate to escape the oppression of extreme boredom and loneliness, but when she asks him if he can try to recreate the experience under her observation, he reluctantly agrees.

They sit together by the campfire on the ledge under a bright full moon. He takes a few deep breaths, half-closing his eyes so that the flames of the fire blur, and tries to imagine himself spiraling up into the night amid the sparks and wavering heat vapors. Nothing happens. He opens his eyes, shakes his head.

"Try once more, will you, dear?" She gives his forearm a squeeze. He shuts his eyes again and tries to imagine leaping up into the air and floating out and away from the ledge on the thermals.

Nothing. He opens his eyes, grimaces, and shakes his head. "I really don't think it's going to work, Nat. It's been years since I've tried this. I might not be able to do it anymore."

"Try just a bit more. Humor me." She gives him an encouraging smile, and he closes his eyes again. Finally, on the fourth or fifth attempt, he imagines himself rocketing skyward, and in the next moment the hallucination kicks in with full force, and he's soaring high above the moonlit mountainside. If anything the vision is *too* vivid, and too realistic. He can see the treetops moving in the slight breeze, the details of every ledge and boulder, the way the moon casts shadows that emphasize the steep mountain topography underlying the forest. Gripped by a dizzying sense of vertigo, he forces his eyes open and is relieved to find himself once again sitting beside Natalie on the ledge in the flickering firelight. She's holding his hand, peering into his face with intense curiosity. "Did it happen?"

"This time, yes." He lets out his breath in a long sigh of relief. The vision had been intensely realistic. It had frightened him.

The next morning he tries again. It's easier this time. The knack is impossible to forget, apparently, like riding a bicycle—although that once-everyday contraption feels more exotic and miraculous to him than do his visions.

Natalie wants to check the accuracy of what he's seeing by having him memorize landscape features that could only be seen from above: a wind-felled oak lying across a remote ravine; the half-eaten carcass of a deer sprawled in the tall grass of a marsh near the lake; an eagle's nest on a cliff beneath the mountain's rocky summit. Upon opening his eyes he describes the thing in detail, then they hike out together to search and verify. His sightings prove entirely accurate (as he knew from experience they would be), though neither of them can precisely explain the phenomenon. Natalie reminds him that out-of-body travel has a distinguished pedigree, from ancient Egypt to ancient India and the shamanic traditions of Mongolia, North America, Amazonia, and elsewhere. She's a good enough scientist to know that the world is full of things that can't be explained by science, especially when it comes to the complexities of the human mind. And she finds it utterly fascinating that the practice seems to have asserted itself of its own accord into Nick's homespun religion.

Her main interest, however, is practical. Because if the visions are at least partially accurate over long distances, as it seems they might be, imagine how useful they could be in their search for a remnant population of humans. Nick has his doubts about this. To him it feels like intuition, some kind of sixth sense triggered by the excessive use he once made of fly agaric mushrooms over an extended period of time. It may have some relation to reality, but is not a direct experience of it, and they have no way of verifying anything he might see that lies beyond walking distance.

Moreover, he no longer finds the practice even slightly exhilarating. It feels like tempting fate. It frightens him in a way it never did before.

At the crux of his anxiety is a doubt so troubling he can barely stand to contemplate it. If his mind is capable of manufacturing such detailed and highly realistic hallucinations of flying above a forested landscape, what's to say that it's not also capable of manufacturing a detailed and highly realistic hallucination of Natalie herself?

43

He keeps these doubts to himself, because Natalie will not be deterred. She encourages him to adopt a methodical approach, extending his range of travel in increments. It seems that the higher he flies in the visions—the more distant he is from the ground—the more ground he can cover. At times he becomes so absorbed in the highly plausible landscapes scrolling out below him—forests, rivers, range after range of low mountains, a connected series of huge lakes—that he'll momentarily forget what he's doing and allow himself to relax into the moment. But then in the next second he'll remember, and he'll start to worry about losing Natalie again, and his heart will pound and he won't be able to breathe. She'll rest a calming hand on his forearm and murmur reassuringly, and he'll keep going—or if his anxiety is severe enough, he'll cut the vision short by opening his eyes to confirm that she's still there.

One day he finds himself farther away than he's ever been. Past the last of the big blue lakes and at the edge of an advancing desert, where a game-filled prairie ecosystem is in the process of being swallowed by a line of wind-driven dunes. The wildlife is easier to spot in this open desert (or to *imagine*, he reminds himself): armadillos; pangolins; a group of boars or peccaries; a huge puma leaving its solitary tracks across the sand that glances up to follow his progress, as if it can truly see him backlit against the sky. Patches of dense vegetation in dried-up riverbeds indicate potential water sources. This appears to be a desert in which a group of humans could easily survive. But he sees no humans.

A few days later he gets his first glimpse of the Rocky Mountains. Free of the ozone smog that used to shroud them, the stone-gray cirques and buttresses of the Front Range peaks are intricately topographical. He knows them all on sight—Pikes, Grays, Evans, Torreys, Longs—and for the first time in weeks of daily hallucinating he knows the coordinates of the location he's approaching beyond the shadow of a doubt. Up ahead, buried under drifting dunes of fine red sand, are the ruins of Denver. He can even make out traces of the city in some wind-scoured patches at the base of the rising foothills.

Curiosity drives him on. This is the setting of his childhood. The houses are gone of course; the whole area was incinerated in the cataclysmic megafires that killed his parents. Swooping lower, he sees that the graceful meadows and ponderosa glades of his youth have been replaced by an unforgiving desert landscape: prickly pear, creosote bush, sunbaked boulders, barren hard-pan gravel. There are patches of darker green on the northern flanks of the mountains higher up—piñon-juniper scrublands of the kind that used to be common a few hundred miles to the south—and higher still, approaching the Continental Divide, he's relieved to see (in his mind's eye at least) that a few sheltered valleys preserve the lush Rocky Mountain ecosystem he remembers from his early years: towering forests of aspen and spruce, wildflower meadows protected by parapets of gambrel oak, stately ponderosa pines with gently swaying boughs like a Japanese woodblock print come to life. But certainly this is just his imagination coloring things in with old memories.

The next day he flies higher than ever, only swooping down to pick up where he left off. The Rockies' Western Slope is even more barren than the desert plains to the east, a bone-dry wasteland of blowing sand, crumbling rock plateaus, and sunbaked, waterless arroyos. Except for the occasional stand of cactus and drought-tolerant shrub, there's little sign of life. It would be suicide to try to cross a landscape like this on foot. Thankfully, he's not on foot. He's not even really here. So he keeps going.

He comes to a prominent ridgeline of bone-white sandstone the wind has sculpted into an intricate latticework of grottoes and false arches. Beyond it the land drops away again, and he finds himself suspended over a yawning fissure in the earth. He recognizes this terrain: the long sweeping s-curve of the canyon; how the river has slashed a cross-section down through layers of colorful stone revealing a three-dimensional record of geological time. This is the Canyon of Lodore, and the river far below, still retaining its distinctive bottle-green color, is the Green. As a teenager he floated this same stretch with his parents, a fleet of river rafts paddled by vacationing petroleum geologists and their families. It was one of the highlights of Nick's youth. Perhaps it's the deeply embedded memories of this trip that are allowing his imagination to reconstruct this detailed bird's-eye view.

Down in the canyon the riverbanks are overgrown with lush vegetation, gnarled old juniper and ash-leafed maple with a dense understory of willow scrub, with the hollowed-out murmur of the river providing a soothing background soundtrack. He sees deer and bighorn sheep, bald eagles and wading herons, and clouds of darting dragonflies. Tiny green lizards skitter across the sandstone boulders. The foraging appears excellent—berry bushes, piñon nuts, crickets, wild onions, and no doubt a good population of trout or burbot patrolling the pools and riffles of the bottle-green river—and it cheers him to contemplate the tenacity of life in this verdant ecosystem cut through the middle of such an inhospitable desert. Even if he's taking it in via nothing more than a memory-informed hallucination. On Earth it seems, barring another asteroid larger than the one that ended the age of dinosaurs, or some volcanic event even more devastating than the continent-splitting flood basalt that wiped out most of the life that existed at the end of the Permian Period, nature will find a way. It will flourish and diversify into the foreseeable future. At least for the next five billion years, until the sun's hydrogen fuel supply is finally depleted.

But then the long-term survival of life on Earth has never really been in doubt, as Natalie reminds him a few moments later. It's the survival of Homo sapiens that has been in question.

Meanwhile Nick and Natalie forage. They play with the cats and invent delicious new combinations of fish and mushrooms, nuts and berries, wild herbs and cattail shoots. They climb the mountain and spend many hours renewing their appreciation for the treeless stone pinnacle. For the abstract designs made by slow-growing lichen on weathered granite; for the surprising tenacity of the US Geological summit marker; for all the familiar crags and escarpments whose shapes remain unchanged after more than ten thousand years. They swim in the brook to refresh their aching bodies, luxuriating in the pool beneath the sheeting waterfall where tiny ginger-ale bubbles tickle their underarms and the gaps between their toes. They laugh and argue, snuggle and sleep, and in the privacy of their own hours find intimate pleasure in ways that only they can know. Time begins to lose its meaning. The days are like weeks, the weeks are like months, and the months, from a certain perspective, begin to resemble something very much like eternity.

On the theory that there might be a population spreading north through Mexico after finding their way across the Darien Gap, Natalie asks him to start directing his attention southward.

"You're remembering that all this is happening in my mind, right?" he says. "The landscapes I'm supposedly seeing are now thousands of miles distant. We have no way of confirming whether any of it corresponds to reality."

"Or of refuting it, right? There's no point in us setting off on foot across the continent, at our age, unless you spot something that gives us at least a spark of hope."

"But you're a *physicist*, Nat. It's part of your training to be skeptical about things like this."

"Skeptical, yes, but also cognizant that there have always been things we can observe without being capable of explaining them. Metaphysics becomes physics once the underlying principles are understood, no? What you're experiencing may well be pure hallucination, my darling, but we've seen with our own eyes that it's strongly correlated with objective reality—at least in this immediate vicinity. Maybe something happened to your brain in the TDS, or maybe it *was* all that *Amanita muscaria* you ate, but whatever the cause, you've clearly connected with *something*. The real landscape thousands of miles away may have nothing to do with what you're seeing, or it may be approximately the same, or it may be *exactly* the same. As you say, we have no way of knowing. But we still have to keep trying."

So they keep trying. Nick has seen the traces of countless ruined cities and highways, but nothing that might indicate a recent human presence, and his long-held doubts about a surviving population have hardened into near certitude. Natalie feels differently. She can think of all kinds of scenarios in which a small population might have persisted, and while it's true that in one period of ten thousand years the early human population spread to every corner of the world, there were much longer periods earlier on when that population probably remained static—just small isolated bands of hunter-gatherers—and other periods in which the numbers likely contracted. She's far from ready to give up, in other words—and Nick, despite his doubts, respects her opinion greatly and is willing to keep going for as long as it takes.

One morning in late summer, ranging far to the south, he sees something in the distance that makes his stomach flip. Rising from a palely scorched plain are three pyramidal structures, clearly man-made and intensely modern-looking. *I've found them*, he thinks. *She's been right all along*. Natalie, watching his face as she tends their breakfast fire, notices the ghost of a smile cross his lips.

Approaching the pyramids, however, he sees that they're not new constructions at all, but quite ancient ones: steep-fronted Mayan temples built of lichen-covered coral limestone, a durable material that is apparently more weather-resistant than the wood, steel, and cement of their own era, and has allowed the structures to retain much of their original height and form. The surrounding jungle dried up and burned away long ago, leaving the trace geometries of the original city-state etched into the desiccated ivory plain. And like everywhere else he's been, the place is utterly devoid of human life.

To cover so much ground, he'd been traveling at a very high altitude. He's gone a bit lower to inspect the position, but now, alarmingly, he notices that his altitude is continuing to drop. This has never happened before. He's always been able to control his movements precisely by the merest thought, but now he feels a distinct dropping sensation, and in the next moment he's entered a full plummet, like a skydiver without a parachute. He kicks and flails, trying to somehow arrest his fall.

Opening his eyes he finds himself lying on his back, gasping for breath. Natalie's kneeling over him with her hands gripping his shoulders, peering concernedly down into his face. "You're right here, Nick. Don't worry. It's okay."

His pulse is racing and he's still gulping air, but it's an unspeakable relief no longer to be plunging toward the ground all on his own. After another moment or two, recovering his equilibrium, he describes the pyramids to her and shares his feeling that no survivors could possibly exist in such a parched desert landscape. It seems that she may finally be coming around to his opinion about the futility of continuing to search these lonely and distant hallucinatory landscapes. He hopes so, because he can't really abide the idea of doing it again.

The sun begins to dispel the cool morning air and the couple heads out for the day's foraging. They've become quite efficient at gathering what they need, and food is plentiful this time of year, so they've finished their work by mid-afternoon. It's a cloudless, seasonably hot day, and they stop to take a dip in the swimming hole. They splash up to the little waterfall, spend a few moments laughing and gazing out through the blurred lens of sheeting water, and take a pleasant nap on the sun-warmed boulders.

"I love you, Nat," he says. The sun is a warm red glow behind his eyelids.

"I love you too."

"I'm so glad you came," he adds. "Having you here has changed everything for me. It's made my life worth living again."

"I'm so glad it has, my darling."

He opens his eyes, sits up on his rock. "I don't know what I'd do if I lost you."

"You're *going* to lose me, dear," she says, reaching for her clothes. "You know that, right? We're both going to lose each *other*, eventually. Just remember this, though. Time doesn't actually exist in the way we perceive it. It's not an arrow, but a river. This is mathematically proven. The water does flow downstream, but if you were to walk back up the river a few miles you would find the same water flowing between the same banks. In a certain sense all the moments that have ever passed are still unfolding. And if you think about it that way, dear Nick, we'll always have each other."

"You really believe that?"

"I really do."

"Well, I guess I'll have to take your word for it. You say the concept is mathematically proven, but I find it impossible to accept intuitively."

"Keep trying, dear. It may be difficult to wrap your mind around, but it's one of the fundamental truths."

They finish dressing and stroll back up to the ledge, where they rekindle the fire and begin to process the day's gatherings with an eye to the coming winter. Afternoon slips into evening, and they watch the sunlight on the forest canopy transition from dazzling gold to a rich, almost liquid golden-red. Neither of them says it aloud, but in their own way they've each come to terms with the likelihood that the two of them, living in this leafy, pine-scented paradise high on a mountainside in the part of the world once known as northern New England, are the last of their species left on Earth. Which means that they're witnessing one of the very last late-summer sunsets ever to be taken in by human eyes.

44

A few days later, as they walk back up to the ledge again from the swimming hole, he asks some inconsequential question over his shoulder—did the water feel a degree or two colder today? Or, did you hear those wolves last night?—and Natalie doesn't reply. He turns, but she's nowhere in sight. His stomach drops. The terror comes flooding back.

It's not that, though. She's not a vanishing mirage, because he can hear her gasping and muttering from somewhere below the trail. She must have lost her footing. There's a gap in the trees, a slab of slippery bedrock slanting down to the edge of a shallow ravine. He scrambles down into the rocky gorge and finds her seated in a jumble of moss-covered boulders, gingerly examining her left ankle. Face pale and clenched in pain.

She greets him with a nod and a sardonic grimace. "Damn it, Nick. I think I've broken my ankle."

He drops down to examine it for himself, rotating the joint gently, and she curses in acute agony. The ankle is discolored, already swelling up. It doesn't take advanced medical knowledge to see that her diagnosis is correct. It's a fracture, not a sprain.

Neither says it aloud at that moment, but both of them understand what the injury could mean, in these circumstances, at Natalie's age, with winter on the way.

With difficulty, he carries her up the mountainside. She's small and light but in order not to cause jarring pain in her ankle he has to cradle her in his arms like a child. They try to distract each other from pain and worry, respectively, by keeping up a running banter. Back at the ledge he covers her with furs and builds up the fire. He goes down to the spring to fill a water skin, cuts a few green saplings for a splint, and peels strips of black birchbark he can use to secure it. By this time it's nearly dusk. The ankle is terribly swollen and discolored. Natalie is trembling uncontrollably, her face pale and drawn and showing her age. As he tightens the splint she clenches her jaw and sucks in her breath through her teeth, managing in the very next moment a remark about the delightful smell of wintergreen exuded by the freshly peeled birch. He thinks she might pass out from the pain.

"I've been meaning to ask you, Nick dear," she says after a time. "Did you get a glimpse of the Caribbean the other day? It can't have been too far beyond those Mayan temples."

He shakes his head. He'd been too focused on the structures to look carefully into the distance beyond them, and then he'd started to plummet.

"What would you think about going back to take one more look, now that you've made me comfortable? There's not much more you can do for me, really. And who knows what you might see?"

All his instincts tell him not to leave her unattended, even for a moment. On the other hand, it's obvious that she's suggesting it not only to satisfy her own curiosity, but to distract him from the intensity of his worry. So he agrees to go back first thing the next morning.

He awakes at dawn, brews an elixir of willow bark and reishi mushrooms in warm hickory milk, helps her swallow a good amount of it, and walks down to the brook to retrieve several strips of deerskin he's left soaking in the cold spring water. She grits her teeth and tries to keep from groaning as he carefully removes the splint and rewraps her ankle and lower calf in a kind of compression sheath. He banks the fire and sits cross-legged on the granite, then clears his mind and visualizes himself leaping up into the rocketing heat vapors.

Several moments later the coastline of what used to be known as the Yucatán Peninsula appears in a low-orbital satellite's view. The shape of it is still recognizable, a pale yellow-brown hitchhiker's thumb of land bounded on three sides by the brilliant turquoise sea. To the north he can make out the faint outlines—or thinks he can, as he never really knows whether it's just his imagination providing him the images his subconscious is looking for—of the immense crater made sixty-six million years before by the Chicxulub meteor, bringer of the catastrophe that wiped out the dinosaurs.

Swooping down to the eastern coast, he zeroes in on a sun-blasted crescent of beach, where a fringe of prickly pear clings to a strip of white sand that darkens to stone-gray where the wavelets saturate the tideline. The seawater is transparent and tinged green in the shallows, transforming to beautiful azure-blue farther out as the bottom falls away to various depths, and beyond that to a reflective, mirror-like silver. It's a virtually windless early morning. Frigatebirds wheel overhead. The sun already beats down punishingly on the beach and the water. He spends a moment gazing out at the empty horizon.

He doesn't stay long. Natalie's worrisome appearance this morning haunts him. That impression of frailty, of brittleness and inward-looking distraction from the world. As if her inner being, shaken loose by the accident, might already be stealing away into the darkness.

Opening his eyes he finds her lying beside him on the comfortable ledge with her head resting on a folded deerskin. If anything she looks worse. Her fingernails have taken on an alarming bluish cast and her cheeks are slack and papery, almost translucent, like the vellum of an ancient scroll. Her breaths are shallow and quick. Beside her on the granite the pictorial codex lies open; he closes it and pushes it away so he can sit beside her. She opens her eyes and greets him with a weak but characteristically cheerful smile. Her lips start moving but her voice is too soft to hear so he leans in, bringing his ear closer to her parched lips. "How did it look to you, dear?" she asks. "The sea?"

"Let's get you hydrated first." He jumps to his feet, agitated, and grabs the nearest water skin. "Then I'll tell you what I saw."

He sits again, and gently adjusts her body so that her head is resting in his lap. Tipping a small amount of water into her mouth, he splashes more into his palm and uses two fingers to moisten her cracked lips. She nods gratefully, then fixes him in a stubbornly expectant gaze. "Well?"

He describes the vision faithfully, adding just one detail. A low dark shape glimmering into view on the line of that empty blue horizon. The impression of wriggling appendages, the limbs or fins of some huge insect-like marine creature glinting black and wet in the morning light as it inched closer across the glassy surface of the sea. As it approached he could see that it wasn't a living creature at all, but a strange-looking watercraft with a prominent raised prow, a centered mast with its sail rolled in the windless morning air, and a rank of oars working.

"It sounds like one of those wooden barques they used to find in the pharaohs' tombs," she observes dreamily. "They were meant to ferry them across the river to the afterlife."

"Yes," he says. "Only this one was filled with living human beings. The most beautiful creatures imaginable, Nat, young and healthy, with well-muscled brown shoulders and long supple hair and teeth that looked strong and white as they laughed and sang joyously to the rhythm of the oars. I thought of calling out to them, but of course they wouldn't have been able to hear me, because it was only a vision."

"A most *wonderful* vision, Nick dear," she exclaims enthusiastically, the words coming out in a hoarse whisper. "Try to make contact with them, will you? Stay with them awhile. Get them off on the right foot." And he agrees. What does it matter? Just the idea of it has made her smile. It has given her a happy tableau to contemplate as she dies.

Later, she gains the strength for one last conversation. She tells him not to worry, that she's actually quite looking forward to the journey ahead of her. Up into the nebulae to join that endless dance across the universe, or wherever it is she's bound. "Enjoy every moment you have left, dear. The forest. The cats. The cycle of days. The moon. The plants. The seasons."

When she's gone, he finds himself right back where he started, alone in an uninhabited wilderness. And it's sad, though perhaps not quite as terrible as he'd been fearing, because in a certain way she's still with him. He can feel her presence, and he thinks he may finally understand her notion of time. Not an arrow but a river. He can feel the truth of that now, almost as palpably as his own heartbeat. All the moments that have ever gone by are still unfolding, just upstream.

High up along the steep mountainside, another outcropping projects out over the canopy of the forest. On the outer extremity of this granite formation a gnarled old redcedar clings to life, like an accidental bonsai corkscrewing out into the vacant air, its roots thrust immovably into the meager soil that has accumulated in a crack in the hard gray stone. Perched on a horizontal branch of this aged conifer, a sharp-eyed predator gazes down upon the pair of elderly primates in the encampment far below, the last of their kind. In its dazzlingly beautiful eyes is a look of something like scorn, and something like pity, and perhaps also a dawning self-awareness of the vital energy contained within it, which runs like a many-forked river from the planet's ancient past all the way to its remote future.

ACKNOWLEDGMENTS

I owe a debt of gratitude to astrophysicist Dr. John L. Tonry of the University of Hawaii at Manoa for his counsel at the inception of this novel. On a spectacular small-ship cruise through Tierra del Fuego—Cape Horn, the Beagle Passage, the Straits of Magellan—Dr. Tonry took my ill-informed questions about quantum physics, interstellar travel, and one-way time travel and ran with them, coming up with a clever way to give one of the novel's central conceits at least a modicum of scientific plausibility. I'm aware that in shaping the narrative I've taken liberties with his original back-of-the-envelope equations, and I would have it known that any of the resulting mistakes and distortions in the math are mine, not his.

On the same memorable expedition Dr. Jesse Farmer, previously of Princeton and now of the University of Massachusetts Boston, introduced me to the fascinating field of paleoclimatology and responded to my questions about the deep-future climate with enthusiasm and grace. Although I suspect that neither of these eminent scientists thought that I would actually end up writing the novel in question, I owe them both a great deal for giving me confidence in the ideas that inspired it, and I thank them from the bottom of my heart for their open-mindedness and willingness to speculate.

My gratitude goes out to Deborah Schneider, Cathy Gleason, and everyone at GSLA, and to Brian Skulnik, Stephanie Beard, Taylor Bryon, and the entire crew at Podium, for believing in this book.

Thanks to Diana Gill and Traci Post for their wise and incisive editorial guidance, which has without question made it a much better narrative, and to the members of the Brattleboro salon who were in the room for my earliest attempts to get the story down on the page. I'm profoundly grateful to Danielle Trussoni, Chris Bohjalian, Angie Kim, and Janelle Brown for their wisdom and support with the first completed draft, and to my wonderful and encouraging friend and talented documentary filmmaker Amy Bucher for restoring my faith in the project's worth at a particularly low moment. Thanks to Dr. John A. Edwards, Frances Hanchett, Chuck Weed, and Susan Edwards Wing, who in different ways taught me how to live well in a world encompassing darkness and light in equal measure, and to Charles, Tom, and Juju for their company and teachings. Above all, so much love and gratitude to my bright beacons in the wilderness, JRJ, LFW, and TJW, whose presence, support, and patience are what have kept me going.

There were a number of nonfiction books that informed and inspired this narrative. The most important were Alan Weisman's *The World Without Us*, Curt Stager's *Deep Future: The Next 100,000 Years of Life on Earth*, Yuval Noah Harari's *Sapiens: A Brief History of Humankind*, Marcia Bjornerud's *Timefulness: How Thinking Like a Geologist Can Help Save the World*, Tim Flannery's *The Eternal Frontier: An Ecological History of North America and its Peoples*, and Peter Brannen's *The Ends of the World: Volcanic Eclipses, Lethal Oceans, and Our Quest to Understand Earth's Past Mass Extinctions.*

If there is one piece of wisdom I would wish for readers to take away from this improbable story, it is that the crisis our species has visited upon the world does not, to use the words of geologist Bjornerud, augur "the 'end of nature' but, instead, the end of the illusion that we are *outside* nature." We are embedded in the ebb and flow, the stew and ferment of life on this 4.5-billion-year-old planet, and the sooner we internalize this basic fact, the sooner we can assume our destiny as its stewards.

ABOUT THE AUTHOR

Tim Weed is the author of *A Field Guide to Murder & Fly Fishing*, *Will Poole's Island*, and *The Afterlife Project*. A sometime international travel guide, Weed serves on Salve Regina University's core faculty for the Newport MFA in creative writing and is a cofounder of the Cuba Writers Program. When not at his writing desk, he can most often be found outdoors.